THE POWER
OF SALVATION

Caterina Passarelli

ISBN: 0692773924
ISBN 13: 9780692773925

Covered designed by Najla Qambers Designs
Edited by Duncan Koerber

For more, visit www.CaterinaPassarelliBooks.com

RECOMMENDED FOR READERS 18 AND
OLDER DUE TO STRONG LANGUAGE, SEXUAL
SITUATIONS AND VIOLENCE.

If you or someone you know is in need of help, please
contact The National Domestic Violence Abuse
Hotline:

(800) 799-7233

www.thehotline.org

PROLOGUE

Luke
10 Years Old

I'm hiding under the bed tucked in between my older sister and younger brother, praying he doesn't come for us. The man of the house. Our dad. He's in one of his moods tonight. We could easily end up getting our heads smashed together if we even look at him the wrong way.

It wouldn't be the first time. My first trip to the hospital was when I was five years old, getting ten stitches across my forehead. I still remember sitting on the white hospital bed while the pretty blonde nurse looked at the blood draining from the gash in my face and asked me what happened.

I remember that was the first time I knew my mom, who I always thought was an angel, was also a liar. She told the nurse I was running around "like five year old boys do," and I fell down the stairs. What a bunch of horse shit. Falling down the stairs looked an awful lot like my dad breaking a beer bottle over my head. He was drunk and angry when I walked into the kitchen asking about dinner.

Now as a ten year old, I know I'm more of the man in this house than my dad. And right now I feel like a piece of shit hiding under this bed in the dark, but I know if I show myself, he'll beat mom worse, and I don't want her to go through that.

"Bill, you don't have to do this," mom says, trying to whisper, but she's loud enough to hear from under the bedroom door.

"What the fuck do you know, bitch?" dad slurs his usual insult back at her.

"Okay Bill, how about we just go to bed? You have to be up early in the morning for work," mom says, trying to end this nasty situation.

"Don't tell me what to do, cunt."

And with that I hear a loud smack. I tug my baby brother in closer to me, trying to tuck his head down and cover his ears with my hands. I should go out there and give him a piece of my mind. But before I can leave, I hear my sister crying as my brother shakes in my grasp.

Why is this our fucking reality?

Other kids have parents who sit down for dinners together and no one gets beat. At least that's what I see on television.

I am too young to be stressed out. Or to even know the definition of the word.

CHAPTER ONE

Ariana

A drunken college student stumbles into the emergency room with shards of glass sticking out of bloody arms. He manages to walk over to me, where I stand at a station of computers. Before I can jump out of the way, he leans over, throwing up all over my hot pink Nikes.

Shit, that's disgusting. Smelling the alcohol on his breath as he takes his dirty hand to wipe it across his mouth, I can guess with 99 percent accuracy this is one of our typical college brawlers. They always look and act the exact same way.

"Dude, you need to pull yourself together. Did someone send you back here or did you just walk in?" I ask.

I surely hope he's not going to become my patient—I don't think I'd be too nice to him with his vomit smell carrying into my nostrils.

"Are you a nurse?" Drunk Boy asks, squinting at me. I wonder how many of me he's seeing right now. By the way he's shifting his eyes from right to left, I'd say at least two.

"No, I'm a doctor." Not that I mind being mistaken for a nurse, but I did just finish medical school and earn my degree.

Dr. Ariana Bellisano.

As egotistical as it is to admit, I love the sound of that. I even enjoy checking off the "Dr." box on forms now— no more "Ms." for me. This has been my big dream since I was a little girl and nothing, I mean nothing, was going to get in my way.

I busted ass to maintain a high GPA through four years of undergrad and four years of med school because I was on a full-ride scholarship. From busting ass to kissing ass, I worked my way into scoring a residency at the best hospital in Chicago—St. Francis.

And now I have to stare at some punk guy, who's about my age, giving me shit. Not tonight buddy.

"Damn, a doctor. You're fine as hell for a doctor. How old are you mama?" he asks.

Mama? I'm going to punch this guy myself.

"You need to walk yourself back to the waiting room for a triage nurse to see you," I say, pointing him in the right direction and taking off before seeing if he makes it there. I couldn't care less right about now; I really need to clean my shoes.

"Hey Ariana, wait up!"

I turn around seeing my best friend, Drake, walking towards me. A few heads turn as he practically glides down the long hallway like an Abercrombie model. This always happens with Drake. He's tall with dirty blonde hair, blue eyes, tan skin, and a Hollywood smile. We met in our freshmen year of college in a history class. Turned out we both clicked over the fact that we were hardcore wannabe doctors—me an emergency room physician and Drake a gynecologist. However, Drake is a little more relaxed than me. You know in terms of still having a social life and friends.

"The guys are meeting for drinks at The Grove tonight—you want to go?"

"Why do you still hang out with those guys? All they do is get drunk," I say, walking towards the staff room where I hope to find an extra pair of shoes in my locker. Drake fully embraced the college spirit and still maintains close friendships with his frat brothers. Me? I avoid most people—except somehow Drake squeezed his way through.

"Getting drunk with the guys will not be looked at as socially acceptable anymore when I'm an attending," Drake says, trying to explain his lame reasoning. Drake and I are both in our last year of residency, and then we'll both officially be what hospitals call 'attendings'— meaning we won't have to work under other physicians. We will have our own patients. "I'm doing it now while I still can. And you should join me. You look like you haven't relaxed since … you were born," he laughs.

"I think getting some sleep sounds much better than getting drinks," I say, slipping out of my shoes, once I realized there were no extras, and running them under the cold water from the sink.

"You've been working your regular shifts plus moonlighting. You look like a goddamn zombie and I'm not even sure if you are showering anymore," he jokes. "Please tell me you're showering still."

"Ha-ha! Yes, I'm showering, you asshole."

A delicious shower at my apartment—that's what I'm about to take. I'm talking a loofah, vanilla body wash, shaving my legs, and maybe even a cucumber face mask. I may have stretched the truth a little when I told Drake I was still showering. I mean, who has time to do that every single day? Or even every other day? Not me. I'm working every possible shift I can at the emergency room. I want to prove myself now among the staff in hopes of securing my spot as an 'attending' once residency is over.

But somehow my best friend got in my head and I'm going to take a shower to show up at that stupid bar. He's right—I do need a break, even if just a short one, then I'm coming right back here to catch up on some much needed sleep.

I pull a cute black dress I've never worn out of the back of my closet, curl my long brown hair, and even put on a little bit of makeup. If I'm going out this once, I'm going to live it up. Mark this date down in history.

"Girl! Where the hell are you going? You look amazing in that dress. I'm borrowing it. Your legs are killer," Serena, my super sassy roommate, says as she walks into our apartment and smacks my ass.

"I'm going to The Grove with Drake and some of his friends. Want to join us?"

Serena puts her purse down in her room directly across the hall from mine. I have to say I'm so glad I met Serena a few years ago. We hit it off when we reached for the same drink in the coffee shop. Normally I'd punch a chick trying to grab my drug of choice, but she was hilarious.

And one year later, roomies. I'm grateful for her rich parents as well. Even though I have a full ride, Serena scooped me up out of the crappy dorm I was living in to let me live in her apartment in downtown Chicago. It's much more than any college student I know could afford, and she could have definitely lived here alone, but she's got a heart of gold.

Our apartment is stocked with top-of-the-line stainless steel appliances, granite countertops, walk-in closets, and a picturesque view of the downtown buildings. Nothing I could afford without her.

Serena is the opposite of me in so many ways—she's nearly finished with her master's degree in business, but she's also a self-described 'free spirit.' She's got blonde hair and blue eyes. Her and Drake would be Ken and Barbie.

"As hard as it is for me to say this, I can't go out tonight," Serena says as she laughs and curls up under her covers. "I'm still hung over from last night. I think I need to stay in. But you can tell that sexy man Drake I said hello and he can drop by our apartment any time he likes," she adds in a wink as if I didn't know she'd love to sleep with my best friend. Serena has been trying to get me to set her up with Drake since she met him.

"Nice try, but you know I don't play matchmaker for anyone. You can get your own date. Just ask him," I say, winking back at her while I grab my red clutch and head towards the front door. I see the notification from the Driver app that my ride is waiting outside of our building. Lael from Nashville is giving me a ride to the bar tonight in his silver Toyota Highlander. No way in hell am I going to walk the cold streets alone, especially in these heels. Chicago winters are not for the faint of heart.

"Alright girl, I hope you feel better. Stay hydrated!" And with that I wish my roommate a good night and get in the car.

Let's get this over with.

CHAPTER TWO

Live band playing rock cover songs—check.
Drunk girls dancing near live band—check.

My friends—no check. They aren't even here yet.

Of course, I'd be the only one to show up on time.
I sit at the bar and shoot Drake a quick text—*'Where are you? I came out to the bar & you're nowhere to be seen.'*

Less than a minute passes by and my iPhone vibrates on the counter—*'You came?! Damn! This is going to be a night to remember. We're almost there! Have a drink to get started—or relax in your case. lol See you in 5!'*

"What can I get for you sweetheart?"

Looking up from my phone I realize the smooth bartender is talking to me.

"Sex on the Beach?" I say more like a question, unsure of my choice. I can't believe it's been this long since I've gone to a bar that I'm ordering my freshmen self's signature drink. He's definitely going to know I'm an amateur.

"I'd love to but there isn't a beach close enough," he says in a raspy deep voice before turning around to start my drink. Luckily with his back to me he doesn't see how tongue-tied I get around men flirting with me … or just men in general that I don't know. I don't really do the whole flirting thing. My friends better hurry the hell up.

Since I've got some time, I decide to do what I do best—people watch. Watching other people and how they interact with one another, or when they think no one is watching them, is interesting to me.

Here's a look around this bar: there's a redheaded woman with an extremely tight green dress trying to press her full cleavage into a balding guy who is staring so hard at her tits that he probably has no idea what her face looks like.

Then over on the dance floor, about 15 ladies clearly enjoying a bachelorette party are dancing with pink boas, plastic tiaras, and penis necklaces. Some creepy guys stand at the edge of the dance floor waiting to pounce on the bachelorette girls.

My eyes scan the dark bar until they land on a pair of eyes staring straight back at me. I almost spill my Sex on the Beach all over myself in shock. I've been caught staring! And caught by an insanely handsome man sitting in a dark corner booth all by himself. Yes, it may be dark in here but I can't pull my eyes away as I take in his thick brown hair, dark smoldering eyes, and get this ... he's wearing a suit that his biceps are straying out of. His eyes remain on mine but he doesn't crack a smile, just continuing to stare. I should look away—I know I should—but I can't. It's like an intense game we are playing with each other. Who will crack first?

Did they turn up the heat in here?

I've never, and I mean never, had the urge to walk up to a man inside of a bar, but I chug my drink working up the nerve to stand up and maybe approach him.

"Ariana! I can't believe you are here!" Drake shouts, showing up out of nowhere, picking me up, and twirling me around.

"Drake, put me down!" I shout at him. "Yes, I'm at a bar, there's no need for unwanted touching." I can't stand being touched, and Drake of all people should know. It's just one of my things.

Drake laughs and gives me a lame ass apology for the touching, and then his friends all say 'hello' before they sit down at a giant table. I turn back around to look at Mystery Man and my stomach drops—he's gone. I quickly scan around the bar to see if he's moved to a new spot, but I come up short.

Oh well, you shouldn't go up to strange men in bars anyway, Ariana! Even if they are drop dead gorgeous.

"Shots my brothers … and sister!" Drake's fellow fraternity brother, Trey, says as he passes me a shot that smells like tequila. Oh god, this is going to be a long night.

More drinks are drunk, stories and jokes are shared, and I find myself having a relaxing time. I don't remember stumbling into my room later, but I'm sure Drake had something to do with my safe passage home. He has no clue how important that is to me.

CHAPTER THREE

The hustle and bustle of an emergency room gets my blood pumping. It's like an adrenaline rush you get when you are about to do something scary yet life changing—like skydiving. When I was a med student, I had to work in all the different areas of the hospital, but this one is by far my favorite. It's where I thrive.

"Bellisano, scrub in on this cardiac arrest in operating room two," Dr. Horton says as he hands me a chart and we stroll towards the operating room.

"We need the resident to stay on the floor. She can't go into surgery with you tonight," says our hospital chief, Dr. Pitters, pulling me away from all the action. Dr. Horton gives me a look of 'sorry kid I tried to help you' as he leaves me standing with the chief—who is nothing short of intimidating.

"Where do you need me, chief?" I ask, totally kissing her ass, and she knows it.

"Can you swing by the nurses' station and see what they are up to. Three girls called in sick tonight and they're swamped—please, for the love of god, help them. The last thing we need are the nurses bitching up a storm," Chief Pitters says in a tone nicer than her normal shouting. I do what she says and quickly head towards where I know the nurses are frantically running around. When the nurses aren't happy, no one is happy.

"Bellisano, can you take room three?" Katie, one of the head nurses, asks while handing me a chart. "A woman in there isn't talking much. All she's given us is that she got mugged. She's beat up pretty badly."

"Got it," I skim through the medical chart, which is mostly empty since the patient isn't talking, and I head towards room three. When I walk in I have to do a mental gut check to compose myself. This woman, who can't be older than 35, is covered head-to-toe in bruises, her right eye is swollen completely shut, her bottom lip is busted open, scratches cover her legs, and she may need stitches in her arm.

Memories of my own past float to the surface, but I push them down before they can creep in to ruin my night. I regain composure, hoping she didn't see my distress. I am normally very pulled together in all situations in the hospital, but seeing women come in here abused—in any way—sets me on edge.

"Hello ... my name is Dr. Bellisano. I'm working under Dr. Horton this evening. Can you tell me your name?" I ask, walking closer to the bed. The woman is shaking. With her one good eye, she's trying to avoid me and doesn't say a word in response to my question.

"Do you have any allergies? I need to know at least a few facts about you if you want me to give you any medication. I think you need some stitches as well."

No answer. I don't know how she made it past the triage team without answering anything; they must have taken pity on her. That's fine—I can wait her out for a few more minutes in uncomfortable silence before I clear up her arm to prep for her stitches.

"Can you please tell me what happened?" Still nothing. I know most doctors wouldn't push this so soon but I'm going in. "Do you want me to call the police? I heard you were mugged." The mention of police must have been exactly what she needed to hear because the mute found her voice—a shaky scared one, but a voice nonetheless.

"Can you please call Luke?" She asks in a mouse-like whisper.

"You're going to have to give me more than a name, sweetie," I say, disinfecting her arm. "Do you want me to get you a phone in here so you can make the call?"

"Yes, please," she whispers.

She seems like a kind person, which I know is weird to say when only meeting someone for a few minutes, but I can just sense it. It's something that comes with the territory. Whoever did this to her, I want to rip off his dick and put it in a blender.

"I can see all your external bruises,"—this part kills me to ask but it's my job to know in case more help is needed—"but do we need to check you for anything else?" She meets my eyes like she's not sure what I'm asking. "Did your mugger … sexually assault you?"

"Oh." Her face drops in sadness, and other than her black and blue bruises, she loses all other color. She looks just like a ghost. "No."

I feel my own sense of relief at her answer. When her stitches are finished I give her some medication for the pain and walk out to find someone to bring her a phone to call whoever the hell Luke is.

The next couple hours go by in a blur—an 11-month-old with bronchitis, an elderly man who fell and broke his hip, a college girl who needed her stomach pumped, and the occasional cases of flus and viruses. It's a very dull night in a Chicago hospital in fact. We are one of the busiest in the nation.

I head back to room three to check on the patient who was mugged. As I slide back the blue curtain, I see a man with his arm wrapped around her in a side hug—they both have their backs to me. They're speaking in hushed voices so I can't make out anything he's saying, but I can tell she's crying. He sweetly kisses her temple and it touches my heart—this must be her boyfriend.

A phone rings. His.

He's off the bed in a second and pressing the phone to his face.

"This better be good news," says a deep masculine voice, a voice that means business, which sets my nerves on fire. And that's when we lock eyes.

It's him. Mystery Man from the bar.

The woman turns around to see us both staring at each other and I blush. Caught staring at this man again … but this time in front of his girlfriend. *He has a girlfriend!* I feel immediate jealously and sadness realizing this. Why do I even care? I haven't even spoken a word to this man … ever.

"I'm sorry … um…" I stumble over my words like the complete hot mess that I've become, "I just came to check on you but I don't want to interrupt."

I turn rushing out of the room. I don't remember the walk from room three to the bathroom but somehow I've made it. I sit down on the floor and think.

He has a girlfriend. And she was mugged tonight. And I think she's kind. What an asshole I am for even being jealous of her.

"Hey Bellisano, what the fuck are you doing in here? Is your shift over?" asks Ben, a nurse who thinks his shit don't stink. That's when I realize I've walked right into the men's bathroom. Of course he would be the one to find me trying to hide out in my time of embarrassment. "Get back out there."

I don't even reply to him. I get up off the floor and push open the swinging door to collide right into a large, muscular person.

"Excuse me," I say, looking up at the person I ran into, locking eyes yet again with the hazel pair I was staring at just minutes ago. "I'm sorry." I try to skirt around him, trying to make a break for it. Get me the hell away from him.

"You ran into me and can't even tell me your name," he says as he reaches around to grab my arm. He's touching me. *Get off me, get off me, get off me!* I pull my arm back as fast as possible and flinch. He notices my freak out and lets go instantly, but not before giving me a quizzical stare down though. "I'm sorry. I didn't mean to startle you."

We are standing so close that if you were to walk past us in this hallway you may not be sure if we were going to hug … or kiss. I'm not a short girl by any means, around 5'7", but I feel so small in his presence. This man … *Luke* … must be over 6 feet tall and extremely well built. I feel boxed in by his muscular chest and arms.

"It's okay," I say, looking down at our feet—me in an ugly pair of Crocs (I can't believe I even own them) and him in a pair of designer dress shoes. He's wearing a finely tailored suit, just like at the bar. It fits his body like a glove … or well a suit I guess.

"What's your name?"

"Ariana," I say at the same time I remember the poor girlfriend sitting in the room on the worst night of her life. "I should go back to properly check on your girlfriend. I got sidetracked last time, sorry." I step out of the area he's got me enclosed in and speed walk towards room three.

Opening the door I notice the girlfriend changing out of her hospital robe. Even more bruises and scrapes cover her back. It's not serious enough to need stitches though.

"Are you sure you don't want to call the police?" I ask, startling her as she spins around to cover herself and knocks down a tray next to her.

"You haven't called the police?" Luke shouts following right behind me into the room. We both bend towards the floor to pick up the contents spilled. We grab the same utensil and I do my best to avoid brushing my fingers near his. He safely keeps his distance this time.

"I wasn't sure if that was the best idea," the girlfriend squeaks out, like she's scared. Sadly, I know how she feels.

"Are you afraid of being judged if you tell someone?" She looks down at her hands in defeat; she knows exactly what I'm asking. We live in a culture where if women speak out to abuse, they are judged.

"Being judged or not … there's a man on the loose right now who could do this again to someone else. Lisa, you can't keep this information to yourself," Luke says, shocking both Lisa and me with his strong stance.

"I think you should listen to your boyfriend," I add.

"Boyfriend?" Lisa asks, and for the first time all night, she smiles. Not only does she smile but also she busts out in a deep laugh that makes tears stream down her face. "Oh my god, I shouldn't be laughing. It hurts my entire body to laugh right now. I don't know if these tears are good or bad."

I look from Lisa to Luke, neither lets on about what's so freakin' funny. Finally Lisa settles down from her fit of laughter.

"Luke isn't my boyfriend … he's my baby brother."

Brother? Baby brother? Why didn't he correct me earlier?

"Maybe because you never gave me the chance. You ran away when I was trying to talk to you," Luke says, intoxicating me with that deep voice.

I said that out loud?

"Yes," both Lisa and Luke reply in unison. I am mortified.

To make matters worse, Ben sticks his big head in the door and says, "Bellisano, you know there are other patients in this hospital. This one was discharged. We need your help for a gunshot to the leg. Hustle your ass."

Ben is the wicked witch of this hospital, worse than the chief even.

"I'm sorry, I need to go. I agree with your *brother*, you should call the police immediately. Don't be ashamed of what you went through." I lock eyes with her as I step towards the door to leave. "You will do more harm than good if you keep this to yourself. What happened, it's not your fault."

And with that I fly out of the room and head towards where I hear Ben shouting at other residents. Can't a house from Kansas fall out of the sky and land on this guy? I could rock some ruby red slippers.

CHAPTER FOUR

Luke
11 Years Old

Mom is sobbing while she holds a pack of frozen broccoli to her right eye. Dad threw her down the stairs before taking off for the bar around the corner to get trashed out of his mind. This has become a pattern for the last few months. Day after day, dad beats the shit out of mom and mom pretends like us kids aren't there to witness it. But we see everything. We hear everything.

"Luke, can you bring me your homework? I want to check it before your big test tomorrow," mom says like nothing crazy took place in our house just five minutes earlier.

I slide the homework across the kitchen table and say, "Mom, dad needs to go." She looks up at me with pleading eyes, like she's the one sorry for me.

"Sweetheart, not again with this. I'm fine," she says, picking up my math homework. "Let's get through the homework and then we'll start dinner with Lisa. We're having macaroni and cheese." She reaches over to caress my cheek with a tender touch. I truly want to kill my dad for what he's doing to her. She's by far the kindest woman alive and does not deserve this life. None of us do.

I've asked her over and over if I can call the police, but each and every time she pleads with me not to do anything. She says he won't do it again, that *'this is the last time'* and he'll change his ways. But those are just empty promises of bullshit. And what upsets me even more is that no one outside of the five of us in this tiny little house knows what the fuck is happening behind these closed doors. I wish someone else knew so that they'd feel the pressure to call the cops like I should. My mom has a brother, where the fuck is that guy? Why doesn't he feel the need to check in on his sister and stand up for her? I could never live with myself if I knew someone was doing this to Lisa.

A loud crash pulls me from my thoughts, as dad stumbles through the front door, knocking over the entryway table. He takes a giant gulp from whatever liquor he's carrying in a brown paper bag. Lisa and Eric rush into the front room to see what's going on.

"Caroline, aren't these kids supposed to be in bed? What the fuck are they still doing awake?" Dad barely even looks at us as he slumps into his lumpy green recliner and throws his feet up, chugging more from his paper bag.

"It's only six o'clock, bedtime isn't 'til nine," Lisa chimes in before mom can shoot her a look to be quiet.

Dad slowly turns his head to look at my sister and his eyes glaze over, like he's not even seeing her clearly. "You want to sass me back one more time you little fucker? I'll get out of this chair and get my belt."

The belt—that's his easiest and most common threat. But he'd never hit Lisa—for some reason she's safe. And at least that makes me feel at ease.

"You don't have to talk to her like that. She didn't do anything wrong," I spit out at him. He doesn't say a word but he's out of his recliner in two seconds flat. Me on the other hand, he will hit.

"Stop! Stop!" Mom rushes into the living room screaming.

Grabbing me by the arm, digging his fingers into my forearm, dad spins me around to hit me across my ass. Once, twice, three times total before he throws me down into the coffee table. I crash down on it and it breaks, glass everywhere.

CHAPTER FIVE

T he line at the Starbucks near the hospital is always so damn long, no matter what time of the day. Caffeine is a priority to college students and hospital staff—it's a basic food group for the majority of us—and we must keep this location in business.

"Next," a peppy girl with a nametag that reads Tricia calls out to me in an extra cheery tone. I want whatever she's drinking. "What can I get for you?"

"I'll take a Starbucks double shot on ice with non-fat milk, *please*." I can't believe I just begged for coffee. I tip Tricia and move over to stand with the rest of the Starbucks groupies waiting for their beverages.

"Did you hear about the lady near campus who got mugged last night?" I hear two girls in front of me chatting loud enough for everyone to hear. They're turning a woman's beating into a topic of gossip.

"I heard she knew the guy. I also heard she's a known slut and was basically asking for it," one of them says in a matter-of-fact tone.

My eyes bug out of my head and my jaw drops. I can't believe I'm hearing this right now. This is why Lisa didn't want to come forward—for the stigma that 'you're asking for it' if something bad happens to you as a woman.

I hope she's okay—I wish there was a way to check on her. But she didn't leave behind much information.

I should hold my tongue, but get the fuck out of here with these bitches.

"Before you spread rumors, you should get your facts straight. If anyone is *asking for it* it's you two ignorant bitches. You should be ashamed of yourself. Congrats on setting women's rights back 50 years. That woman had nothing to do with that man—it was completely random."

Both of them look at me with a deer in a headlight stare. And to save the day, my drink shows up on the counter, and I take it and walk out without them saying a single word to me.

On my walk to the hospital Drake shows up next to me. "What's with the sour face?" he asks. I'm sure my pissed off attitude is radiating off me for everyone on this block to feel.

"It's nothing—just two stupid girls talking crap in the coffee shop. I can't believe the human race sometimes."

"It's because under that 'I'm a badass' exterior you display for everyone, you're a big softy and you care about what's right," he teases me.

"Can you keep the 'softy' remarks between you and I? I have a reputation to uphold," I laugh. We part ways upon entering the hospital. I stay here on the main floor of the E.R. and Drake heads upstairs to the land of bringing cute babies into the world.

Another day of living the dream in the hospital. Luckily for me, Ben and the chief are both off today. It's like a Christmas miracle. Everyone is in an upbeat mood and nothing too serious has walked through the doors—yet.

I make my rounds checking on my patients and head towards the front station when out of the corner of my eye I see him, Luke, standing at the desk talking to Sheila, the head nurse tonight. She's looking up at him with dreamy 'fuck me' eyes, and I instantly want to punch her in the face for flirting with him. *What's wrong with me?* Sheila is the nicest girl ever.

Why is he here? Please tell me Lisa is okay!

"Hey," I say, walking up behind him and putting my hand on his strong back. "Is everything okay?"

I must have a concerned look on my face because he goes to reach out to me but when I flinch he pulls back.

"Yes, everything's okay. Do you have a minute?"

"Umm ... sure," I stumble out my words; my confidence from a minute ago when I thought there was an emergency has clearly diminished. We walk to a corner out of the way, and I notice Sheila has a huge smirk on her face. She actually winks at me. Great, let the office gossip begin.

Again we are standing a little too close for my comfort. I notice just above his mesmerizing hazel eyes a small faint scar running from his hairline to his temple. I don't know what comes over me—something protective—but I reach out to touch it. This time he's the one who moves back, and I instantly feel like an idiot. I know what it's like to not want to be touched—why the hell did I just do that?

"I'm sorry," I say, looking down at the floor. Why is this a pattern with me when I'm around him? He catches me off guard and then I need to look away. Normally I back down for no one. What happened to that tough-as-nails person Drake was just talking about?

"It's okay," he says, touching the scar on his face with his tan hand, "sometimes I forget it's there. You just startled me, that's all."

"How did you get it?"

"I fell down the stairs when I was a boy." He says the sentence as if he's said it a million times. Even though it came out as repetitive, for some reason I get the feeling he's lying. I tilt my head to question him, but he cuts me off quickly.

"Are you seeing anyone?"

His question catches me off guard. Of course, my awkwardness saves the day by repeating his question, "Seeing someone?"

"Yes, seeing someone. Do you belong to someone?"

I've never heard that question worded in that way— *belong to someone.* Who says that? I'm not a dog.

"No, I don't *belong* to anyone." I fight the urge to say that I never will belong to anyone but I keep quiet for once.

"What about the guy at the bar?"

Now I'm confused again. What guy is he talking about? Then I remember the night I first set eyes on him at The Grove.

"Oh, Drake? Hell no, he's just my friend."

He looks relaxed at my answer. "Ariana, do you want to get a drink with me?"

"I'm kind of in the middle of a shift," I say, sarcastically waving my hand around to remind him we're standing in a very busy hospital.

Do I want to get a drink with him? I don't know anything about this man, well except for he must have an important job because he's always wearing suits tailored perfectly for him.

He has a sister who he cares a great deal about.

Has a set of hazel eyes that can pierce your soul.

And a body that can make your panties wet.

Whoa. Where the hell did all that come from?

"I know you're working. I didn't mean we would have a drink right this minute," he smirks at me. "You have to leave here at some point. And you can't tell me you don't like alcohol. I saw you down that drink at the bar."

How embarrassing. I have a flashback to the moment I downed my Sex on the Beach when I felt all-powerful, about to go over to the sexy man brooding alone in the corner booth. How childish. This guy is way out of my league.

"Yes, I want to get a drink with you." My confident answer even surprises me, but he smiles. Why did I say that?

"Good, here's my number," he says, handing me a thick black business card, "call me when you're ready for that drink." And just like that he turns around and walks out the emergency room doors.

Sheila rushes over to me, shrieking at a very high pitch rate, "Girl! Who the hell was that? He's the hottest guy I've ever seen—in a dark and dangerous kind of way."

Dark and dangerous—that's the vibe I get from him too. And it's kind of hot.

I flip the business card over and over in my hand debating whether or not to throw it out. Black with red font and it's heavy. The card is freakin' heavy—it must be at least a pound.

Lucas Vulcano
Vulcano Vodka, CEO

I've had the card in my possession for about a week and done nothing with it.

Luke is apparently the CEO of one of most profitable high-end liquor companies in the world. I don't know much about liquor, other than occasionally drinking it, but I do know Vulcano Vodka is what the rich kids and businessmen order at the bar when they are trying to impress someone.

I can't call him. No way Jose. Dark and dangerous is not what I need right now. I need to focus on finishing my residency. I've avoided guys for the most part in school, now is not the time to let one slip into my life. Even if it is just for a drink.

My phone rings and Drake's name flashes across the screen.

"Hey dude. What's up?" I ask while tossing the card into the trashcan. Decision made: I need to avoid Luke and all other romantic ties. Avoid them like the plague, just like I've been doing for years.

"You coming to the coffee shop? My treat! I'm sitting here bored out of my mind."

"Oh man, you are the best. I could use some caffeine!" I grab my purse and head towards the door. "I'm on my way."

Drake has scored the biggest table in the coffee shop, right next to the electrical outlets. It makes me proud to see he stalked us out the best spot in the place. I'm super picky about my coffee shop seating. I smile when

Drake looks up from whatever paper he is highlighting like a crazy man.

"Thank you, thank you, thank you!" I say while picking up the iced coffee he had waiting for me.

Drake laughs as he pushes aside a study guide I see him creating for a class. Along with being a resident, Drake is a professor's assistant at our university. How the hell does he find time to do this? I literally would pull out all of my hair if I had any more responsibilities on top of my residency.

"Not a problem, sister. You basically helped me get through med school. Without you I wouldn't be here," Drake says, surprising me with his compliment.

"When you put it that way—you're right. You owe me more." I laugh.

We sit for awhile chatting about our goals for after we finish this last year of residency and what we want our lives to look like—with the occasional break to scroll Facebook and gossip. What are best friends for?

We start packing up our laptops when a stranger pulls out the unoccupied chair at our table and takes a seat.

Wait a second, this is not a stranger: Luke is sitting at our table. My jaw drops at the surprise of seeing him here. He looks so out of place in this casual environment with him, yet again, looking like a model in his suit.

"Did you misplace that card?" Luke asks, raising an eyebrow at me. I can't tell if he's mad or trying to be a smart ass.

"Excuse me, who the hell are you?" Drake interrupts. Luke does not even tilt his head in Drake's direction— only keeping his gaze on me. Locked on me.

"No, I threw it out," I say, now annoyed he just showed up after I made the decision I wouldn't see him anymore.

His eyebrows perk up at my remark and he surprises me. Luke starts laughing. He's laughing at me? This is not how I thought this would go. Well I never thought I'd see him again; *this* interaction I never saw coming.

"What are you even doing here?" I ask with attitude.

Drake is glued to this conversation waiting for me to let him in on the identity of this man at our table. No one comes to this coffee shop except for students at the university around the block or hospital staff. I'm telling you, we run this place. It's rare a stranger sneaks his way in. Leave it to Luke.

"I was on campus as a guest speaker for Professor Hasting's class. He's a good friend of mine. I was walking by this coffee shop and who would I happen to see through the giant windows … you. The girl I can't seem to stay away from."

Drake pushes his chair out and motions for me to stand up.

"Okay man. I don't think it's healthy for you to stalk my friend. And she clearly threw out something you gave her—so I'm going to guess she couldn't care less about you." He puts his backpack over his shoulders and heads towards the door. "Let's go Ariana."

"I'm sorry but I thought you didn't have a boyfriend?" Luke asks, he is standing now as well, shoulders squared ahead. "This guy seems to be awfully controlling."

"Controlling? What the fuck do you know man?" Drake walks back to our table, his hands clinched in tight fists. Their confrontation is like a dance. Two steps forward, one step back. Before this little show of macho men becomes something it doesn't need to be, I need to do something.

"Excuse me," I say, putting myself between them, "this little show of masculinity is adorable but you need to cut it out because people are now staring."

No one is studying anymore and I don't blame them; if crazy people were having a showdown when I was studying I would stare too. Hello juicy gossip. But I hate being the center of attention—it makes my skin crawl and causes anxiety. In public I want to be invisible.

"I don't care if people are staring. This guy needs to know his place," Drake says as he pulls on my arm to try guiding me towards the door. I have never seen my super chill friend act like this before.

"You don't need to put your hands on her," Luke growls. But instead of pulling me towards him to continue this ridiculous battle, he respects my space and does not touch me.

"Drake, it's okay." I pull my arm away from his gentle grasp. "I do know Luke. We'll just be a few minutes and then I'll head out too. You don't need to wait for me."

Drake looks shocked and a little defeated. I've never picked anyone over him. Now that I think about it, I've never had to make a decision like this before either.

"Fine. I'm going to guess you know what you're doing. Call me when you get home," he says while giving Luke one last evil stare before leaving the coffee shop without saying goodbye.

"Want to get out of here?" Luke asks, nodding towards the door. I don't know where the hell we would go but I agree that we need to get out of this place. I feel trapped. Luke walks extremely close to me as we head towards the front door. We step out into the cold air and I wrap my black zip-up jacket a little tighter around me.

"So …" I say self-consciously, turning to walk in the direction of my apartment.

"Would you like to get that drink with me?"

I keep walking with him right by my side. "I don't drink often."

He raises his eyebrow and laughs a raspy laugh. "Says the girl I witnessed down a shot like a champ."

Busted.

"That was a rare occurrence," I say, which sounds super lame.

"Well I'd invite you to coffee but I'm not sure we should go back in there. The room was a little tense."

"You noticed that too?" I laugh, realizing he's said exactly what I was thinking. "Okay fine, one drink then."

I caved. I threw out his business card thinking there would be no chance for me to ever see this guy again. I mean Chicago has more than two million people in it, what are the chances? And I do want to know how his sister is doing; it's not often I can follow up with someone who has come into the emergency room.

He doesn't say a word but turns our direction to walk across the street. I don't realize where we are going until we are walking the steps to enter The Grand Plaza's hotel lobby. My face must have shock written all over it because he laughs at me and nods his head in the direction of the hotel bar.

"Don't get the wrong idea. I don't fuck on the first date," he says with a smirk as we approach the bar.

"Who said this was a date?" I tease as we take our seats at an intimate looking table tucked in the back of the bar. The lights are dim and a candle sits between us, casting flickers of light across his refined face.

"I'm sorry. I don't fuck on the first whatever this is."

"Well as long as we got that cleared up."

A waitress approaches our table with her eyes glued to Luke. She looks like she may drool. Has she never seen an attractive man before? I mean damn lady, pull it together.

"What can I get you?" she asks as she turns her body to face only Luke. If this were an actual *date*, then I'd be a little pissed, but since it's not I guess she can eye fuck him all she wants. I'm trying my hardest not to do the same thing from across this too small table.

Luke surprises me by reaching across the table to put his hand on top of mine. The shock causes me to forget

I don't ever let men touch me. The waitress's eyes land right on our joined hands and she turns just slightly to face me as well—probably sizing up her competition.

Luke orders us both Lemon Drop Martinis with Vulcano Vodka—his company's brand.

"What was that all about?" It didn't escape me during the weird waitress confrontation he took the liberty to take away my option to choose my own drink. I'm an independent woman, damn it.

You'd order another lame ass Sex on the Beach.

"You made it very clear you didn't like her staring with your not-so-subtle eye rolls. I figured I'd put her in her place. And as for the drinks, I'm used to most people letting me pick when it comes to that area."

I smile back at him teasingly. "Because you're the big bad CEO of Vulcano Vodka that means people automatically let you make decisions for them? What if I hate vodka?"

The waitress returns with less pep in her step, placing our martinis down in front of us and saying, "Let me know if I can get you anything else." Then she takes off before we can even thank her.

"So you've been researching me?" He studies me with quizzical eyes.

"Don't flatter yourself. All it took was reading the business card you handed me to know you're the CEO," I laugh.

"So you read it then threw it away because you couldn't possibly be seen with the vodka guy when you hate to drink?" he asks with a smirk before sipping on his own drink.

I laugh at his teasing and then finally sip my own drink, making a slight face because it's strong. How much vodka did they put in this martini?

Luke tosses his head back and lets out a deep laugh. "Too strong for you? I should be offended to see someone make that face when drinking our vodka."

"I think that's a drink that could put hair on your chest," I say with a blush, feeling terrible for dissing his work right in front of him. I wonder if he feels a sense of pride when he drinks his company's creation? I would.

"I could check for you," he says in a serious tone.

"Check what?"

"Your chest ..." His hazel eyes turn dark.

"Oh um, no, no thank you," I stumble over my words. Despite my absolute embarrassment, I feel heat between my legs at the thought of Luke's hands on my breasts. Would he like what he sees? *Wait, what?* Why do I even care if he likes what he sees? I've already decided anything between us is a bad idea; that's why I threw out his business card in the first place. And intimacy is so far from being my strong suit—I avoid it at all costs—and that would be hard to do with a man like him. Someone who seems so experienced. I'm sure the eye fuck he got from the waitress happens to him all the time. A man who's powerful and handsome—he must get his pick of any woman he wants. That definitely outnumbers the few men I've been with. I need to get the hell out of here.

This is a bad idea.

"You know I'm so sorry to do this to you, but I need to cut this short. I just remembered I have an early shift tomorrow morning," I say, collecting my jacket as I stand up from the table. Even from the few sips of the martini I feel a little off balance.

He doesn't miss a beat. Luke picks up his own jacket and throws a hundred dollar bill on the table to follow me as I hightail it out of the hotel. I step outside and the cold Chicago air slaps me hard across the face. Just the slap I need to wake me up from this ridiculous fantasy I was falling into.

Wake up Ariana! This isn't a life for you. This isn't what you need. You don't do men. You avoid men, you know what happens. Your focus is your medical career. Making your own way. Making a difference without a man.

"Are you okay?" I feel his hand on my lower back before the words even register in my mind. I jump back out of fear and shoot out some kind of lame ass apology over this situation. I grab my phone to find the Driver app for a ride home; I don't want to walk tonight, not with my head all over the place.

"Wait," he says as he tries grabbing my hand when he sees the app open on my phone. But I quickly move out of his grasp. "Let me give you a ride home. It's the least I can do. It's freezing out here and I don't want you waiting for someone to show up." As if on cue a black

Lincoln rolls up to the curb to meet us. A middle-aged man dressed like a chauffer gets out of the driver's seat and tips his head at Luke.

"Mr. Vulcano, Miss, lovely night," the driver says with a smile as he opens the back door looking at us both.

I hesitate for a moment, debating my next move, as Luke stands next to me patiently waiting, not saying a word to persuade me. I feel like he's trying to assure me that the decision is mine to make. I push the 'cancel ride' button on my app and climb into the back of the car alongside Luke, giving a small smile to the driver before giving him my address.

I'm sitting as far from Luke as I possibly can in the backseat but it's still not as far away as I'd like. My knuckles look white as my hands have a death grip on my phone.

"I'm sorry if I offended you with that comment about your chest," he says, turning his body to face me. I don't move but continue facing forward as a divider goes up between his driver and us. I'm afraid to look him in the eye, yet I'm in shock over the fact that he apologized. I would assume a man like him takes what he wants and asks no questions—especially with women. No need for apologies.

"Thank you. I'm sorry, I freaked out. I …" I mumble, "I'm just not used to this. I don't even know what I mean by *this* and now I feel extra stupid for saying that." I let out a breath and squeeze my phone even tighter.

"I really want to reach out and grab your chin. Turn your gorgeous face to look at mine," he says in a deep sexy voice that has my panties wet, "but I notice how you react when I touch you, so I won't. I'm not going to pretend it doesn't upset me that you flinch. Do I repulse you?"

My heart sinks as tears pool in my eyes. Damn it. He notices it's extremely hard for me to let men touch me. Most people don't notice. No one has ever said anything about it before except for Drake and Serena.

I turn to face him, giving him what he wants without him having to take matters into his own hands. Literally.

"It's not you … that makes me flinch. I just don't do well with being touched. It's 'my thing' I guess." I try a half-ass attempt to laugh it off like it's no big deal.

"I don't believe that it's 'your thing.' "

"Why not?" I whisper.

"You don't seem like the person who would naturally want to keep people out. I saw you at the hospital—with my sister and a few other patients. You care about them; your eyes say it all. You are a natural nurturer."

I'm stunned. No one has ever read me. I don't think I've ever even identified myself that way—a natural nurturer.

"Wait. With other patients? Were you researching me?" I smile, turning the tables around on him.

There's that laugh again. "I guess so. You intrigue me. Since that night at the bar, I've wanted to know more about you."

"I'm sure you want to know more about all kinds of women." I can't imagine a man like this being genuinely intrigued by a skittish doctor who avoids men when he could land a model who would sleep with him this instant.

"Not true. Most women I meet do not intrigue me. They put it all out there in every way—their emotions are easy to read, their thoughts are not deep, and their bodies," he pauses to scan my body with his eyes, "they leave nothing to the imagination. You seem to be the opposite."

It's like all the air is sucked out of this car and I'm gasping for a breath. I've definitely never been left breathless by anyone before. Someone check me for a pulse.

"Maybe you just aren't meeting the right kind of women. I can assure you, I'm not the only one who is like what you just described," I say as I try to blow off the compliment. I can think of many smart women with deep thoughts at the hospital that could prove his theory wrong.

The divider comes down between us as the driver lets us know we are outside of my apartment. I reach for the door handle at the same time the driver opens it, causing me to fall forward out of my seat. I almost hit the ground but a pair of strong arms wrap around me. My mind is completely devoid of any thoughts of being annoyed by his touch. Instead I'm grateful to feel ... *protected* by him.

Luke sets me up straight in my seat and takes his hands off me as rapidly as they reached out to grab me.

"I'm sorry," he apologizes again.

It bothers me I evoke so many apologies from him. He shouldn't have to feel sorry for saving me from literally falling on my face, but I'm at a loss for words; my mind is in utter shock.

You let a man touch you several times tonight and you didn't feel like throwing up.

"Don't be sorry," is all I manage to spit out before bolting from the car and into my apartment building. I climb the stairs two at a time to the fifth floor, out of breath but feeling alive. So alive, like adrenaline was just shot into my veins. I slam the door behind me and take a second to just stand there trying to collect my scattered thoughts.

"Hey, are you alright?" Serena asks as she comes out of her room. "You look like you've seen a ghost, and if there are any ghosts in this damn building, we are moving the hell out of here, now."

I laugh! It's much worse than a ghost—it's a man.

CHAPTER SIX

Luke
12 years old

Rushing home from school I'm excited to show my mom my spelling test. There's a red A+ on the top of the page and a yellow smiley face sticker looking back at me. I'm proud and I know mom will be too. We spent hours studying at the kitchen table the night before. She always makes me feel smart, even when I spell the words wrong.

I throw my Power Rangers backpack on the wood bench in the foyer, and I take off towards the kitchen.

"Don't go in there," my sister whispers at me from the couch in the living room. I didn't even notice her over my excitement. Lisa's face is red and tears are streaming down her face. Before I can ask what's the matter, I hear my dad shouting in the kitchen with mom.

Why is he home already? Dad is a government official for the city. A corrupt government official.

"You stupid fat bitch! Who the fuck is John? Tell me now, goddamn it!"

His slurred words prove he's drunk in the middle of the day. I spot three empty Budweiser bottles on the table next to his recliner—probably his lunch.

"John? I don't know anyone named John. Bill, what are you talking about?" Mom's voice is pleading. Dad is always asking her about random guy names—and mom always lets him know she has no clue what he's talking about. He thinks she's a cheater. What a fucking bastard. That's one word I know how to spell clearly—b-a-s-t-a-r-d. And that's exactly what my dad is.

Eric quickly throws the door open and tosses his backpack into the room. His smile drops from his round face when he sees Lisa and me huddled together. He knows the drill.

Screaming. Fighting. Hurtful words. Hitting. Hiding.

But tonight is different. Looking even more pissed than he was originally, dad stumbles into the living room and notices us kids

"The fuck you runts looking at?" He slurs at us before downing the beer in his bottle.

"Surprise asshole, we're your kids, and as much as you want to get rid of us, we come back every day. We have to live here," I shout. Lisa cries harder, letting out a sob. Eric is tucked behind me out of sight. Mom hasn't come out of the kitchen yet, so we are on our own against him.

"You think you're funny you little smartass?" He reaches out for me but completely misses his target and ends up grabbing Lisa by the shirt collar. He pulls the wrong kid off the couch and starts choking her. He never hurts Lisa—this is not good.

He's lifting her off the ground with his hands tightly around her neck.

"Stop! Stop you asshole!" I scream as I push into my dad from behind with enough force that he loses his grasp on Lisa and she breaks free, running out of the room, not before grabbing Eric and pulling him out of the way.

It's me and him now.

Dad reaches for one of the beer bottles, and before he can grab it, I get low to the ground and run after him. I grab on to his legs and tackle him to the ground. With him being this drunk, I can overpower him—that's rare.

I've knocked the wind out of his lungs with our fall and take the opportunity to start pounding my fists into his smug face, over and over.

A beer bottle is for pussies; I fight with fists. He should know—he taught me.

"That's enough!" my mom shrieks, louder than I've ever heard before. I turn towards her noticing see she has a huge cut down her cheek she's trying to hide with a washcloth soaked in blood. My dad must have cut her with a knife. He's never done anything like this before to mom. He leaves bruises; never cuts. My poor mom— this one looks deep. "Go to your room, now!"

I never did get to tell mom about my spelling test that night. It just seems so stupid now. I rip it up into pieces and toss it in the trash on the way to check on my brother and sister.

F-u-c-k t-h-i-s.

CHAPTER SEVEN

It's a slow morning in the hospital, which is always a bit eerie. The calm before the storm, maybe? I switched shifts with another resident. I'm here during the day, instead of pulling the vampire night shift. After checking in on my assigned patients I head to the computer station at the whiff of bagels. That's one good thing about the morning shift—they bring food.

"Ariana, are you going to tell us about that Mystery Man?" Katie asks, passing me the garden vegetable cream cheese for my plain bagel.

"Mystery Man! Do tell. I don't think Ariana has told us anything about guys in the past," Tara, a fellow resident, says between sipping her black coffee—eyes bright and ready for any gossip. Women are vultures when it comes to gossip.

I try to play it off like it's no big deal, feeling a sense of protection when it comes to Luke.

"There's no Mystery Man. Don't get your panties in a bunch, ladies. He was just here to ask me some follow-up questions about his sister who was here before."

Tara seems to accept my lame ass answer but Katie will not let it go.

"Bullshit! I saw the way you two were huddled close together; you couldn't keep your eyes off each other. That was a pretty intense follow-up. What kind of care did you give his sister? I'll be happy to help her next time if it will get him to look at me like that," Katie says with a laugh.

"What did he look like?" Tara asks, turning to face Katie, blocking me out, clearly not wanting me to add anything more to this juicy conversation.

"Girl! He was handsome. He looked like a business man in a very expensive suit … that he wore well," she says with a wink, "but when he came up here to ask for Ariana, his eyes set off this dark, smoldering look. Very intense." She pretends to fan herself with her hand.

"Okay this is a little over the top. Yes, he's good looking, but you don't need to drool over him," I chime in.

Both women look at me and burst out giggling. *Are you kidding me?* We are professionals here. We save lives. Why are we gossiping and giggling? And why before breakfast?

"You *like* him!" Tara exclaims.

"What? No I don't!"

I shove my bagel into my mouth.

"Oh yes you do. That was totally a 'don't drool over him because he's my man' type of comment. You can keep your claws down. We were just kidding," Tara jokes.

Is she right? Am I jealous of the other women drooling over him? It did kind of piss me off, just like when the waitress was doing it at the bar. Jealousy. It's not an emotion I feel often—never when it comes to men.

Before I can add anything to quiet down these two smartasses, a paramedic flies around the corner with a man bleeding out on his stretcher.

"Drive-by shooting," he says, "three more guys are on their way in now. All shot multiple times."

And just like that—the storm hits.

The drive-by shooting victims ended up being a whirlwind experience. After the four men were brought in, my heart sunk when a small boy was also admitted. He was shot by accident, in a home riddled with bullets in a dangerous part of town. It makes me sick. I can't even watch the news anymore—it's death, destruction, and danger every minute.

I stumble out of the hospital heading towards the subway to get home. My bed is calling for me. I can't wait to slip under the covers, let my head hit the pillow, and crash for hours upon hours. I don't have to work tomorrow. I am going to sleep until my body says it's time to get up.

It takes my phone vibrating in my hand to get my head out of the clouds, dreaming about my bed. I've got a text message from an unknown number.

You left your jacket in my car. I would love to return it. —L

Damn it, Ariana! I didn't notice when I ran from his car like it was on fire that I left behind my jacket.

Thank you! You can send it to my apartment or the hospital. :)

Instantly he replies …

I would love to return it in person. —L

Do I even really need that jacket? I have plenty of jackets. Old Navy always puts them on sale.

You can keep it. I'll get myself another one.

I should know by now my attempt at a blowoff was not going to be the end of this conversation.

You really don't want to see me? I thought we had a nice time. —L

I don't know what to say next. I want to keep him at a distance, but I equally don't want to be an asshat to him.

Caterina Passarelli

Okay fine. I'm going home to sleep the day away after a rough shift. What about tomorrow?

Maybe I can wake up with some ridiculously nasty cold tomorrow that I can use to avoid seeing him. I mean he wouldn't argue with that? I can only hope the sickness gods would do me a favor and bless me with the flu.

You got a flu shot you dumbass!

Ugh, there goes that wish.

Sorry to hear you had a rough shift. Tomorrow it is. I'd like to take you to dinner. 6p? I'll meet you at your place. —L

And just like that, Luke is back in my life. With his brooding, masculine, sexy self making all the decisions again. Double ugh.

⇒++⇐

"Wake up sister!" Serena pokes her head into my bedroom shouting. Didn't she get the memo that I wanted to sleep for a good 12 hours?

"What the hell do you want?" I growl at her, not even bothering to open my eyes.

Serena flops down on my bed causing me to stir.

"I need you to come out with me tonight."

"Are you crazy? I don't even go out with you on nights when I'm well-rested, I sure as hell am not getting out of this bed."

50

"Please, pretty pretty pretty please," she begs, bouncing up and down on my bed, forcing me to open my eyes. She doesn't normally beg. Serena has a long list of friends she can call at any moment to hang out with her. She's the kind of girl people want to be spotted with on the streets of Chicago.

"You're begging? What's the deal? Where do you want to go?" I glare at her, still upset she woke me up from my coma.

"I'm going to a tarot card reading and I don't want to go alone. Will you please come with me? I'll pay for you to get a reading too."

"Ha! Hell to the no," I say, flipping over and pulling my comforter up past my head. Serena reaches for my comforter and gets it in a death grip before pulling it down, leaving me blanketless and freezing. "Give that back!"

"Nope. You will get your comforter back *after* the reading," she says, strutting out of my room with my blanket trailing behind her.

She is clearly out of her damn mind. Maybe I should be there for this.

"Gemini Goddess," the red sign above the door reads. It's a small building in a hipster part of town, tucked away in an alley of cobblestones. As soon as I open the door a strong smell of incense tickles my nose. It also takes a moment for my eyes to adjust to the dim lighting. My senses are in despair right about now.

I didn't tell Serena this, but this whole 'tarot cards / seeing the future thing' kind of creeps me out. It's not that I don't believe, which is what Serena thought her other friends would say; I'm afraid someone will read me correctly. No one needs to know what I've pushed down years and years ago. I do not want to burden this baggage on anyone else.

An attractive petite woman strolls up to us with her hair in long blonde braid. She's wearing a topaz-stoned headband and long flowing green dress. She's striking, and I can't take my eyes off her.

"Hello," this fairy-like woman says in a surprisingly strong voice, "you must be Serena?"

"Yes," Serena whispers at her. I think she's equally nervous about this experience, something we have both never done before.

"I'm Renee. Is this your first reading?" the fairy woman asks, eyeing us both intensely. She's reading us like books already. Get me the hell out of here.

"Yes," we both squeak out. She smiles a warm smile and then turns to walk through sheer drapery into a small back room. We both look at each other, passing off an 'it's now or never' face, and follow the fairy.

"Please have a seat," Renee says to Serena, pointing to a chair at a small table directly across from where she is now sitting. "You can sit there and watch until your turn," she says to me, pointing to another chair against the wall.

The room is dimly lit, like the entire store, and on her round table sit glistening crystals of all shapes, sizes, and colors. The table is draped in a gold tablecloth, and on the opposite wall from where I'm sitting I see an altar of candles.

Without asking us any questions, the woman shuffles a deck of gold tarot cards. Renee looks slightly away from Serena as if there were a figure just off to the right of her head. The psychic concentrates hard until she stops shuffling, looking directly at Serena before laying down three cards face up. I can't see the cards from where I'm sitting but my friend looks as white as a ghost; clearly she doesn't like what she sees.

Renee points to a card that I cannot see before saying, "You are lost when it comes to the direction of your life."

This can't be right. Serena is the most confident person I know. She told me she knew she wanted to go into business since elementary school when she started selling candy to kids at recess. I lean forward in my chair, ready to get up, because Serena will surely call this woman out on her lies.

Instead, I'm shocked.

Serena nods her head and replies, "Yes."

What?

The psychic shuffles the cards and flips over three more. "You have many strengths and it's hard for you to pick which one will make you the most successful. Being a powerful leader is what you want more than anything, but it upsets you that you feel this way. You think that is not noble or humble," the woman continues while Serena keeps nodding her head yes.

Flip, flip, flip. More cards are laid out on the table.

"Don't worry. You will find a charitable calling in business that will do good for others and leave you high-paid—as well as challenge your strengths in leadership."

Serena's shoulders relax and the tension floats away from her body. She smiles from ear to ear.

"Thank you."

The tarot card reader continues the reading for a good 45 minutes. They talk about her relationships with men (she's having plenty of fun but *the one* hasn't shown up her life yet), health (no one in her inner circle will die within the next 10 years), and her relationship with her parents (her mom will continue to nag her for the rest of her life but only out of love).

"Time is up," Renee says and looks away from the table towards me. "It's your turn, young lady."

I don't know if I'm imagining it, but it's as if her face takes on a questioning look as her head tilts to the side. My stomach drops. I feel like I'm going down the first loop on a roller coaster—and my gut instinct says *don't do this*.

"You know what, that's okay. I came here to support my friend. I didn't sign up for this for myself," I say, bolting from my chair and moving towards the drapery to leave the shop.

"Wait! You can't leave here without your own reading," Serena says, looking at me like I'm insane. "I made you come all this way. Please, it's my treat."

"I'm sorry. I just can't."

The two women look at each other and then back at me before realizing I'm serious. I will not be having my cards read. Over my hopefully not dead body.

We all walk out of the room. Serena pays Renee for her reading, and we head towards the front door.

I'm caught behind Serena but in front of Renee. She grabs my arm gently and whispers into my ear, "Don't continue to live your life with a guarded heart. What happened to you is not your fault, and you do not need to continue shutting people out. Let him in. He faces battles too, deep and grave, but you need each other."

Chills run down my spine listening to her hushed message. I walk out the door without even making eye contact with Renee and bump right into Serena's back.

"Hey! You alright?" my friend asks with concerned eyes.

I nod 'yes' without saying a word. Serena looks like she's on cloud nine after hearing all this great news with a big smile on her face, having no idea what happened after with me. But I can't tell her; that would mean answering questions that I don't want to talk about.

How did Renee know all that stuff?

Goose bumps break out across my arms. This is all too much. I didn't want a reading; why did she do that to me?

"You sure you're okay? You look sick," Serena says, waving her arm in the air to catch the attention of a taxi driver. I give her a questioning look; we normally walk most places or take the subway or a bus. "Girl, I want to get you home as soon as possible. I'm sorry I made you get out of bed for this. I had no idea you didn't want to have your own reading. I'm kind of bummed. I bet yours would have been really cool to hear about all your future success."

If she only knew.

"That's okay. I was happy to go with you," I say, getting into the back of a yellow cab.

The entire ride home Serena is talking and I must be replying, but my mind is replaying what Renee, the magical fairy, said over and over.

Don't continue to live with a guarded heart.

What the hell does she know? Nothing good comes from relationships. My heart needs to be guarded for my own protection. The one time it wasn't, look what happened.

What happened to you is not your fault.

Then whose fault is it?

You do not need to continue shutting people out.

I only let the few people I trust in—picking and choosing what information they'll receive. No one knows the entire story, and I'm going to keep it that way.

Let him in, he faces battles too, deep and grave, but you need each other.

I highly doubt she's talking about Drake. So then is this about Luke? I barely even know the guy. Why the hell is he showing up in my reading?

My heartstrings pull—what kind of battles is he carrying around with him? Something in me needs to know. I have an immediate urge to take care of him, to protect him from whatever deep and grave stuff she's talking about.

Could this explain his scars?

I need to go back to bed—my head isn't thinking clearly. I've never felt the need to protect someone else—I barely do an okay job protecting myself. And what would a man like Luke need me for anyway? I'm sure he can do a fine job of protecting himself. I saw the way he cared for his sister, the love in his eyes when he talked to her, and the concern for other people when he knew that cops weren't called yet.

That's a man who does the protecting, not a man who needs to be protected.

What the hell is going on with me? Why do I care about any of this stuff? I don't even believe in psychics; this is all hocus pocus bullshit.

CHAPTER EIGHT

Music is blasting as I dance around my bathroom to get ready for this dinner Luke is taking me to. I wanted to blow it off, but I can't get what Renee said out of my head—I need to see him at least one more time to get my jacket and get the hell out of this mess. I'll explain to him that we can't keep seeing each other because I have to focus on my career, which someone running a company should understand.

There's a pause in the music and my phone beeps, letting me know I've got a new email.

Email from: Gina Potter
   Subject: This year's benefit
   Hey Ariana,

How are you doing? Hope you're fabulous! I wanted to send you this year's flyer for the "Stand Up Against Abuse" charity benefit. Does it look okay? It will be going out in two days, so if you see any changes, let me know. We can count you in for attendance, right? This year we've added in a silent auction, so if you know any wealthy people who want to be donors, invite them. ;)

See you soon!

xoxo

G

I shoot Gina a quick email back, letting her know the flyer looks incredible and that, of course, I'll be at the event. I wouldn't miss it. I've been donating my time and what little extra money I have to the Stand Up Against Abuse campaign for the last eight years. Their main focus is helping women who are victims of domestic abuse or sexual assault. We go to soup kitchens, collect and deliver food, raise money for medical treatment, and offer anonymous counseling. Many of these women are mothers, and the organization does what it can to make sure their kids are taken care of as well. This charity means the world to me.

My phone vibrates again and I glance down at the screen to see Luke's name.

5 minutes away

I give myself a quick look over in the mirror, making sure my long sleeve black dress is in place. I spritz some hairspray into my light brown hair, which is down in long curls tonight—a change from my typical messy bun. A quick swipe of peach lipgloss and I hear my doorbell ring.

He came to the door. How sweet!

I bolt from my room, but I'm not quick enough as I round the corner where I see Serena making small talk with Luke. When I walk towards them, they both look up and Luke smiles at me. I watch his gaze travel the length of my body, stopping on my bare legs.

"You look marvelous," Serena says as I blush while quickly pulling Luke out the door. "You two have fun. Don't do anything I wouldn't do. Wear a condom!"

"She seems … fun," Luke laughs once we've made our way down the stairs and into the back of a stretch black limo.

Even though there's plenty of room to spread out, we are both sitting next to each other, extremely close. Luke reaches across my body and grabs two glasses of champagne waiting on ice for us.

He really knows how to take a woman out on a date. Is this what all of his dates are like?

"You look stunning," he says, interrupting my anxious thoughts with a champagne flute.

"Thank you. You look very handsome yourself," I say, drinking in the view of him in a dark blue suit. I have yet to see this man in anything but a suit. Does he even own a pair of jeans? He smirks, clearly seeing me check him out before taking a sip from his drink.

I down mine a little too quickly; I'm a big mess of nerves. I feel my face flushing, a sign I'm drinking too fast. I would bet any money underneath all this brown hair my ears are shining bright red. That happens every time I drink too much. I definitely get that trait from my dad.

"You seem nervous," he says, taking my empty glass to refill it. "Tell me something about yourself to relax a little."

Talking about myself won't make me relax, but I decide to go along with this. "Like what?"

"Anything—I'm all ears."

"I'm in my last year of my residency at the hospital. Just a few more months and it will be over," I say, taking the refilled glass from him but giving myself a mental reminder to only take small sips or this is going to be a long night.

"You seem to shine in the hospital. You took great care of my sister."

"Oh my gosh, your sister!" I turn my body to face him, grabbing on to his arm desperately needing to hear his answer. "I've been meaning to ask you: how's she doing? Did you end up contacting the police?"

"She did contact the police and the asshole is now behind bars." He pauses for a moment too long before saying, "You did the right thing by encouraging her."

"It's my job. And you encouraged her too. Much more than I did."

"You seemed a little close to the case. Have you seen this many times?"

My hands shake as I bring up the glass of champagne and take a drink. If he only knew how close.

"You could say that," is all I can manage to squeak out. "Okay, now tell me something about you. Do you have any more siblings?"

"Oh yeah, a crazy younger brother, Eric," he says with a proud smile that lights up his entire face. "He's going to school to be a lawyer."

"That's incredible. How much more schooling does he have left?"

"He's in his last year as well." Am I the same age as his *younger* brother? I figured Luke was older than me based on his success alone—probably mid-30s—but I wasn't sure until now.

"How did you get started in the alcohol industry?" Since our drinks at the hotel, I will admit to doing a quick online search on his life. I came up pretty empty. Much of his life before starting his vodka company is blank; the Internet seems to be in agreement that he's a Man of Mystery, just as the nurses at the hospital said.

I did, however, see several paparazzi photos of him with women at parties—one in particular kept showing up, a breathtaking blonde. I'm going to push that finding aside because I'm the one here on this date.

"I used to work in bars when I was young. Bar back, stock boy, bartender, bouncer, until I became a manager. All the ins and outs fascinated me. I worked my way up the ladder until I was able to open my own high-end club. That's where my current business partner approached me about creating our own vodka. He was pretty into the idea, and I'm pretty unwavering if I decide to commit myself to something," he says as he locks eyes with me—is that a look of warning? "My partner, Wayne, needed me for the money and my willingness to bust ass, but I became much more involved. I sold my club and became the majority owner of Vulcano Vodka a few years ago."

And one thing my Internet search can confirm, Vulcano Vodka is highly successful. Ambition, goal-oriented, and extremely handsome—how is this guy not already with someone?

"I'm sure you saw some wild things working in a bar. How old were you when you started?" I ask, curious about all that he's gone through to get himself to the man he is today.

Luke runs his hand through his dark hair thinking about his answer. "I don't know … maybe 14 or 15 when I got my first job?"

That's so young. What kind of parents let their 14-year-old son work in a bar?

"You can say I didn't have the typical upbringing," he says. He turns away from me to face the divider now; I guess we're clearly done with this topic. From this angle the lights of the night sky light up his face, revealing the faint scar I noticed at the hospital on his temple.

He has battles too.

There's a loud beep and the divider comes down. "We are here, sir."

I just realized I never asked where we were going. The driver opens the door for Luke, and then Luke comes around to open the door for me. He extends his hand and looks at me, daring me to touch him.

Can I do this?

"You don't have to if you don't want to," he says in a gentle voice, yet his hand remains there for me to take.

"I'm just not ready," I say. I feel terrible as he pulls his hand away as if it's not a big deal, but I know it is. No man wants to feel like he's just been rejected—especially from physical touch. Maybe this will be the straw that gets him to lose interest in me? I can only hope.

Climbing out of the limo by myself, I crane my head up to take in the sight of the Willis Tower. I've been inside before, but I don't tell him. I smile as we walk towards the doors. A man at the front greets us with, "Good evening Mr. Vulcano, miss."

He nods at us both as he opens the door, escorting us inside where we are greeted by a woman.

"Good evening, it's a pleasure to have you here tonight," she says. Her Willis Tower nametag reads *Pamela*. She presses the button to the first elevator and we wait just a minute for it to arrive. Once the elevator door opens, Pamela extends her arm to indicate we should get inside, and then she follows behind us. We are up the first elevator in what feels like seconds to then get into the second elevator that takes us up the last few flights. My ears pop from the pressure change.

We're at the 103rd floor. It's not until we step out of the elevator that it hits me—we are the only people here. The last time I came to the Willis Tower it was still named the Sears Tower and I was on a ninth grade field trip. The place was jam packed with tourists but I didn't care. I was so grateful to be away from my parents.

This time, other than the few staff members, Luke and I are the only people in the building. I look around the 103rd floor and see a dinner table in the center of the room. Luke starts walking towards it, and I follow behind him in awe. I've been on very few dates, and not a single one of them as nice as this.

On the table sit vanilla-scented candles and a bouquet of hot pink roses. Luke pulls out my chair and we take our seats.

"You sure know how to set the bar high on a first date," I say, taking a sip from the much-needed water glass in front of me. Hydration, I've needed you after the champagne on the limo ride over.

"Are you saying that means there'll be future dates?"

Am I saying that?

"Let's play it cool, Luke. I don't even know how I feel about you yet."

He smiles at my smartass answer just as a waiter approaches us carrying yet another bottle of champagne. I don't think I've had this much to drink in such a long time—not even that night out with the fraternity boys.

"Good evening Luke and Ariana, it's a pleasure to have you here," our waiter says as he pours our drinks. "Your food will be ready shortly."

He turns to leave and Luke lets me know he took the liberty to order for us. He seems to do that often. I'm not sure if it's an alpha male trait or that he's trying to be considerate. I'll figure him out.

"I've got an idea," I say, feeling a little too brave after a few too many sips of bubbly. "Let's ask each other questions and we have to give the *honest* truth. No 'first date let's pretend we are cooler than we actually are' bullshit. No facades. Okay?"

A huge smirk breaks out across Luke's ridiculously handsome face. "Game on. Ladies first."

When I threw the idea out for this game I didn't have any questions in mind. That was a mistake. I take my time looking around the room and out at the picturesque view, while I stall and think.

"What are three things on your bucket list?"

That's a lame question, but it's all I can think of in this moment. The pressure is on.

Luke pauses for a brief moment while studying me, giving away no sign of emotions on his face. "I don't have a bucket list."

"That's it? 'I don't have a bucket list' is the lamest answer, ever. That's not how you play the game," I say, pouting at the fact he's already giving me a hard time on this. "If you aren't going to take this seriously, then we don't need to keep playing."

I don't know why I'm getting so defensive over a silly game of question and answer, but his non-response pisses me off.

"I don't have a bucket list because I do the things in my life that are important to me right when I think of them." He drinks from his water now. "Life is too fucking short to wait around with ideas of 'I'd really like to do this' left in your mind. There's no guarantee you'll get another day, another moment."

Well, damn. Now look who made a joke of herself.

"Okay, I accept your answer. Your *good* answer." I smile back at him with a blush and say, "It's your turn."

The waiter shows up at just the right time to bring our food. He places a plate of pan-seared scallops with a bacon cream sauce in front of me. This is definitely not something I'd order for myself—I stick to the cheap basics—but my first bite confirms it's absolutely delicious. In this moment I appreciate Luke ordering for me—showing me things outside my comfort zone.

We enjoy our meals in a few moments of silence and then just as I'm bringing a bite of scallops to my mouth, Luke asks, "What's your biggest turn on? Sexually."

I fumble and the bite drops off my fork and back onto my crisp white plate. "I, uh, I don't know."

"It looks like we aren't very good at this game. How can you not know what your biggest sexual turn on is? Maybe you have too many to pick just one? You can say a couple." He teases me with a deep laugh.

Just be honest with him. You made the rules of the game.

"I wish that were the case," I say, putting my fork down and looking up at him. "No, if we are going to be honest, I don't have the best track record of stellar sexual experiences. None to be exact."

It feels like an eternity until Luke finally speaks again. "Are you a virgin?"

"Oh no, that's not what I meant. I've had sex before, yes," I confess, laughing and feeling like a loser. "I just meant no experience was that great."

"That's an absolute shame. A beautiful, kindhearted, smart woman like you deserves to be treated like a goddess in the bedroom … in all areas of life."

I laugh at this ridiculous notion that I'm a 'goddess,' but Luke doesn't join in on the joke. "Oh, you're serious?" My laughing slowly comes to a stop. "I don't think anyone has ever referred to me as a 'goddess' before."

"Maybe you should think of yourself that way," he says as he looks at me with true concern; I break our eye contact because it's all too much. Looking down at my plate, I pick up my fork to continue eating this delicious meal.

"Okay, enough with this question. My turn. How would you describe your perfect day? I know you said you go out and do everything you want, but there's got to be a day that sounds amazing to you," I say, just after the waiter clears our plates and promises to be back with dessert.

"My perfect day … no one has ever asked me that before." Luke takes a moment to think of his answer and then continues, "I'd do many of the things I do right now. I'd wake up in my penthouse overlooking the Chicago skyline, just like I do now. I'd eat the healthy breakfast my private chef prepared, and then hit the gym in my apartment building. After I'd head to work for the majority of the day—which can be stressful and overwhelming at times but I love it. In the evening, I'd spend it with friends or my siblings. Taking them out to dinner, a show, museum or we can catch a private jet and leave Chicago."

His day sounds wonderful, but very different from mine. And there's one thing he seems to have left out.

"There doesn't seem to be any mention of a woman by your side in this perfect day."

"I'm going to be honest with you. I don't think about sharing my life with a woman. Dates, companions for business events, a fuck, yes. But anything more than that, never."

I should be comforted to hear this. I've never once seen myself with someone long-term—or even married—either. I don't know if my perfect day would include a man by my side. But why does it make my stomach feel slightly sick at the thought of him being alone … specifically … without me?

"Well, that's very interesting, because I don't see sharing my life with a man either. Which makes me wonder, why are we here together right now? Aren't we just wasting time?" I ask with a cold edge to my voice.

Luke stares at me so intently I feel like he's peering into my soul. Then says, "I don't think we are wasting time. Maybe we are just figuring out that we might not want what we believe we always have. Or shit, if we don't want to end up without anyone that doesn't mean we have to be lonely right now."

Before I can ask more questions, the waiter brings two pieces of tiramisu to our table. I drop the subject and dig into my cake.

Once we finish eating, we walk over to the Sky Deck hanging off the Willis Tower. This is a new feature since the last time I was here. Glass box ledges extend about four feet from the building. Luke walks out onto the glass floor and looks back at me with a wink, "Are you afraid of heights?"

"Shouldn't you ask someone that before you set up a date like this?" I laugh and join him in the glass box. "No, I am not afraid of heights, but it's still slightly unnerving to do something you've never done before."

"Doing things you've never done will help you grow as a person."

It's such a simple statement, like it could be on a Pinterest quote somewhere, yet his words mean a great deal to me in this moment. Everything about knowing him seems like I'm experiencing something new.

I look out towards the dark night shining bright with twinkles of lights from the buildings in the city. It's truly a breathtaking view. I've never seen anything like this. I've never taken the time to stop to see anything like this either—cooped up in the hospital taking as many shifts as I can get—there's not much time for fun or views.

"The view is striking," he says, breaking our silence, reading my mind. I turn to face him to agree and notice he's not looking at the view in front of us; instead his eyes are on me. "Yes, I mean you. I'm going to be bold here and try one more time. If it's okay, I'd like to kiss you. Normally I'm not a man who asks, but I don't want to take any part of you that you are not comfortable giving … yet."

He wants to treat you like a goddess.

And with that it feels like a piece of my heart melts into a big gooey pile of mush. Damn it. My hands are sweating and my breathing is so quick—I bet he's regretting his question, considering my awkward state.

Do you want to live the rest of your life shutting people out? No. Do you want to be lonely right now? No. Do you want to continue to do the same things you've always done? No. That's not how you grow. You can do this, Ariana. Try. He has battles too.

Turning my body to face his, I suddenly feel small as I look up to him. Surprising us both, I reach my shaking hand out and place it on his chest, right over his heart. I feel it beating beneath his black suit—a suit I have a sudden desire to rip from his god-like body. I lick my lips, "You can kiss me."

I don't have to give permission twice; he gently cups my face and slowly brings his luscious mouth to mine. Luke's being very sweet and patient with me. My body reacts to his kisses and I surprise myself, taking matters into my own hands. Reaching up, I grab onto his shoulders and slam our mouths together with more intensity. He pulls back for a split second, to look me in the eyes, as if to double check I'm sure about all of this. He sees my desire and then returns to devouring my mouth. Luke sucks on my bottom lip and my body gives in. I moan, a reaction I've never given a man before.

We hear the sound of someone clearing her throat, and we both push apart from each other as if we were high schoolers caught making out. We look towards the woman who sent us up the elevator, Pamela, who equally looks embarrassed for catching us.

"I'm sorry, but we are closing for the evening now, Mr. Vulcano," Pamela says in a sweet voice.

Luke slips his hand into mine and tells her we'll be right down.

"Thank you for this gift," Luke says as he brings my hand to his lips to place a kiss on top of it. The fact that Luke sees me allowing him to touch me as a gift makes my heart swell.

Once down the two elevators we thank Pamela for being a gracious host as we leave the Willis Tower. This is a visit I'll never forget.

CHAPTER NINE

Tonight is the night of the Stand Up Against Abuse charity benefit and I'm already dragging ass. I've been at the hospital for ten hours—just two more to go! My bed is calling my name, but it will have to be for just a quick nap—I promised Gina I would help set up the banquet hall at the Grand Plaza Hotel before the event kicks off. Each year the event gets bigger and bigger, which is amazing but a lot of hard work.

Stand Up Against Abuse is entirely run by volunteers—myself included. I found out about the organization during my first year of college and immediately joined—I felt I had a duty to the cause.

Quickly pulling my head out of the clouds, a screaming man frantically carries a pregnant woman into the emergency room. "Help us! Somebody help us. My wife." He looks toward the woman in his arms who is extremely pale. "She's pregnant and she's bleeding ... a lot!"

Instincts kick in and the team gathers around to care for this woman. It's moments like these where I'm proud to be a physician; I know we have one of the best medical teams in the country working here. All hands on deck.

I end up staying at the hospital an extra hour; I couldn't leave the pregnant woman behind. She was bleeding a lot, like her husband said. We ended up delivering her daughter, Eloise, by emergency C-section. Watching Drake and his team place baby Eloise into her mother's arms almost brought me to tears. Almost—it takes a lot for me to show emotion in the hospital setting—but on the inside I felt the joy. I wish more than anything that my mom and I had a good relationship, but we don't. We barely have a relationship at all. Same goes for my dad. Not since ... anyway.

"It's been real, it's been nice, it's been real nice, but I've got to go, ladies and gentlemen," I say, grabbing my jacket out of the locker room and waving goodbye to this wild group of people I'm lucky to call coworkers.

Once in my apartment I don't even make it to my bed—I crash on the couch. My feet couldn't carry me those extra steps. Not today.

It's not until I feel Serena shaking me to 'Wake up! Wake up!' that I realize I've been asleep way too long. I check my phone's clock and bolt off the couch and jump into the shower like a crazy person. I've got to hustle my ass or I'm going to be late—and Gina will kill me.

I shower quicker than I ever have and grab my dress, shoes, and backpack with some makeup—I'm going to get ready in one of the hotel rooms with Gina after we set up. I wave goodbye to Serena who lets me know she already alerted the Driver app to come pick me up.

"You are the absolute best! Thank you. I'll see you tonight?" I ask her with one foot in the door, the other out.

"Of course! See you then. Call me if you need anything."

And just like that, I'm out the door and getting into a BMW driven by Dante from California who takes me to the Grand Plaza Hotel.

⟞⟝

With strands of flicker lights hanging from the walls, gold and red martini glasses being passed around by waiters, red tablecloths, and gold vases with roses—this place is breathtaking. If I wasn't down here running around to set it all up with Gina and the other volunteers, I would never know all the work that went into it. It's like a fairy tale party.

I match the room's decorations in a long red evening gown that's very slimming and backless. I love this gown and Serena who forced me to buy it. Sometimes I'm so indecisive when it comes to this stuff—I wear scrubs all day long and then switch into workout clothes. That's pretty much it. But I do admit, I love doing girly things too.

Speaking of Serena, I see my friend walking towards me with Gina. Serena's wearing an emerald green gown with lace sleeves. I need to borrow that when she's done with it. Gina looks remarkable in her little black dress paired with some purple pumps. I see a few guys turn their necks to get a glimpse of my friends. That's right boys, these are rock star women.

"This place looks da bomb! You girls did a fantastic job. Can I hire you out as party planners?" Serena eyes us both.

"Count me down for no on that," I say with a laugh, knowing I'd be no help in planning any parties. "The decorations are 100-percent Gina's doing. She gets all the credit."

Gina smiles at us and says, "You guys, stop. You're going to make me blush." She looks around the room and I see pride in her eyes. This event raises a ton of money each year, and Gina works hard to make sure it helps as many people who have suffered domestic or sexual abuse as she can. "I have to go look for our keynote speaker—he's the biggest donor we've ever had. Also, check him out when he's on stage; he's *very* easy on the eyes. I'll see you girls later, have fun!"

And just like that she takes off to do more work.

"Martini?" asks a gorgeous waitress, who lowers her tray so Serena and I can grab drinks. Taking a sip, I immediately know this vodka. "Is this Vulcano Vodka?"

"Yes, all of the alcohol tonight is from Vulcano Vodka," the blonde hair, blue-eyed waitress says.

"Are you a Vulcano girl?" Serena asks the woman.

"A ... what?" I ask in utter confusion. *What the hell is a Vulcano girl? Sounds like something you'd see in a porn.*

"Yes, I'm a Vulcano girl," the waitress says with a smile on her face and a hand on her hip. It's then I really take in her appearance and all of the other waitresses in the room. They're all tall with long blonde hair wearing tight black dresses and black high heels. And they look the exact opposite of me with my long light brown hair and gray eyes. They look like they should be models, not waitresses.

Maybe they are also models?

That I don't know. What I do know is they work for Luke. How often does he see these Vulcano girls?

Okay nerves, calm the fuck down. I'm going to need to finish this drink, stat. I sip the martini as I head over to the silent auction section of the room. I need to step away from the hot waitress before my mind thinks the worst.

Many of Chicago's most talented artists have donated their artwork for this event. I scan my eyes down the row of paintings, sculptures, and ceramics. I place my bid on a few pieces that speak to me. I can't bid a lot. I'm sure I won't win anything, but I have to try. The money is going to a good cause anyway.

"There are way too many hot guys in this room," Serena squeals into my ear as she joins me in the bidding section. She turns my body towards the crowd of people now filling up the room; I scan my eyes around and confirm she's right. I know she'll stake her claim soon enough. But no one catches my attention like the man who took me on a private date at the Willis Tower. And his stupid 'girls' are also filling up this room of hot people.

I haven't heard from Luke since our date and, to be honest, it makes me a little bummed. I thought we had a good time, but it's been a week and a half. Maybe that's a normal time to wait before calling someone again? I'm not familiar with dating, and I sure as hell am not going to ask Serena because she'll make a huge deal about it. I'm also not going to be the one to reach out to him first. If he didn't have a good time, I'm not going to make myself look like an idiot by reminding him I still exist.

"Let's take our seats. It looks like Gina is about to get on stage," I say, pulling Serena away from a few guys staring at her.

"You are no fun!" she protests but gives the guys a little wave and follows me to our seats, which are a few rows back, center to the stage.

"Good evening ladies and gentlemen. My name is Gina Potter, and on behalf of the Stand Up Against Abuse organization I'd like to thank you for spending your Saturday evening with us. According to the latest statistics, one in four women aged 18 and older in the United States have been the victim of severe physical violence by an intimate partner in their lifetime. Like many of the people our charity helps, I too am a victim of abuse."

It makes me heart swell with pride to hear Gina share her story. She's incredibly brave; it's something I could never do. Open my wounds up like this in front of anyone, let alone so many people.

"But like many of the people in this room, I don't use the word victim anymore. I'm a survivor. This charity means the world to me and I know it means the same to those we help. When I needed support, there was a helping hand reaching out, but for many they have no one—and that's where we try to come in.

"Tonight we are having our first silent auction." Gina points towards the artwork and announces, "Please take a look at all of the pieces of art that so many talented Chicago artists have donated. Your donations will be going towards providing food, shelter, health care and basic needs to many abuse victims and their families. As well as for helping to keep our advocates highly trained in providing lifesaving tools and immediate support to those who need us.

"And now, without further ado, I'd like to introduce our highest donor ... *yet.* I asked if he'd share a few words about why this charity means so much to him as well. Please give a warm welcome to ... Mr. Lucas Vulcano."

The room erupts into applause as Luke strides up the steps to take the stage next to Gina. My jaw drops. Serena turns to me to give me a "did you know he would be here?" look and I shake my head no.

Luke is here? Stand Up Against Abuse means something to him too? Why didn't he tell me?

And good god, does he look marvelous. He's wearing a black tuxedo with his longer hair styled back. He looks like James Bond.

"Hello," Luke says in his deep voice commanding the attention of everyone in the room—if they weren't already staring because of how sexy he looks, they would be now. "I had no idea that I was the highest donor for this organization—hopefully someone else can claim that title this evening," he says as the crowd laughs.

"Abuse can happen to anyone and, from my experience, I know most victims suffer in silence. They carry their shame alone." His eyes grow dark and then he spots me in the audience staring so intently at him on the edge of my seat. He smiles and cocks his head to the side. He's just as surprised that I'm here, as I am to see him.

"We have to do our part to give a voice to those who do not have one. To lend helping hands to those who face hurtful ones. Stand Up Against Abuse has been doing just that for years, and I know they will continue to. Thank you."

He nods his head and walks off the stage to join a table closer to the front of the room. I watch him take a seat next to yet another gorgeous blonde woman and she whispers something into this ear. *Is he on a date?* I'm an idiot; he never said we couldn't date other people. Actually he specifically told me he didn't want to end up with anyone.

Gina introduces a few more speakers who quickly say their speeches and then the live band takes over playing music. People dance, drink, bid on artwork, and have a great time. I should be happy for another successful event under our belt, but I can't get a certain man's belt out of my head. It's then I notice Luke walking directly towards me—as the crowd in the room parts for him.

"Hello Ariana. I'm happy to see you here. Serena, you both look lovely," he says.

"Thanks! We clean up well," Serena jokes before excusing herself to find those cute guys from earlier as I head towards the bar. I don't know what it is about Luke, but he drives me to drink. Maybe that's a sign I should stay away.

"You did a great job with your speech. I had no idea you were involved with this organization," I say, waiting for the bartender to make my drink.

"I haven't taken part in many of the volunteer activities, but I do what I can in donating. I know it's not enough, but that's what I have time for right now," he says with a shrug and a look of sadness in his eyes.

"Hey," I say feeling brave and putting my hand on his bicep, "that's okay. Your money is going to be put to good use to help so many people. Gina knows what she's doing and she does it well."

"So you volunteer? How did you find this organization? Through the hospital?" He asks the questions so innocently. I could easily blow it off and say yes, but his quote about doing things you've never done—and Gina's admission to the entire room—ring true in my ears.

"No, I found the organization before the hospital. I was looking for something to do with my time when I was in my early years at college, and this one stood out as something I should care about."

"Why?"

I take a deep breath in, noticing my hands are shaking as I bring my glass up to my mouth for a quick sip of liquid courage. "Because it's something I wish was around when I could have used someone to talk to."

I've never spoken to anyone but Gina, Serena, and Drake about this stuff. But none of them knows the entire story. I did tell my parents after it happened, but that was a huge mistake. I look up to meet Luke's eyes and they grow darker than I've ever seen them. A mix of anger and grief flash across his face.

"Someone ... abused you?" he whispers in an angry growl. "That's why you don't want to be touched?" A look of understanding flashes across his face as he works out what he just said.

I don't think I can do this—keep sharing my history with him. And I don't have to worry about this conversation going any further because the blonde from his table walks up to us and slips her skinny arm around

Luke's waist, pulling him close to her side. It's then I recognize her as the notorious blonde he is seen in Internet pictures with.

"Where did you run off too?" she practically ogles at him while fluttering her fake eyelashes, completely ignoring me standing right in front of them.

"Excuse me," I whisper, ducking away to dash to the bathroom. I fly into the first open stall and take deep breaths as I'm having a panic attack. I feel intense pain all over, and it's extremely hard to get in any air, so I lean over the toilet and throw up all the liquid courage while dizziness washes over me and panicked tears roll down my cheeks.

"Ariana? Are you in here?" I hear Serena's voice from the other side of the door. "Come out, please. Luke told me you ran in here. I can see the bottom of your dress under the stall. I know you're in there."

I open the door and she sees my face. Hers looks back at me in shock. It's very rare when I show emotion of any kind. She hesitantly opens her arms up to me, offering a hug, yet knowing I don't like touching.

"Can I?" she asks. I nod *yes* and she embraces me quickly while I keep my arms limp at my sides. This is what I can give and she understands—this is probably the most touching we've done, ever. She knows this is a very big deal, but she doesn't point it out, probably not wanting me to change my mind.

"What happened out there?" Serena asks as I calm my breathing down while she rubs my back.

"I started to…" I pause as I catch my breath, replaying the fact I was going to let Luke in, completely forgetting that he is here with another woman. *This is not your guy. Don't share your battles with him.*

"You started to…" Serena pulls back from the hug to study my face. "You started to let him in? Into your life. That's good Ariana. You've been carrying this around by yourself for far too long."

I remove myself from her grasp to look in the mirror. I look terrible—the color completely drained from my normally rosy cheeks, my eyes are bloodshot from vomiting, and I think my heart is about to explode from my chest as it's beating a million miles-per-hour.

"Serena, he's here with someone else," I barely whisper the words out, embarrassed I have to say them. How stupid do I look? I surely feel stupid.

"That blonde lady? We have no idea what she is to him. I know you don't want to hear something like this, but maybe she's just a friend?" Serena tries to give him the benefit of the doubt to ease my anxiety, but it only works a little.

"Friend or not, he could have asked *me* if I wanted to come with him." I want to take my words back as soon as they escape my lips. I've never wanted to be *that girl*.

"Ariana, you really like him? I can see it on your face and the fact that you're hiding out in this bathroom confirms it. I've never seen you interested in a guy in all the years I've known you. Don't let this blonde chick ruin anything. Talk to him. Let him explain," Serena says, grabbing a tissue to clean up my smeared mascara. "If he says something idiotic, then we kick his ass and move on."

She hands me a bold red color lipstick, forcing me to put it on. I fake a smile in the mirror while she's still watching. Okay, whatever, it does look good. She's always right.

"Let's go tell blondie to take a hike," Serena says before looping her arm through mine and guiding me out of the bathroom.

My eyes scan the room until they land on Luke. He's standing in a group of people with the blonde lady still by his side—it looks like he's telling a story. His eyes spot mine. Luke strides away from the group, clearly in the middle of whatever he was saying. The group eyes him as he walks towards me. I look around to give Serena a *can you believe this* look, but she's nowhere to be seen. *Where the hell did Serena go?*

Luke is now standing right in front of me and I feel like I did in the hospital when he cornered me: small under his giant height. But I force myself to look up to meet his eyes.

"Are you okay?" he asks with concern written all over his face.

"Yes, I'm sorry I wasn't feeling good and I just needed to splash my face with some water." I look down at my hands, not feeling right about lying.

"Tell me the truth."

"What are you talking about? I wasn't feeling well, that's the truth."

"Ariana…"

"Okay, fine. Who is the blonde hanging on your arm?"

Ouch, why did it have to come out so … jealous?

"Monica, she's a woman who helps me out by attending events with me." He says it in such a monotone way, like it's no big deal. That's a bullshit answer.

I move away from him and grab a martini from the nearest Vulcano girl, taking a swig. Darting my eyes around the room, I spot Serena and start walking over to her. We are going to need to catch a Driver home together. I do not feel like walking in these crazy stilettos.

"Can you not walk away when I'm trying to talk to you?" Luke asks with a bit of attitude in his voice. And that's when I lose it.

"Can you go bother someone else? Like your *date*? You know the woman who attends events like this with you?" My words come out super fast as I get more worked up. Gone is the panic attack feeling; now I'm just angry. "Can you lose my number while you're at it? I don't think this is a good idea. I need to focus on finishing up my residency. I can't handle whatever this is with you right now. This isn't good for me."

And just like that, I walk away from him in a hurry and he doesn't chase me. Serena is nowhere to be found so I get into a cab and ride home … alone.

———

My roommate stumbles into the apartment a little after midnight with a dark-haired man who I haven't seen before. They are kissing as she undresses him on the path to her bedroom until she realizes I'm still wide-awake and watching TV in the living room.

"Ariana!" She squeals out in a drunken banter. "This is … what's your name, cutie?"

"Jack," *cutie* replies, looking equally drunk and not an ounce bothered that Serena has no idea what his name is.

"Yeah, this is Jack. Where's Lukey?" She looks around the apartment, like I'm hiding him somewhere. I'm sitting in the living room in a pair of Wonder Woman pajamas eating Mint Chocolate Chip ice cream out of the carton. Where does she think I could possibly be hiding a man? And why would I let him see me like this?

"He's not here. You guys have a great night," I say as I nod my head in the direction of her room, letting her know she's off the hook and doesn't have to hang with me. She takes the hint and pulls Jack into her room by his tie.

I fall asleep on the couch and wake up to Serena shaking me yet again. This is becoming a pattern between us.

"Ariana, calm down, please wake up," she pleads. I open my eyes and see my friend in my face. "Oh thank god! You were screaming. Bad dream?"

I sometimes have nightmares about a time in my life I'd like to quickly forget. It's been a long time since I've had one of these; last night's events may have triggered something.

It's always the same nightmare and I always wake up screaming with sweat dripping all over my body even though I'm shaking from feeling so cold. My throat is sore from the screams and I feel my face is wet from tears. I know I should call my therapist, but she'd want me to come in for an appointment and I just don't have time to schedule anything. I also don't want to talk about feelings.

"I'll make breakfast. You feel like French toast?" Serena asks as she heads to the kitchen, giving me a minute to recoup, which I'm grateful for.

"What happened to your guy?"

I join her in the kitchen, taking a seat at our wood table.

"He left around 2 a.m., I called him a cab after … you know," she says, winking before cracking some eggs into a bowl. I look at my friend in awe. She's so relaxed about her life, no one gets on her nerves, she makes friends very easily, and she manages her stress with sex. Again, the opposite of me.

We girl talk about our lives—her work, my residency, our families, the latest gossip on Facebook—all over a delicious breakfast. My friend can cook! Another thing I'm not that great at. My head is always in my books; where it should be.

I go to my room to get ready for tonight's hospital shift and think about how foolish I've been lately. Why am I letting a guy control my thoughts? I know better. I need to focus on finishing this residency so I can apply for a job or at least snag some killer references. I can't screw this up—I just can't. Luke can take all kinds of women to whatever the fuck events he wants to now because I don't give a shit anymore.

Stand your ground Ariana.

CHAPTER TEN

Coming out of a hospital room with my scrubs covered in blood—someone else's, but still—I see Katie walking towards me with a bouquet of lilies. They remind me of my Grandma Betty—she was the only person I've ever felt a connection with. She would always have fresh flowers on her kitchen table, she knew just the right comfort food to bake to make you smile, and she had a good listening ear. Grandma Betty passed away when I was 12—before my life turned upside down.

"Those are lovely," I say as Katie approaches me with a huge grin on her face.

"Well I'm glad you like them; they're for you," she says, handing me the bouquet. "I wish someone was sending me gorgeous flowers like this too. Don't tell me they are from Hot Mystery Man?" She eyes the little white envelope that will answer her question. I know she's dying for me to open the card in front of her but not a chance in hell.

"Thanks Katie!" I say as I dart into the break room. And rip into the card—

A,

> *I need to see you again. We ended things on a bad note + I'd like to explain.*

L

My heart sinks. I didn't know what I was expecting, but it wasn't that. Shouldn't cards with beautiful flowers hold romantic words? This one doesn't even include an apology. No "I'm sorry for being a jackass." Just he'd "like to explain." I think he explained himself very well— he wants to date me *and* other women. That was made clear. I'm not the girl he wants to take to events with him. Also noted.

I rip the card into a million little pieces and toss it in the trash. I really want to do the same with the flowers but they are just too gorgeous to abandon. I know what I'll do with them! I jump in the elevator, pressing the button for the ICU floor, and head into the room where one of my trauma patients rests.

"Hello Ruth," I greet the 20-year-old perky redhead who is lying in the room hooked up to a few machines. She was in a car accident when another driver blew through a red light and smashed into her car. Ruth has a broken collarbone and blood in her spleen—we are watching the spleen to make sure it heals itself before we can operate on that collarbone. She's a brave girl though. I haven't seen her cry once; instead, she's always got a smile on her face when we enter her room.

"Stunning flowers!" Ruth says, putting the T.V. remote down in her lap.

"They're for you!" I say, putting them on the tray next to her bed, where I see she's left most of her food. "Girl, you know you need to eat this."

Ruth looks at me like I just told her the most obvious thing ever and then makes a face of disgust. "You know that stuff tastes like crap."

I bust out laughing. She's right, I can't argue with her.

"Are you hungry? I can see if I can find something else in this place that doesn't taste so bad. The options are slim but …"

"That's okay." She puts her finger to her mouth to indicate she's about to tell me a secret: "I have food on the way."

I throw my hands up in the air, "You did not just tell me that!" I put my fingers into my ears. "I didn't hear that. But if you are going to sneak in food, make it good." I wink and walk out of the room, not before sticking my hands under the hand-sanitizing machine.

Ruth is one of the few happy people on the ICU floor. This floor can sometimes be sadder than the emergency room; it's full of doom and gloom. I jump back in the elevator and stroll back to our computer station to get my next round of patients.

My night continues as normal as working in an E.R. can be until a few hours later I spot the girls huddled together gossiping. Tara spots me and her eyes light up like a freakin' Christmas tree.

What the hell are they doing now?

It's not until I get closer that I see exactly what they are so excited about ... Luke is here. He's in the waiting room talking to a little boy who has a big bump on his head and a lady, who I'm guessing is the little boy's mom or babysitter. Luke is crouching down eye level with the boy and they both start laughing.

So cute. Damn it heart, don't be a traitor!

Luke spots me as I walk into the waiting room and stands up tall, towering over everyone else.

"It was nice to meet you, Max. I hope you feel better real soon," Luke says towards the little boy, and then he sticks his hand out and Max gives him a high-five.

"Mommy, he's funny," I hear Max chuckle as Luke and I walk away from the waiting room towards an empty corner around the hallway. I stop abruptly and Luke bumps into my back—if this could get any more awkward I think it just did.

"What are you doing here?" I grill him with attitude.

"Did you get my flowers?"

"Yes, I gave them away, right after I ripped up your card. You shouldn't be here. You can't keep showing up where I work. People are going to get the wrong idea," I plead. I cannot let anything get in the way of this residency ending smoothly. Better than smoothly, it needs to end with me getting hired as a permanent doctor.

"When you didn't answer my phone calls or text messages, I decided face-to-face was how to go about this," Luke says matter-of-factly.

"Go about … what? This," I say waving my hands in between us, "is nothing that needs to be discussed further. We can just end this. We *need* to."

"That's bullshit. You don't want that," he says with such confidence that even I believe him for a brief moment. I know I don't want to never speak to him again, but I also know I have to keep my eye on the prize—my career—and not let whatever I was feeling at the charity event consume my life.

Jealously, embarrassment, longing, need.

"Please just go," I say as I try to break free and round the corner, but Luke stands in front of me, blocking my path to escape. He looks me in the eyes silently, letting me know something is about to happen.

And then … he shuffles towards me, backing me up against the wall before pressing hot, open-mouthed kisses onto my mouth. Both of his hands are on the wall framing my head, and I close my eyes and give in. This is nothing like the soft and patient kiss in the Willis Tower—this is urgent and demanding. He thrusts his seductive tongue into my mouth and I let out a moan, reaching my hands up to grip his shirt to pull him closer to me.

My body is definitely betraying me as electricity sparks through me.

"Well, well, well, what do we have here?"

The sound of Ben coming towards us brings me back to reality, and I push Luke away, wiping my hand across my lips as if rubbing off the kiss ... *or rubbing it in?*

"Should residents be standing in the middle of the hallway making out with their boyfriends? I don't think so," Ben utters in his usual demeaning tone, reminding me of my place.

"I, uh, we aren't in the middle of the hallway," is the only thing I can spit out at him. He raises his eyebrows at me as if I shouldn't even have said that much.

"Hello, I'm Luke Vulcano, it's nice to meet you." Luke reaches his hand out towards Ben. I see a quick flash of shock cross his normally smug face and then a smile takes its place.

"Mr. Vulcano, it's so nice to meet you. I've heard a great deal about you. My cousin works in television marketing and she's always going on and on about you and your company's ads. I'm Ben Carter," he says as he returns the handshake.

What the hell is this about?

"If your cousin would like to set up an interview, have her call my office and ask to speak to my secretary, Tracy. Let her know you are Ariana's friend," Luke says, putting a little emphasis on the word *friend*. What is he doing?

Trying to save your ass from whatever Ben could possibly do to ruin your reputation at this hospital in a matter of seconds.

"Wow, thank you so much. I'll tell her right away. She's going to be thrilled. I'll leave you two alone." Ben nods at us and walks away with a little extra pep in his douchebag step. This leaves Luke and I alone again, huddled close in the corner of the otherwise empty corridor.

"Thank you for that. But you know I wouldn't need your help if you weren't here making things difficult for me in the first place," I explain. "I don't mean to sound like a total bitch, but this residency is the most important thing I have in my life."

It's the truth. Outside of the residency and the charity, I don't have anything else. Yes, I have a few friends, Drake and Serena, but even with them I only let them in to a point, keeping my private thoughts just that, private. I don't even speak to my family anymore. This is it.

"I understand being passionate about your career. Trust me, I'm one of the few people who gets it and I admire that about you. I don't want to stand in the way of that," he says as he inches closer yet again, "but what would a few more dinners hurt? You have to eat, right?"

I laugh. "Yes, I have to eat but that doesn't mean I have to eat with you. I'm perfectly fine eating dinner alone."

Even saying that sounds terribly sad.

"Come on, that's ridiculous. Why eat alone when you've got this devastatingly handsome guy begging to take you out and buy you dinner?"

Is he joking with me? Mr. Serious? I bust out laughing!

"Okay but one question," I say, "will you also be having dinners with other women at the same time?" I feel a sense of embarrassment that I even feel the need to ask it, but I really want to know what's going on between us. Not that I'll be dating other men, I still think it's respectful to know what's going on.

"No, no other women, just you. It was stupid of me to take Monica to that event after our lovely date. I should have asked you to join me. It was already set up that Monica would be attending and I didn't even think about changing it."

"Fine," I say, moving around him to head back to the nurses station. "And I never said you were devastatingly handsome!" I shout back towards him as I leave him standing alone in the corridor. That's when I hear him laughing behind me.

CHAPTER ELEVEN

Luke
13 years old

Mom doesn't leave the house much anymore; her face is always covered in bruises that are too hard for her to cover with makeup. I called the police the last time my dad came home in a drunken rage and beat her up. They came to the house, I told them what happened, and then my parents told them I made the whole thing up. It hurt that my mom called me a liar. Really hurt.

Are you fucking kidding me?

I don't even know what to do. I want to help her so bad and get her out of here, but she won't give up on my dad. She says he wasn't always like this, that he doesn't mean to be like this, and that there's a lot of pressure on him at work.

This family is a fucking joke.

My brother and sister try to stay out of the house as much as possible, but I can't leave mom alone. She encourages me to go with my siblings but I refuse. What if he comes home and hurts her? I mean really hurts her. She won't call for help. I need to stay. I have to protect her.

CHAPTER TWELVE

Luke and I are going out to dinner again, but this time I'm in charge of our evening's activities. I loved the date he planned, but I want to show him a more laid back version of Chicago. Has this guy ever not had the best of the best? Doubtful. Let's see if he can hang with the middle class.

My phone vibrates on my dresser, a text message:

I'm outside, whenever you're ready come down. Don't rush.

Even though I'm in charge of this date, he still insists on picking me up and using his car. I guess if I had a private driver I wouldn't want to slum it around the city either, so I won't call him out on this one. And I like not having to find my own way home when I'm with him.

I look in the mirror for a last minute check to see that everything is where it should be. I leave my hair down in long waves, swipe some lipstick on, and grab my clutch as I head towards the door. Serena is out for the night, so I can slip out without any harassment about having a good time and giving him some sex.

Rushing out the door I bump into my neighbor, Linda, an elderly woman who's carrying a bunch of groceries up the stairs. She refuses to take the elevator— she says she's fighting the aging process. But before I can offer to help her, I notice Luke coming up behind her with his arms full of grocery bags.

"Hello Ariana, your kind boyfriend here offered to help me with my groceries. What a sweetheart!" Linda exclaims.

"I'll be down in a minute," Luke says, trailing behind Linda, looking like a man on a mission to get these groceries into her apartment. It looks like they've got things covered and I would just be in the way, so I head downstairs—skipping the elevator myself so Linda doesn't yell at me—and meet Luke's driver on the curb.

"Hello, we've never officially been introduced. I'm Ariana," I say, sticking my hand out towards the middle-aged man with short red hair and green eyes. He extends his hand and takes mine into a firm grasp.

"Pleasure to meet you. I'm Ryan," he says. I give him the directions and then he walks towards the back door to open it for me. It feels so weird being treated like royalty—something I'm not. I want to tell him I can get my own door but he looks like he takes his job seriously—which is something I can admire in any person.

Climbing into the backseat, I pull out my phone to browse social media while I wait for Luke to finish helping my neighbor. In just a few minutes, he's in the backseat next to me. He takes my phone and puts it inside my clutch and then sits the clutch back on my lap. I'm in shock—no one touches my phone—and I think my jaw drops. What the hell just happened here?

"We don't need something like that to be a third wheel when we are together. So many people are obsessed with their smartphones and social media—it's ruining real-life interactions."

Well, damn. He's right, but I didn't see something like that coming from him.

"You run a massive company—how can you not be in support of the Internet?" I laugh at this ridiculous conversation.

"I didn't say I don't support the Internet. Vulcano Vodka has an entire marketing department that consists of people who solely work on online advertising and social media. But outside of the office, that's useless to me."

"Enlighten me—what is useful to you then?" I lean in, touching his arm while I tease him.

"Right now … being present in the moment with you," he says, turning to face me.

As we pull up towards the bar, which I think is a hidden sports gem in Chicago, I laugh now realizing how opposite we are going to look tonight. I told him to be casual, but he's besides me in a black dress shirt and black dress pants. At least he ditched the full suit. I'm walking in next to him wearing dark ripped jeans and a green T-shirt paired with a brown bomber jacket, but I did pair the outfit with a cute pair of heels.

"What's so funny?" He looks at me quizzically.

"Do you know what the word *casual* means?" I ask, pointing to his clothes as the hostess takes us to our booth.

"This is casual for me," he replies, not even looking fazed that we don't match. This is probably another one of those things he just doesn't think twice about. I wish I had such a carefree attitude when it comes to caring what people think.

"Is this booth okay?" The peppy hostess asks, placing the menus on the table.

"Perfect," I say, sliding into the booth.

This is where true sports fans come to watch the game or eat the best deep-dish pizza in the entire state of Illinois. I love sports; they are so cut and dry—there's a winner and a loser. Tonight there isn't a local game playing, but we can still enjoy the atmosphere.

Our waiter takes our drink orders. I wisely pick water this time and Luke gets a beer. I'm not going to be off my game on this date. No chugging champagne or martinis like they are going out of style.

We chit chat about how our days went—his in the office and mine in the hospital. It's a very easy conversation—talking about the vast personalities of the people we work with and why we do what we do. This date is going well until moments after our check arrives—Luke pays it even though I fight him on it since this was my idea. We are relaxing at the table before we head to our second location when I spot Drake and a few of his fraternity brothers pile into the bar. Drake eyes us and strolls over, not even stopping to talk to the waitress who tries to get his drink order.

"Ariana, how are you doing?" Drake asks, not even glancing in the direction of Luke. I spoke to Drake a few nights after the weird confrontation in the coffee shop to clear the air—he said everything was fine but apparently that was a lie.

"I'm doing good, Drake. You remember Luke?" I ask, extending my hand in Luke's direction to bring him into the conversation. I feel a little weird about all of this.

"Of course—the guy who wanted to start a pissing match with me in the coffee shop over my best friend," he says, still staring at me, and then he turns his body to face Luke. "Yeah how you doing?"

Luke breaks out into a shit-eating grin, clearly not phased by how rude Drake is treating him. Before I can swoop in and correct the conversation, Trey walks over to our table and drapes his arm around Drake's shoulders. Clearly these guys have already been drinking before coming to this bar—a Friday night ritual.

"Ariana, girl, it's good to see you! Is Drake interrupting your date?" Trey shouts—I don't think he knows how loud he's talking but the fellow patrons have as they glance our way. "Have we seen her go out with other guys before?" he asks, turning his head towards Drake to get an answer. Drake just nods his head 'no' and doesn't say a word. "Oh damn, I thought you two would always end up together," Trey slurs; clearly indicating he means Drake and me.

"Okay fellas, it's time you go back to your own table. Ariana and I would like some privacy," Luke orders.

"Privacy? She's our friend. What the fuck? Are you going to let him talk to us that way?" Drake asks me. Now he's the one raising his voice. This is déjà vu of the coffee shop with all eyes on us yet again. Why can't I be in the room with my two favorite guys and have nothing go wrong?

"I think you guys should go back to your table. Luke and I were just about to leave anyway," I say. A flash of hurt and confusion crosses Drake's face and then it's gone in an instant—replaced with anger. He clenches his fists and puffs out his chest.

Drake leans into the booth, crowding my personal space. Before he can say anything else, Luke eyes him with rage. Luke's hand, already wrapped around his beer bottle, squeezes it a little too hard in his grasp and shatters the glass.

Drake's eyes go from me to Luke's broken bottle.

"What the fuck man?" Drake asks. Pushing past him, I slide out of the booth.

Drake turns to me and grabs my upper arms a little too tightly. "Ariana, I don't think you should keep seeing this guy. I've looked him up, he's not right for you. And what the hell was that with the bottle?"

Drake's fingers dig into my arms and now I'm uncomfortable, trying to weasel my way out of his grasp.

"Drake, you're hurting me, let go."

My friend doesn't seem to comprehend what I'm saying and it's only a matter of seconds before Luke is out of the booth and pushing Drake's hands off me.

"You heard what she said, asshole. I don't want to see you put your hands on her ever again," Luke commands, taking a stance right next to me like a guard dog on duty.

"Or what?" Drake shoots his mouth back at Luke.

"Or you'll answer to me," Luke growls between clenched teeth, his hands clenched in fists as well.

"Okay boys, I think this has gone on a little too long. Luke, let's just go," I say pulling on his arm.

"Ariana, what's wrong with you? You used to care about your friends and you'd never let a stranger control your life," Drake snaps, shaking his head with disappointment all over his face.

"I don't want to have this conversation right now," I say towards Drake. I then turn to Luke and say, "Let's go."

"Whatever," is all I hear Drake mutter under his breath. He drops the conversation and lets us leave without causing any more of a scene—thank god! We walk outside and I pull my jacket a little tighter as the Chicago chill hits me deep in my bones. I grew up in Florida, only moving to Illinois when I started my undergrad, yet I feel like I will never get used to these winters.

Luke notices my shivering and puts his arm around me before pulling me into his chest. Since we so abruptly left the sports bar, Ryan wasn't ready to pick us up and is driving over to us now. I take the time to nuzzle myself as close to Luke as I can. He smells absolutely heavenly. I need to find out what his body wash or cologne is so I can bathe in it.

Ryan pulls the car up to the curb and we climb into the backseat, thankful he kept the heat on full blast. I gave Ryan the rundown of the night's locations earlier so he doesn't need to ask me as we take off towards the Navy Pier, which is a surprise to Luke.

As I regain feeling in my fingers and toes, I get a little courageous with the man sitting next to me. He did just stand up for me against Drake's grabby hands, which was kind of sexy.

"So tell me something about you that no one else knows?"

"You always seem to come up with questions I've never been asked before," Luke says, taking a moment to think—is he considering his options? "I sleep in the nude."

He flashes a big grin at me.

"Really? That's all you're going to give? And I said something *no one else* knows," I sass back at him.

"No one else knows that."

"You've never had a sleepover with a woman? What are you going to say next—you're a virgin?" I laugh.

Luke fiddles with the zipper on my bomber jacket and looks up to meet my eyes. "I'm definitely not a virgin. I lost that title many years ago. But I was telling the truth—I don't let women spend the night with me. I always leave or ask them to go. Now tell me something about you that no one else knows."

Okay, I wasn't expecting that answer. *Why doesn't he stay with them?* I guess that's something I don't really want to know the answer to anyway; I don't want to imagine him having sex with anyone else.

Else? Where are you going with this brain of mine?

"Let's see." I pause thinking of what to share. "I have a tattoo."

His face lights up eagerly. "Go on ... where is this tattoo no one knows about?"

I point towards my jeans. "It's pretty low on my hip bone."

His eyes dart right to where I pointed. "Wouldn't that show if you are wearing a bikini?"

I fidget in my seat feeling a little uncomfortable with him clearly imagining what I must look like in a bikini.

"Since I've gotten the tattoo I haven't had many opportunities to wear anything revealing in public. I can't remember the last time I was on a vacation or even at a beach." As I talk, I realize just how sheltered I've kept myself. "It's always been school, working, part-time jobs, and then throwing myself full force into my residency. Does the idea of a tattoo on a woman turn you on or gross you out?"

I'd hate to hear that it grosses him out, but before he can answer I notice we've pulled up to our location and I hear a tap on the window—it's Ryan letting us know he's about to open the door. I remind myself I'm going to ask him that question again later. I'd love his opinion.

"The Navy Pier?" Luke asks as he turns to offer me his hand. It's such a simple act, to place my hand in his, but I have to remind myself that I can do this—let him touch me. I reach out to slip my fingers into his.

"You're very observant," I tease.

"How late is it?" he glances at his watch. "Isn't this place closed?"

I grab a tote bag that Ryan helped me store in the trunk and head towards our destination: the Ferris wheel. Luke doesn't let me carry the tote bag very long; he's taking it from my hands to carry himself.

"Serena is good friends with the Public Relations manager for the Navy Pier—she pulled some strings. Don't look so surprised. You aren't the only person who has connections in Chicago," I tease, nudging him as we approach a teenage boy standing by the Ferris wheel looking down at his phone.

"Miss Bellisano?" the teenager asks apprehensively.

"That's me! Nice to meet you." I extend my hand towards him, he shakes it, and then he gets right to work by opening the cabin door to our seats on the Ferris wheel. Once we are tucked inside, I take a minute to enjoy our view before reaching inside my tote bag, pulling out a huge fleece blanket that I wrap us up in then I grab two thermos with spiked hot chocolate. Luke takes a whiff and immediately laughs.

"What are we, in high school?"

"Hey now Mr. I Own The Fancy Liquor Company, this is what some of us can afford," I say, taking a sip from my thermos. His face changes into a more serious expression but he's hard to read as he sips his drink. I was completely joking, considering Serena said the same thing about my alcohol of choice before I left. It's partly because I'm cheap and it's partly because I have no clue what kind of alcoholic beverages I even like.

With the blanket wrapped around us and sitting in such a close space, we have nothing to do but be in each other's arms. It still makes me slightly on edge to let someone touch me, but as I continue to let my guard down with him, the fear goes away more and more.

The teenager must have pressed some button or another because the giant wheel rotates.

"Will you ever tell me what happened? What exactly lead you to not letting people touching you?" He breaks the silence of us staring out at the nighttime view.

I debate whether I want to get into this, but there's no point in keeping it hidden. I've come to terms with it a long time ago; it's just not something I like to share. I've started once before with him at the charity event, but that was cut short. He already knows I was abused, so I might as well give him the rest.

I take a deep breath in and out, trying to calm my nerves. My hands are shaking and I feel uneasy. This is something I've never fully told a guy before except my father, but that doesn't count.

"When I was 14, a friend of my parents ... raped me," I say as matter-of-factly as I can. I've convinced myself if I put no emotion into what I say, I won't feel anything. I won't cry, shake, want to throw up, or hide my head in shame—what I felt like for years upon years after what happened to me. That's what I try to tell myself at least.

I feel Luke's entire body stiffen beside me; he doesn't say a word.

Should I have kept this to myself? I mean, he did ask. This is why I've never told anyone all of this before. I don't know what they'll think of me. I don't want this moment in my life to change the way someone sees me. I don't want it to define me.

Is he not going to want to do anything sexually with me now?

Am I too damaged for him?

Before any more ridiculous questions fly through my brain, Luke finally speaks, "Did you tell your parents?"

That's not the question I expected him to ask.

"Not at first. I was really scared and really confused. I didn't know much about sex other than the stuff we learn in school. Which isn't really anything when you go to a private Catholic school. I had never even kissed a boy before…"

It's like I'm instantly brought back to that moment.

Allen cornered me at my family's house during a Christmas party, which he was attending with his wife, Sarah. My parents were known for throwing big parties. It was always so much fun. *Was* is the keyword here for me now.

"I was in my father's office getting a special Christmas CD that I left in his computer. I burned it earlier that day and was so excited my parents said I could be the DJ; they normally never gave me responsibilities. They are kind of the people who think children are better seen, not heard."

I grip the fleece blanket a little tighter to my chest, feeling the Chicago winds picking up as the Ferris wheel continues to roll slowly around. Luke says nothing, giving me time to collect myself before I continue.

"Allen walked into the office and I didn't think anything of it at first, until he closed the door behind him. I felt so out of place, even in my own house. I had never been left alone in a room with a grown man before who wasn't my dad or grandpa. I felt uncomfortable, but I tried to play it off like it was no big deal, like I was mature."

I wasn't mature; I was a 14-year-old innocent girl trying to enjoy her family's Christmas party.

"Allen came stumbling towards the desk carrying a drink in his hand, whiskey. To this day, just the thought of whiskey fills my nose with the vilest smell and brings me back to this moment. I asked him what he was doing, saying my parents would be back to check on me at any minute. It's like I knew danger was coming."

I look intently into Luke's eyes.

"He came up behind me, pinning me against the desk and …" a tear slowly falls from my eye, sliding down my pink cheeks. I take a deep breath before finishing my story. "I was wearing a knee-length velvet red holiday dress that my mom helped me pick out. Allen reached up the skirt to pull down my underwear. I tried to fight him off, tried to scream, but he shoved me down on the desk so hard he knocked the air out of my lungs. He ripped off the underwear and covered my mouth with his rough hand that was almost the entire size of my little face.

"After he was … finished, he told me if I ever told anyone he would tell them I was making the entire thing up. He said no one would believe a little girl over a judge—that I was a liar and that I would get into a lot of trouble. He said I'd be taken away from my family. I look back now and think that was so stupid for me to believe him, but I was young. I didn't know any better."

Luke pulls me closer to him—if I were any closer, I'd be on top of his lap.

"You are brave," he says, lifting my chin to meet his eyes. "When did you finally tell someone?"

I don't know which part of the story makes me feel more embarrassed. The fact I was raped or what happened next. This part I've never told anyone, ever.

"I told my parents a year later. I lived the entire year after in fear of everyone. I felt so many emotions but didn't know how to express myself—fear, anger, embarrassment, shame, and guilt. I saw every person I came in contact with as a threat to me and I shut down completely. My parents asked me what was wrong, but I said nothing and they never pushed me for more information. I know now, they don't give a shit about what happens to me, as long as I'm quiet, well mannered, and don't cause any trouble for them."

I shake my head thinking about how little my parents paid attention to me when I was silently screaming out to be noticed.

"I finally worked up the courage to tell my parents before the Christmas party the following year. I knew Allen would be on the guest list, and I wanted my parents to remove him from it. I told both my mom and my dad at the same time—they looked shocked. Then my mom said in her pristine voice, *'We'll take care of this. Tell no one else,'* and that was the last time we spoke about it.

"I overheard my parents whispering in the kitchen a few days after I told them. My mom said I probably made the entire thing up, claiming no one could keep something like that a secret for an entire year. They thought I was trying to get attention after my year of hiding. My dad said something along the lines of *'this will ruin our reputation if this gets out.'* I stopped speaking to my parents around that time."

Knowing your own parents think you are a liar, that cuts you deep. Allen wasn't at the Christmas party, but I never found out if they took him off the invite list or if he decided just not to show.

Downing the rest of my drink, I lean my head against Luke's shoulder. I feel exhausted all of a sudden, but I also feel a sense of relief to have said it out loud. No matter what Luke's reaction is going to be, I told the truth. I shared something that's been kept locked inside of my soul for years.

"Ariana," Luke cups my face between both of his hands, "what happened to you is not your fault. That man was a monster preying on a young girl. And your parents are disgusting pieces of shit. They should have been in your life to protect you," Luke spits out. Something tells me this is more than just about my parents, but I don't press him. I appreciate him for listening. "Thank you for telling me your story, for trusting me with something so important."

He picks up my hand and kisses the top of it—making me feel like a queen. I smile, and if my cheeks weren't already red from the frostbite, I may be blushing.

Turning to him I lose myself in his warm hazel eyes. At the top of the Ferris wheel, with the lights of Chicago glistening all around us, I kiss him. I've revealed the worst part of me to this man and he's still here by my side. He didn't judge me for anything I said.

I pour my soul out through hot kisses to his addictive mouth. My body quivers with desire for him I've never felt before.

"Excuse me, we need to close the Ferris wheel now," I hear the pimpled faced teenager say from his post as our cabin makes its way back to the platform. Damn it, are we ever going to move past kissing? My body is all too willing to let this man show me what intimacy is supposed to feel like. And I trust that he can.

Deciding that's what I want for myself, I feel a sense of power. I want to give myself to Luke—nothing being taken away from me, everything given.

CHAPTER THIRTEEN

"You told him? Are you serious?" Serena shrills; looking shocked as she corners me on the way to the bathroom the next morning.

I tried to tell her that it was no big deal, but we both know I'm lying. This is a big deal, enormous even. When I told him I felt scared but after I felt so free, not having to walk around carrying this disgust inside of me. Not disgust for being raped because I know that was not my fault—which took me years of therapy to come to terms with—but disgust in the fact that my parents don't believe me.

They were supposed to protect you.

His words haunted me last night and I woke up having a nightmare, but not like my usual nightmares about

Allen—this one was concerning Luke. Was he not protected from someone who was supposed to be there for him?

He has battles too.

Renee's words continue to haunt me, and now that I've revealed myself to him, I want to calm his battles if he'll let me in. That's the mystery—will he?

After we got off the Ferris wheel, we left the Navy Pier and simply enjoyed sitting together in silence, cuddled up into one another on the drive back to my apartment. I didn't invite him up—I wasn't ready for that—and he didn't pressure me to. The night had its ups and downs, but I'll look back at it as one that changed my life.

"Yes, I told him. Yes, I'm an idiot for falling for this guy," I say to Serena who hasn't closed her gaping mouth since she heard the news. Serena doesn't understand how significant this is. She is one of the few people who know about the rape, but she doesn't know what I heard my parents saying behind closed doors or that I stopped speaking to them that moment. She does know I hate them though. I kind of skate around telling her all the details and she has never pushed me.

"An idiot? No, you are finally coming out of your shell and living the life you deserve. I'm really proud of you!" Serena exclaims, letting me sidestep her to finally get into the bathroom. I have an afternoon shift starting at the hospital in an hour and don't really have time to fan girl over Luke with my too excited roommate.

"Don't close yourself up Ariana. You deserve this, I'm telling you!"

"Okay, okay, leave me alone. Can't a girl take a shower in peace around here?" I laugh, shutting myself into our bathroom. I'm through talking about this subject for now; it's weird for me to be this open with others that it has me second-guessing myself.

After I step out of the shower, I throw on a pair of maroon scrubs and toss my hair up in a wet messy bun—that's my uniform and I wouldn't have it any other way. I quickly glance down at my phone on the bathroom counter and notice a text message waiting for me from Luke.

Last night was perfect! You are perfect. Care for round 2 tonight?

Yes, yes, and yes! I would love round two—I'd love a chance to get past first base with this guy. I can't believe I'm even thinking about this stuff.

I've had sex with two other guys during my undergrad when I lived in the dorms. It was super awkward and I made sure I was in control. I was on top, I picked the pace, I picked the guy, and I kept the touching to a bare minimum. I basically had sex so Allen's assault wouldn't be my last time. I wanted to erase that entire experience and I thought another guy would be able to do that.

But it didn't. The sex was never anything I truly wanted. Those guys weren't horrible—in fact they were very nice guys—but we didn't share anything special. I wouldn't let them.

Coming back to reality, I speedily type up a reply as I head towards the front door to dash to the hospital and whatever awaits me there.

I'll see if I can fit you in to my busy schedule. ;)

I hop on the bus and see Luke's already sent a message back. Doesn't this guy have a company he's supposed to be running right now?

I have something I'd like to fit in you.

My eyes must bug out of my head in shock as I feel myself flush with a mixture of embarrassment and need. No one has ever spoken to me like this before. Luke is one dirty man, and I can't say I hate it.

How bad do you want to fit it in??

I immediately hit send and immediately feel a sense of regret. Why did I say that? I drop my head in my hands and wish I could delete the text from the universe. Before I can sit stewing in my own embarrassment for much longer, Luke replies.

Are you provoking me Ariana? I want it bad & I think you know that. I'm hard at my desk right now thinking about you.

My embarrassment flies out the door knowing this is turning him on, knowing that I have the power to turn him on through just a few words ... or thoughts. What is he thinking about at that desk? Do I want to know? Yes, I do. Is it getting hot in here? I look up from my phone and scan the other people sitting on the bus—feeling like they know exactly what filthy words are displayed on my phone ... and in my head.

Round 2 tonight—I'll be out of the hospital around midnight. Is that too late?

The thought of finding out just what would make Luke's cock hard drifts to the side when I think about him not being able to hang out because it's too late. Doesn't he have to be up early to go into his company? I want to know so much more about what he does at work. Does it bother him that I have a crazy schedule and that it will probably never be normal?

He swiftly puts my rambling thoughts to rest with a reply.

It's never too late for spending time with you. I'll be there to pick you up.

I smile at his cute reply until I notice we are at my stop and the bus is starting to pick up speed to pull away.

"Wait!" I scream, running towards the front of the bus to catch the driver's attention so he'll let me off. Well that's an easy way to work up your heart rate. I probably just burned 2,000 calories in anxiety.

It's the night from hell! After I ran into the emergency room like a crazy person from the bus, I was thrown into the operating room with Dr. Horton. I helped him with surgery on a boy who was thrown from the windshield of his mother's car when a drunk driver hit their SUV. An older man with a heart attack, a college student with a respiratory infection, and two different patients with sprained ankles followed up the boy's successful surgery—I am absolutely spent!

I grab my coat from my locker in the staff room but sit down on a bench and take a minute to do some breathing exercises, gathering my thoughts, and that's when my phone beeps.

I look at my phone and see it's after 1 a.m. and I never texted Luke. My stomach drops and I feel terrible.

I spoke to Katie—I know you're having a long night. I'll be out here waiting when you are ready. Don't rush.

He's been sitting out there waiting for an hour? Bless his precious heart. I don't think I'd sit and wait an hour for anyone. *Okay maybe him.* I grab my backpack and dart towards the emergency room exit. Katie smiles at me with a knowing grin. I just wave at her and make my quick escape before she can question me—I'm sure the girls will be talking tomorrow. Let them.

I spot Ryan hanging out next to the black town car and run over. He sees me crossing the street and opens the back door for me. I thank him before flopping into the seat noticing Luke has a laptop on his lap. He's been working while waiting for me. It makes me feel a little better that he had something to do. And it doesn't escape me that he's wearing a suit yet again.

"Thank you for waiting for me. It's been a crazy busy night," I say as I lean in, planting a kiss on his cheek. Luke looks back surprised by my action, which equally surprised me. Affection doesn't come easy for me—it never has—and I think that's because I've never been shown any. My parents were never affectionate with me. Then after what happened, I closed myself off from any emotions anyone wanted to share with me.

"I don't mind, Ariana. You're doing important work. I'd wait for you forever," he says, closing his laptop and putting it out of the way.

"I hope you don't mind, but I'm so tired. I don't think I could do anything fun tonight—no breaking in to a place that's supposed to be closed," I laugh, scooting myself a little closer to him now that his computer is gone.

"I figured that. We are just going back to my place."

His place.

"I like the sound of that," I say as he opens up his muscular arms and I curl myself inside them.

I tell him about the night at the hospital and he tells me a little about his day at the office—minus the parts about him getting hard at his desk and my panties getting wet on the bus. He tells me about the process of making vodka—I'm sure a "For Dummies" version—and I explain some of the basics about hospital work. Our work environments are completely different; our lives are completely different. How are we finding so much to talk about?

Ryan pulls the town car into a private garage off Lake Shore Drive into an impressive looking apartment complex. I never knew where Luke lived—I imagined it would be nice, but just from its location I know this place will make me feel so inferior.

Ryan opens the door for me and helps me out before we head towards a private elevator. Luke pulls a keycard out of his suit jacket, slipping it into the card reader. A button for the penthouse suite lights up on the elevator's display panel.

My family was on the higher-end of the middle class in Florida. My parents sent me to private school and whatever I asked for, they provided. That was until I stopped asking for things—they'd still manage to get things for me because they wanted to put on the show that we were really well off. How lame. Even though I wanted for nothing, I know my family was nothing like what I'm about to walk into.

Thinking of my family makes me wonder what Luke's family is like? Has he been rich his whole life? I know he said he had his first job when he was young, but that might have been out of the fun of the hustle, not because he needed to work. I don't want to ask about that now. I just want to see where he leads this night. *Hopefully into his bed.*

The elevator doors open up and I see a white, clean lobby area with a large round black marble table in the middle of the room with a vase of red roses. Just past the table are two double doors that Luke walks towards. He sticks another key in a slot next to the door before it opens.

I step into the room and my breath hitches. My eyes instantly dart to the floor to ceiling windows ahead of me showing off the lit up Chicago skyline, I would bet good money this view is better than the one we saw at the Willis Tower.

"You like what you see?" Luke whispers into my ear, pulling me closer to his side.

I turn to face him, "Is this where I give you a cheesy line about loving the view as I stare at your body?"

He busts out laughing. He remembers that cheesy line he pulled on me on our Willis Tower date.

"No, you don't need to tell me anything about my body. I don't need a confidence boost," he winks at me.

"Who said that? Maybe I'm grossed out by what I see. I mean who wants to stare at a guy in finely tailored suits all the time. I mean who the hell knows what's under there?" I tease, giving his bicep a playful shove. I definitely do like what I see—and I'm dying to see more of that handsome body ... without the suit. He must feel my eyes drinking him in.

Luke instantly pulls me into his chest, I grab onto his chiseled arms, and I'm pressed full body against him. We lock eyes and then he brings his lips to mine. His tongue darts inside my mouth and I feel him pull on my lower lip with his teeth. Vibrations tremble throughout my eager body—needy for whatever he has to offer me. I'm terrified but I'm equally excited.

"Still grossed out?" he growls into my ear as he pulls my scrubs and tank top off, tossing them to the marble floor.

"Oh yeah, repulsed," I say, pushing his suit jacket off and throwing it on the growing pile of clothes. I slowly unbutton his dark blue dress shirt, and as I push it off his firm chest, I step back in absolute shock.

Now I know what he's been hiding under these three-piece suits ... Luke is covered in tattoos!

My eyes scan the full sleeves on each of his arms up to the large piece on his chest. Just knowing he hides these pieces of artwork from the public, but is sharing them with me, makes my panties even wetter. Our sexy little secret.

"Damn, you're so hot," I pant without realizing how stupid that must sound. Of course he knows he's hot. "Why didn't you tell me about all of your tattoos when I confessed to having one?"

I feel like a complete idiot. He strides over, closing the gap between us to pick me up, wrapping my thighs around his waist.

"I thought it was cute that it was your secret. I didn't want to take that away from you. And I knew I'd eventually show you," he confesses, carrying me out of the living room, pushing open a door, and throwing me down on a big bed. Stripping off my pants, he stands back admiring my body as I lay in my underwear. Seeing him stare at me makes my body tingle from head to toe.

"Ditch the pants, Luke," I command, hearing my voice take on a husky tone I've never heard before. He smiles a wicked grin at me before unbuckling his belt and sliding his pants and boxer briefs down. My hungry eyes take in his body, stopping to stare at his massive cock. I'm not going to be dumb and question if it will fit—I know how anatomy works—but I'm still scared.

"You keep staring at me like that and I won't be able to make this gentle."

"Do I look like I'm going to break? I don't think so, I want you inside of me … now."

He cocks his eyebrow up at me, testing me with his stare, but I don't back down. When he sees I'm truly serious, Luke climbs on top of the bed and presses his luscious lips to mine as he turns our bodies to lay on our sides. He skims his hands over my shoulders and around my back to unclasp my bra. With that out of the way, he cups my breasts, which are heavy and tender at his touch. He massages one breast and then the other while devouring my mouth with deep strokes of his tongue. Our tongues dance together as our bodies sing out in delight.

My body trembles before I regain my confidence and pull myself closer to him, running my fingers up his muscular tattooed arms.

I'm going to have to study these in the daylight.

His skin is hot against mine. Luke moves his hand down my stomach towards my inner thigh, lightly caressing me as he makes his way towards my sex.

He pushes my underwear to the side running his fingers through my most sensitive spot.

You can do this—give yourself to him.

"You are so wet for me. God, I want to bury myself so deep inside of you." He rolls me onto my back and slowly trails down my body, leaving gentle kisses along his path. He stops at my hipbone to plant a kiss on my small tattoo that seems silly next to all of his.

"I love this," he says, appreciating the small tattoo of a heartbeat rhythm—or EKG strip—that connects to a heart on my hipbone.

When he gets to my underwear, he looks back up at me with questioning eyes—he's asking for permission and I nod at him.

"Please, don't stop, Luke," I beg, knowing what he's going to do next. This is something I've never done before. I've never given myself to a man like this, so intimately. He doesn't make me repeat myself as he rips my underwear from my body and throws it on the floor.

He brings his mouth between my thighs and blows on my clit, sending chills through my body. I arch up as he brings his sensual mouth to my nub and circles it with his tongue.

I think I see stars!

Burying my fingers in his thick hair I push him closer towards my sex, silently begging him not to stop. He sucks on my clit as he brings his finger towards my entrance and ever so slowly pushes one inside of me. I moan out in pure ecstasy.

I have never had an orgasm before; I'm a little scared of how my body will react. What will happen to me?

Again, you know how this works. Calm down. Enjoy him.

I feel myself on the verge of losing control; my legs shake as Luke sucks hard on my pussy. I close my eyes, letting my body do what comes natural. After I stop shaking, I look down at Luke who is staring up at me from between my thighs.

"God, you're incredibly sexy," he purrs as he makes his way back up my body.

It's time I repay his very generous favor. Another first for me—I'm embarrassed to say I've never given a blowjob. Should I tell him? No, that's even weirder.

I push Luke back on the bed and position myself straddling him. I alternate between sucks and nips as I trail my way down his chest and rippling abs. I'm now eye to … dick … with him. I start off with something I'm familiar with and stroke him up and down with my hand.

"Tell me what you like," I say, hoping my inexperience will shine through as curiosity to please him the best I can. He doesn't question me even if he knows.

"Run your tongue up and down it."

Okay, I can do this. I lick my lips and then trace my tongue up and down this shaft. Once I get a little more daring, I add in my hand and gently massage his balls. I hear him make a ridiculously sexy noise, which encourages me to keep the slow and steady motion, sliding up and down his throbbing manhood.

"Stop," he commands, pulling me away from his cock. He flips me over to position himself on top of me; I feel the dampness return between my thighs just staring at his gorgeous face.

He reaches for a condom from his dresser and positions his tip at my entrance.

"Are you okay?" he asks in all seriousness. My heart melts that he cares about how I'd feel about sex, but my pussy is begging for him at the same time.

"Yes, I want this." I arch my hips up towards him to rub on his shaft.

And with that he thrusts his hips down and sinks into my entrance ever so slowly until my body feels adjusted to his size. I let out a breath of air as I try to relax.

He doesn't move until I lock eyes with him and nod—he needs to know that I'm okay.

With my nod, Luke starts rocking his hips back and forth. The slight pain from adjusting to his size turns into a tingling sensation and a deep pull in my stomach.

I don't ever want this to stop. I grip onto his broad shoulders and pull him down harder into my sex. He takes my hint and works his powerful hips faster and harder. The next thing I know, Luke's mouth is sucking on my neck, sending chills down my body. I rake my hands down his back, feeling more scars, but stop when I get to his muscular ass—I think even his muscles have muscles. I grab on.

He stops sucking on my neck and growls, "I'm going to come," before he pumps hard into me one last time. As if my body knew it was time, I join him in an intoxicating orgasm. I've gone my whole life without having any to experiencing two in one night.

"What are you doing to me?" I ask as he pulls out of me and heads towards the bathroom to dispose of the condom.

He crawls back into the bed, reaching his hand out for me to hold his. I take it in mine without a second thought. We are both staring up at his ceiling, catching our breath after what feels like running a marathon.

"That's how you should feel after sex," Luke says pulling me into his side, "my goddess."

I cuddle into him before we both drift off to sleep.

CHAPTER FOURTEEN

Luke
14 years old

We sit together for a family dinner around the table—minus dad, of course. He is out at the bar ripping cigarettes and getting drunk beyond belief—his usual after work routine lately. Can't say I mind one bit because that means less time he spends here making our lives a living nightmare.

Mom asks us all about our schoolwork while setting down a plate of chicken nuggets and French fries. She brushes a piece of hair out of Eric's face and he gives her one of his goofball smiles. Eric is the clown of the family.

Lisa, Eric, and I go around the table telling mom what we are working on in school as she listens intently to every word. This would be the picture perfect Brady Bunch shit if we weren't ignoring the fact that mom has a black eye and split lip that bleeds every time she smiles too wide.

Before we can get up from the table, we hear dad stumble into the house. Drunks are never quiet even though they think they are. He staggers his way into the small kitchen carrying a brown paper bag reeking of whiskey. Dad tries to put it on the counter and instead drops it to the laminate floor in a loud crash.

"Look what you made me do!" he shouts to no one in particular. My brother and sister look down at their plates, trying not to make eye contact with him, but I stare at him good and hard. I burn his picture into my memory—what I promise I will never fucking look like. I'm 14 years old and I know that I will never be like my dad. Ever.

He reaches into the pocket on the front of his blue T-shirt, looking for his pack of cigarettes, but comes up empty.

"Did you smoke my last cigarette?" he slurs towards the dinner table. Who the hell is he even talking to?

"No one smoked your cigarettes, Bill," mom explains as she gets up from the table, collecting our empty plates to take towards the kitchen sink.

Dad gains super strength and smashes his fist into the stack of plates mom is carrying, sending shards of broken glass all over the floor. Mom's hands bleed as she tries grabbing a piece of paper towel to clean herself. It doesn't slip my attention that she didn't even scream or cry—she's so goddamn used to this. I wish so very bad that weren't the case.

Dad leaves the room and we hear our parents' bedroom door slam shut. *Did he finally give up?* He's never backed down from a fight; he usually fights it out until he passes out or tires out. But he never gives up without the last word.

Lisa, Eric, and I all jump out of our seats and rush over to mom. Lisa begins picking up all the broken plate pieces to throw in the trash as I clean up mom's hands.

"I fucking asked you pieces of shit, did you smoke my last fucking cigarette?" Dad shouts into the kitchen and we all swing around looking towards him. That's when panic sets in. He's holding a gun. Lisa gasps and drops all the pieces of plate.

"Bill," mom tries saying in a calm voice as she puts her body in front of all three of us with her arms outstretched. This has never happened before. I didn't even know he had a gun in the house.

"Caroline," dad says in a mocking tone, "don't fucking protect these little shits. One of them," he says, swinging his nine millimeter at each of us, "smoked my last cigarette. And I will find out who. No one disrespects me in my own house."

"Bill, please put the gun down." Mom's voice takes a higher pitched tone.

"Come over here bitch," dad slurs with the gun still making its rounds to point at each one of us. Mom does what he says and stands by his side. "You want to protect them? You want to teach them to lie to me?"

"No, Bill, that's not true," she says while standing next to dad but keeping her eyes glued on us. "They aren't lying. You probably smoked your last cigarette; let's leave them alone. Kids, go to your rooms."

Dad's eyes go from full of rage to an eerie icy glare—no emotions at all reflected in his hazel eyes that miserably reflect my own. I hate that I have his eyes.

Oddly enough, dad lets us kids pass him and we go into Lisa's room to hide out together. But that was too easy.

That's when we hear dad start screaming at mom. It's the usual stuff at first about how she's a dumb bitch, a terrible wife, a cheater and an incompetent mother—which are all drunken lies. She's the best thing that's ever happened to him or us kids. We can't hear mom's replies, but I assume she's trying to calm him down. Then I hear a blood curling scream like I've never heard before.

Fuck this.

I run from Lisa's room after telling my siblings to stay back. I round the corner and I'm frozen in my tracks. Dad has mom picked up by her throat and he's choking the life out of her—mom's face is turning purple. I spot the gun unattended on the kitchen counter but it's still closer to him. I don't think dad even knows I've left my room.

Mom can't take much more.

"Stop!" I scream, charging towards dad, knocking into him, and causing him to lose his grasp on mom's neck. She falls to the floor clutching her throat. As she gasps for air, I start pounding my fists into dad's face. I'm coming out on top until dad regains that super strength—probably from the alcohol—throwing me off his body. I slam into the kitchen wall. As I stumble to my feet, dad takes this time to grab his gun again.

Mom screams, I scream, and then the gun rings out as the first shot is fired into the kitchen.

CHAPTER FIFTEEN

Waking up with the sun shining across my face, I slowly pull my eyes open. I know I'm in Luke's bedroom but the man of the house is not here—I'm alone. Before I can stew for too long about being left by myself, Luke walks in the bedroom wearing only a pair of black basketball shorts and a gym towel wrapped around his neck. His chest and abs glisten with sweat. Seeing the tattoos covering his arms in the daylight causes me to lose my breath.

On his right arm I spot an angel wearing a long, flowing white robe. Underneath the angel there's a woman's name—*Caroline*—written large in cursive. Her face is soft and beautiful, very real looking. I don't have it in me to ask who she is or what this is about. It's too much, too soon. Clearly this is a tribute to someone who means a great deal to him. Enough to put her on his body for life.

Around the angel and trailing down his right arm I also spot a giant eye towards the inside of his bicep followed by an hourglass, lotus flower, and dove.

On the other arm, it's an entirely different theme. Dark. To oppose the angel and her beautiful light on his right arm, his left showcases a grim reaper and a demon like figure. Polar opposites reflected on his skin.

Luke notices me sitting up in the bed and takes his earphones out.

"One day we are going to talk about all these tattoos," I say. He smirks as he eyes my body, reminding me how naked I am. I pull the sheet up around my body, suddenly feeling a little self-conscious in the daylight. Luke strides over to the bed, drops the towel on the floor, and pulls the sheet away to display my bare breasts.

"Good morning, Ariana. I wanted so desperately to wake you up, but I couldn't do it knowing how hard you work," he says as he cups my chin, planting a deep kiss on my eager lips while taking a hand to massage my tender breast. I moan into his mouth, pushing my breast out even more, begging him with my body to keep going. "Are you sore?"

That's a question to kill the mood.

But am I? I guess slightly between my legs, yes, but the need to have him again is overruling the aches and pains.

"I want you," I say in my raspy morning voice, reaching my hand out towards his shorts where I find his throbbing erection.

I don't have to ask him twice. Luke jumps in bed with me for his second workout of the day. And this time he isn't the only one to work up a sweat.

Walking into our apartment, I trip over a stack of boxes Serena hasn't picked up yet. No doubt stacks on stacks of designer clothes. She's definitely got a shopping problem, but with her parents' money footing the bill, she doesn't seem to care. I don't care either because the offer always stands for me to borrow any clothes I want. And sometimes I do, usually when she forces me.

I spot my roommate in the living room curled up on the couch with her laptop while some trash TV plays in the background. Flopping down on the chair opposite her, before I even say a word, she flashes me a grin and screams, "Oh my god! You got laid!"

I blush and that's all she needs to confirm her accurate assumption.

"How did you know?"

Serena laughs and puts her laptop to the side, focusing her attention solely on me. I know she wants the dirt on the down and dirty.

"Your face is glowing. He was good, wasn't he?" she asks. Not even waiting for my answer, she pretends to fan herself with her hand and continues her daydream. "He looks like he'd be an animal in the sack. Please tell all the details. I'm so jealous."

Now it's my turn to laugh.

"Get real! A lady doesn't have sex ... twice ... and tell."

Her mouth drops and then she's flying off the couch and running into the kitchen. In a flash she's back with a wine bottle and two glasses. "Twice? You were gone for one night. I'm so proud of you. Let's toast."

It's noon on a Saturday and I have a shift tonight, but toasting to having amazing sex with Luke is just what I need. I take the glass from my roommate and we both raise them in the air.

"To hot guys," Serena says.

"To passionate kisses," I add, which gets a smirk out of Serena.

"To blow jobs."

"To massive cocks."

Serena's eyes perk up, clearly approving of where this toast is going.

"To sex ... with massive cocks." We both giggle at that one.

"To letting your guard down and letting someone in," I say. On that note, we click our glasses together, sipping our chilled white wine.

We continue to chat about what we've been up to as we finish our wine. I then excuse myself to take a much-needed shower. It's time I wash away Luke's delicious smell from my entire body or else I'll be too distracted at work to save any lives—and that sounds dangerous. Not the fun kind of a dangerous either.

While the water heats up, I hear a ding from my phone. A text from Luke—

I miss that hot ass already! What are you doing to me woman?

I smile knowing he's had the same effect on me. Before I can second-guess myself, I snap a quick picture of the 'hot ass' he's referring to and hit 'send' as I hop in the shower. Me sending a nude picture? Looks like we are both doing things that shock us.

The shift goes by smoothly, and I think it has something to do with me feeling like I know what the hell is going on … finally. I'm comfortable in the emergency room. The chief even complimented me on how well I handled a disgruntled family member today who was losing his cool in the middle of the waiting room. She had no idea I used to work in a restaurant when I was a teenager. It would fill up late at night with drunks—who would get in fights every chance they'd get. I learned how to master a headlock or two.

I step outside of the hospital to see Luke waiting by the curb next to an insanely hot silver Jaguar. Of course, he's still wearing a suit, but now that I know what's lurking under there I can't stop picturing his muscles and tattoos.

"I didn't know you were picking me up tonight."

"Can't a guy surprise his girl?" *His girl?* I don't address his word choice, not wanting to draw attention to what it's doing to me. Drenching my panties that is. "Want to grab dinner?"

"Hell yes!"

I think since meeting Luke I've had more decent meals than in the last eight years of med-school and residency; I've been living on cheap junk and energy drinks just to get me through to the next shift.

"Any place you'd like to go?" he asks. I'm surprised he doesn't just take the lead like he normally does.

"Whatever your heart desires," I say, climbing into the most expensive car I've ever seen. The gorgeous leather seats smell new, and even though I don't want to imagine how much this car costs, it's cozy.

"My heart desires eating …" he trails his hand down my thigh and cups my sex. I squeeze my thighs together, trapping his hand, and close my eyes before he can see the lust in them.

"Don't tease me, I'll make you deliver on your word," I pout, unclenching my thighs while he places his hand on the steering wheel.

"My word is good, always. I will eat that pussy later, but first let's get you some real food," his sensual mouth smirks at me before we head away from the hospital.

We sit in silence during the ride, enjoying the sound of the car's engine and just being in each other's presence. I notice we are turning away from the hustle and bustle of the downtown Chicago streets into a nearby neighborhood. As we pull into a small family diner, I shoot Luke a questioning look but he smiles without saying a word. This is not what I pictured for a man in a suit, but I'm all for it. This reminds me of that place I used to work at back in Orlando. It was all the rage with the senior citizens of Florida.

Walking into Molly's Diner, a waitress shouts from behind a counter that we can sit wherever we want. Luke walks like he owns the place towards a booth in the back of the restaurant. This place screams 1970s with its pink and teal furniture and fake potted plants—but it feels homey. I slide into the worn-in booth, sinking down in the middle. It's definitely had its fair share of customers.

An older waitress with grey hair tied into a low bun walks over to our table and a big smile breaks out across her wrinkled face. "Luke! It's so good to see you, sweetie. And who's the pretty lady?"

It surprises me that he's on a first name basis at place like this—I think he stands out in his three-piece suit but apparently that's not the case. Another waitress walks by and waves at our table. But unlike the 'I want to fuck you' glares we get from women in other public places, these ladies look at him with caring eyes.

"Kathy, this is Ariana," Luke says, waving across the table towards me.

Both Kathy and I realize Luke did not give me any kind of title—just my name. She doesn't say anything and neither do I—Ariana it is. Luke takes charge, like always, telling her we'll have coffees and waters. As Kathy scurries away to get those ready, I pick up my menu.

Kathy is back in the blink of an eye and before Luke can try to order my food, I spit out that I'd like French toast and bacon. He smiles at me across the table and sticks with the 'breakfast for dinner' theme ordering their biggest breakfast special—eggs, bacon, silver dollar pancakes, and hash browns. And just like she appeared in a flash, Kathy takes off towards the kitchen to put in our orders.

"Do you come here often?"

Luke sips his black coffee and then replies, "You could say that. I got caught stealing some food here when I was around 15, and instead of turning me in, they let me work here part-time along with the bar I told you I worked at. They are good people here."

"Why were you stealing? Were you a rebellious teen?" I ask, smirking at him, thinking of a young Luke getting into trouble just to get into trouble.

"I was stealing because I was hungry ... starving actually."

My hand shakes and some of the coffee I was bringing towards my mouth slips out of the cup and onto the table. *Starving? This handsome CEO with his Jaguar and penthouse suite was starving?*

"Why were you starving?"

He sighs, but before he can answer Kathy comes to our table. She places down more plates of food than I could imagine. I'll say this about family diners—the portion sizes are always out of this world.

Luke switches gears from talking about being a starving teenager to asking me how my day at work went. We chat about his marketing meetings and my shift of chest pains, stomach bugs, and the usual emergency room visits. We don't touch back on the earlier subject and I get the feeling that's for a reason. Luke opened up as much as he was going to for today. As much as I want the answer to why he was starving, I don't want to push someone to talk when they aren't ready.

It does hurt me a little to know he isn't ready, especially after I shared something so deep with him.

After Luke pays our bill, we get in the car and I notice we are heading towards his penthouse. Relaxing into the comfortable seat, Luke blasts the heat on this cold Chicago night, and I drift to sleep. It's not until I hear the elevator door ding that I realize Luke has carried me out of the car, into the elevator, and now across the threshold into his home.

"Put me down. Are you crazy? What if you throw your back out carrying me?" I scream, trying to get myself out of his arms. But he squeezes me even tighter, refusing to let go.

"I'm definitely not weak, Ariana. I can carry my woman anywhere she wants to go."

Earlier I had no title and now I'm his woman. I'm confused. I know we will need to discuss this … by 'this' I mean whatever the fuck it is that we are, but tonight is not the night.

Even though this is such a caveman move to carry me into his apartment, I'm extremely turned on. Forget the bedroom! I need him and I need him now. As he places my feet down on the grey tiled kitchen floor, I attack his mouth with such intensity that he cups my face with his hands to hold my head still.

I can't be held down. I need to move. I need him to move.

"Do you want to fuck me?" I beg. With his hands still holding my face he scans my eyes to make sure I mean what I'm saying. Hell yes I do. I pull my scrubs off my body and stand in front of him in my underwear. "Well, do you?"

He doesn't say a word; instead he shows me his answer. He rips his dress shirt off, letting buttons fly through the air. In a matter of seconds, he has all of his clothes off and he's standing in front of me in full glory. I lick my lips, swollen from our passionate kisses, while I slowly scan his body. Perfect: everything about him from those sexy tattoos to the scars. I wouldn't change a single thing about this man. *My man.*

Luke stalks towards me as if I'm his prey and then cups my sex while pushing me back towards the black kitchen counter. Thrusting my fingers into his brown hair and pull hard. This earns me a little bite on my lips, which makes me moan.

Luke lifts me onto the counter and I wrap my legs around his waist. Pulling myself as close to him as I can get, I grip a handful of his muscular ass. He squeezes my breast before devouring my mouth with deep sweeping strokes of his tongue. I grind my sex into his hard cock. I rub against him, getting us both wet. When he must not be able to take much more, Luke slams into me and I have to hold onto the wall or else I'd slam backwards.

He's driving into me so hard. Bottles shake and who knows what falls from the counter to crash on the floor—we are rocking everything in this kitchen.

Luke cups his hand around the back of my head and buries his face into my neck as he slams into me one last time. I feel his rock hard manhood pulsate inside of me and I come with him. We both try to catch our breath, as we remain clung to each other's sweaty bodies, coming down from the ride of my life.

"I'll never be able to look at this kitchen the same way again," Luke growls into my ear and I bust out in a fit of laughter. I shove his chest, and as he pulls out of me, it's only then it hits me, we just had sex without a condom. Luke looks down and must have the same realization. "I'm so sorry, I was caught up in the moment."

"It's okay, I'm on the pill. But we never had the oh-so-sexy STD talk, which is embarrassing considering I'm a doctor," I say, burying my face in my hands.

"Hey," he says pulling my hands down from my face, "I'm clean. But I'll gladly get tested again if it will make you feel better."

"I trust you," I say, hopping down from the counter heading towards the bathroom to clean myself up. He doesn't block my path but lets me go to the bathroom alone to collect my thoughts and get dressed.

I trust him.

That's true. I don't think I've ever trusted a man before. I vowed I never would. I'm breaking my vow for Luke, and as much as that scares me, I think I'm okay with it.

I hear a light knock on the door after what must be a good ten minutes, "Ariana, you alright in there?"

Opening the door I see Luke standing in front of me. His pants are back on but he's still shirtless. He looks at me, trying to read my face. I instantly wrap my arms around him and bury my face in his chest mumbling, "Yes Luke, I'm okay."

We stand there in each other's arms for what feels like eternity, holding onto each other as tightly as possible. I don't know when Luke breaks the embrace, but it's only for a brief moment to pick me up again and carry me to his bed.

CHAPTER SIXTEEN

The sound of a door slamming in the distance jolts me awake and again I find myself asleep in Luke's bed … alone. One day I'll wake up and he'll be next to me—that's something I'm waiting for. At the thought of Luke striding around his apartment just home from the gym, I jump out of bed, wrapping the white sheet around my naked body and head out to find my man.

I'm almost into the living room when I hear a woman's voice and I stop in my tracks. Who the hell is here? I want to backtrack towards the bedroom, but before I can move a muscle the voices get closer to me. Luke and Lisa walk around the corner to catch me awkwardly staring at them from the hallway.

Lisa's jaw drops upon seeing me. "I didn't know you had company." Then realization sinks in: "Wait a second. You're the girl from the hospital?"

I pull the sheet a little tighter to my body and I extend my hand towards her, "Ariana."

She shakes my hand. "Lisa, but you already know that. I'm sorry to act so shocked. I've never seen a woman at Luke's before."

Lisa glares at her brother who is looking down at the floor. Is he embarrassed to have her catch me here?

"It's nice to see you again Ariana. I hope we can catch up one day," she says as she heads towards the front door, "but I have to dash off now. Bye brother!"

And just like that, she's gone. I don't say a word to Luke instead I rush back to his bedroom to put on some clothes, feeling like a damn fool.

"I didn't know she was coming," Luke says, appearing in the doorway just as I'm throwing my scrub top over my head and searching for wherever the hell my shoes are. The kitchen! Then the memory of last night's sex in the kitchen causes my face to heat up. I push past Luke but he blocks my path in the hallway.

"Luke, I don't care that you didn't know she was here," I say, faking as if I'm going right but quickly dart left and make my way around him. I'm in the kitchen in a hurry, slipping on my sneakers and barreling towards the front door.

"What's wrong then?" Luke stops me, gently grabbing on to both of my arms.

"What are we doing?" I ask, moving out of his grasp.

"We are dancing around my apartment apparently," he sighs as if exhausted by my question.

"That's not the answer I was looking for. I'm sorry. Can you get out of my way? I'd really like to leave."

Luke follows me on my mission to get to the front door. "I don't understand your question then. What are we doing … about what?"

I stop and face him, "About *us*? You introduce me to the waitress last night by just my name. You didn't even say 'my friend' … then you call me 'your woman' later when we are alone… and now with Lisa you stand there looking down at your feet in embarrassment she caught you with me. You didn't even bother to introduce me yourself."

My face falls after getting all of that out, bearing myself so vulnerably. I'm sick of feeling like I'm not what Luke is looking for—first with the girl at the charity event and now all of this crap.

Why don't I measure up?

"You think I'm embarrassed to be seen with you?" he asks, looking straight into my eyes, not backing down. "Are you fucking serious? I'm honored to be seen with you, Ariana. I'm sorry I didn't introduce you with any special title. I haven't had to do this before. This is all new for me."

"Well, what about with your sister?"

He runs his fingers through his hair, looking frazzled. "I didn't like having her catch you here for the first

151

time wrapped up in a sheet—it's pretty obvious we were fucking."

"So you don't want her to know we're having sex?" I ask clearly annoyed.

"Goddamn it," Luke says looking defeated yet angry. "I want better for you than that."

"Thank you for wanting better for me," I say, thinking his confession was cute, "even though we are adults and it would be okay if she knew we are fucking. What would you want me to introduce you as to the people in my life?"

"Your sex slave," he grins, which gets a laugh out of me.

"I guess I could make that happen ... after my shift that is—I have to go back to work," I say, reaching the door handle. Before I can twist the knob, Luke has me pressed against the door with his chest on my back.

"I hate to see you go," he says cupping my ass. "I will have this ass on my mind all day long without you."

"You can use that picture I sent to keep you company." I blush at the memory of sending it.

He nuzzles his nose to my ear and sucks on my ear lobe. "That was a lovely surprise, Ariana."

I smile, imagining what it must have been like for him to get that text message. I wonder where he was when he got it?

"Okay sex slave boy, I really have to go," I say as he gives me some space to open the door.

"I won't be able to come pick you up tonight. I have to stay late at the office and then catch a flight to Detroit early in the morning for back-to-back meetings."

He's leaving? I feel sadness deep within my heart thinking about him not being right around the corner if I need him.

You've never needed anyone right around the corner before. Not even your parents.

The thought wakes me up to the realization that I can't put all my happiness on Luke. I also have to realize I am a big girl and needing a man around was never what I wanted.

I lean in to kiss Luke on the cheek and tell him to text me when he lands safely in Detroit before I head out the door, where I find Ryan waiting for me by the curb to drive me to my apartment. I laugh because I was planning to walk, but of course, Luke is always one step ahead of me. When did he have time to alert Ryan? I'll never know his mysterious ways.

⇥+⇤

Standing at the computer station, I scan through my patient files while I have a few minutes to catch my breath before my shift starts. I've got about fifteen minutes until it's go time. With my headphones in, I escape to my own little world and it's not until Drake touches my arm that I look away from the computer.

I jump back a little from his touch. I don't know if that's because he surprised me or if unwanted touching from people I don't approve of still is a concern of mine? I don't have long to think about it because Drake comes bearing gifts, placing an iced coffee on the counter in front of my now empty cup.

"Thank you," I say, slipping my headphones out of my ears.

"I haven't seen you in days. What have you been up to?" Drake asks.

I take a sip of my coffee before replying, "Working every shift they'll give me and then hanging out with Luke or Serena. What about you?"

We both work in the same hospital but our floors are both equally busy; sometimes we can go days without seeing each other. But in the past, we'd never let that happen. We saw each other daily or at least would send text messages.

I feel weird with how he treated Luke at the sports bar—which he has not apologized for. He should know how hard it is for me to open up to guys—he should be supporting me, not trying to sabotage me.

"You're still seeing that guy? Wow. Ariana, for someone I consider my smartest friend, I don't think this is smart at all. What do you even know about him?"

And just like that, he sets me off.

"What do *you* even know about him? Why are you being so judgmental Drake? As someone I consider one of my kindest friends, judging someone so harshly isn't kind at all."

"I don't want to be kind to someone who has a reputation of fucking around with women—he's seen with all kinds of different girls. Someone like him doesn't seem to fit with the girl who guards herself so cautiously. You are not a match and this will not last long."

So he's done one Google search and he thinks he knows everything about my boyfriend? He's basing his opinion on rumors. Fuck this.

"I understand you are trying to look out for me. I can see that. But you need to give me a chance to figure out who is a fit for me or not by myself."

"And what if you get hurt?" He asks, reaching out towards my hand, but I pull it back.

"Then I get hurt, that's life. And that will suck big balls," I laugh, "but it will be my own mistake, and I'm okay with that."

He stares at me for a moment, as if daring me to back down, but I don't. Then he changes his tune: "Ariana, you're a pain in the ass. But you're still my friend and I don't want to fight with you. Want to get some lunch later?"

And just like that my best friend is back to being his normal, laid-back self.

"Yes! I'll meet you in the cafeteria later."

━━┽╋┾━━

Luke hasn't been a part of my life for long, but a night knowing I absolutely can't see him makes me sad. After lunch with Drake and a few of our coworkers, I finished my shift and then went back to the apartment to see if Serena was there to lounge around with.

But the place is empty. I don't like how quiet it is so I dash back out of the door as quickly I came in. I have no direction to go; I just set off and walk. It's freezing, but I don't even care that my body is probably going to go into shock.

Walking up and down each street, I look around at my neighborhood's surroundings. It's sad that I've never done before. I've never taken the time to give a shit about anything but school or my residency. Me, me, me—wow, I'm a giant asshole that's for sure.

I walk past a man on the street peddling flowers. He's dressed in a light winter coat with some holes in it and his shoes look very worn—he must be so cold.

"Beautiful flowers for a beautiful girl?" He pushes a bouquet of red roses at me.

"How much are they?" I shock myself by answering him. Normally I am a 'head down, don't talk to me' type of person. I don't get asked much by the homeless people. I think my 'back the fuck off' vibe intimidates some.

"Five bucks," he says, holding an open palm out to me. It's filthy.

I reach in my pocket—grateful I grabbed some cash, my ID, and my cellphone, and I hand him some money and take the flowers before walking away.

"Miss! Miss! You gave me too much! Way too much," I hear him calling out to me as. "Come back for your change!"

I turn around and wave at him. I don't want the change. He waves back at me and yells "Have a blessed day!"

When I stroll into the apartment after my walk, Serena is in the kitchen making something that smells delicious.

"Those are a lovely," she says eyeing my flowers, "are those from Lukey boy?"

"Lukey boy? Ugh—we are not giving him a nauseatingly cute nickname." I grab a vase from one of the cabinets and put the roses in some water and then hand the vase off towards her. "No, they're for you."

"What? Who are they from?"

"Me silly!" I laugh—my roommate looks like she's in shock.

"Thank you," she says, putting the flowers on the kitchen island before walking over to give me a hug—this time without asking me if it was okay.

"Okay, get the fuck off me," I joke after the hug goes on for much too long. She laughs at me, not even complaining that I swore at her. "What are you making for dinner?" I try moving the conversation away from Serena smothering me with love and affection.

"Pot roast with mashed potatoes, garden salad, and chocolate cake for dessert." Serena lists off the foods like it's no big deal she's cooking a feast, something I could never do. She says it's because she hung out in the kitchen with her chef and nanny who taught her how to make all these meals. Her parents were too busy building their careers, not raising their own daughter. Her words, not mine. Compared to my parents, hers don't sound all that bad, but I do not tell her that.

As she pulls the pot roast from the oven, I get a whiff of the scent. My stomach knows what's coming and lets out a little noise. I'm forever grateful for Serena's chef abilities in this moment. I take out plates and silverware for two as I set the table—I mean it's the least I can do.

"Can you set it for two more?"

"Two? Who's coming over?"

I grab two more sets of everything and walk towards the table. It's rare that we have anyone eat with us except for Drake on occasion. Serena doesn't make big sit down dinners often.

"Remember that guy from the other night … Jack?" Her face turns red when saying his name. I've never seen this confident girl blush before. What the heck is going on?

"The guy you were making out with and didn't remember his name? Cutie?"

"Yeah, that's the one," she says as she finishes chopping the raw vegetables for the salad. "We've been talking almost every day since then."

This is big news! Serena goes through guys like she does toilet paper, but I keep my opinion to myself because I definitely do not want to get uninvited to this feast.

"Okay ... so Jack wants to sit in two spots? What's the deal with the other plate?"

She turns around quickly to avoid looking at me when I hear her say, "He's bringing a friend. I'm sorry."

"Wait, what? What kind of friend and why are you apologizing about it?" I ask, clearly confused by everything that's taking place since I've walked into this Twilight Zone of a kitchen.

"When I invited Jack over for this dinner you were still moping around about Luke. So when Jack offered to bring a friend for you, I said sure. Now I know you are talking to Luke again, but I didn't know how serious you were. I couldn't bring myself to ask Jack to tell his friend to fuck off. So just be nice. Okay? We'll explain when he gets here that it's not a double date."

It's really cute—my friend is trying to set me up with someone but this couldn't come at a more terrible time. Luke and I are back together, kind of? He still never said he would introduce me to others as his girlfriend, but he did say he was honored to be seen with me. An innocent dinner with some friends isn't going to break any rules, right? I mean it's in my own apartment for Christ's sake, so it's not like I can ditch out, plus Serena's cooking is a treat.

I head to the bathroom to freshen up since I went on my walk through the neighborhoods. While throwing my hair up in a quick bun, I hear a knock at our door followed by a loud crash in the kitchen accompanied by a few choice words from Serena. She really wants this to go well. I rush out of the bathroom to get the door so she doesn't get stressed.

Swinging the door open I come face-to-face with two very handsome preppy looking guys: Jack, who I recognize from our quick encounter the other night, and his friend.

"Come in," I say, moving to the side gesturing them into the foyer. "I'm Ariana," I say, extending my hand to Jack who takes it and smiles.

"Nice to meet you again, under much better circumstances," he laughs as he nods towards his blonde friend. "This is my friend, Paul."

"Nice to meet you, Ariana," Paul says, taking my hand in his. I collect their coats, and as I'm putting them in the closet, Serena prances into the living room looking stunning as ever—when did she freshen up?

"Gentlemen! I hope you're hungry!"

She kisses Jack on the cheek and Paul makes his introduction again. The guys sit down at the table, which I see Serena has transformed into a masterpiece. Her table display could rival the works we see at major high-end functions; it's like Pinterest exploded in here. She's a wizard. Little do these guys know we eat off paper plates most days. I highly doubt they'd care either.

Dashing to my friend's side, I offer to help but she tells me to sit down and chat with the guys, giving me a serious 'stay out of my kitchen' stare. I take her orders and do exactly what she says. Taking my seat across from Paul at our four- person table, I learn he's a banker, like

Jack, and they went to college together. They also both played college football.

He's a nice looking guy—blonde hair, green eyes, and an athletic build—but I still feel weird sitting here knowing he's thinking of me as a potential date. How do I bring up the fact that I'm not? Or what if he's looking over at me thinking about how to get out of the double date too? This is extremely weird—especially for a girl who is already awkward around the opposite sex. Serena needs to hurry her ass up and sit down at the table with us before I turn into a complete clown.

And just like that she saves the day, carrying in the pot roast and placing it in the center of the table, next to the salad, garlic mashed potatoes, and dinner rolls. "Dig in, please!" she says, handing a carving fork to Jack to take the first slice of pot roast.

As we bite into our first mouthwatering pieces, Jack, Paul, and I say at the same time with mouths full of food, "This is amazing." I think all three of us moan a little too—it's really that good. Serena's face lights up as she takes her first bite. She really is a great hostess; I should take mental notes on how she does everything.

The conversations flow easily with Serena here directing the topics, along with making lovey dovey eyes at Jack, so it doesn't feel so much like a double date. It's more like a few friends catching up over a delicious meal. That is until we hear another knock at the door. It's rare we have visitors; it's even rarer that we have unannounced visitors.

Serena excuses herself from the table and comes back in the room, giving me an apologetic glance as a very stern looking Luke trails right behind her. At first I'm in shock to see him and then I realize how much I've truly missed him these last few days. I want to eat him up, staring at his handsome body in yet another finely tailored suit, which only I know holds beneath it sexy works of art.

"Luke!" I jump up from the table and run over to give him a hug. I squeeze him tightly but do not feel the same tight squeeze in return. He just gave me a half-assed hug—what gives?

It's not until Jack and Paul get up from the table to introduce themselves that I put two and two together. Luke must think he just walked in on what clearly looks like a double date. I need to get him alone for a brief moment to explain.

"I'm sorry I didn't mean to interrupt your dinner. I'll leave you to it," Luke says, heading towards the front door.

"You don't have to go. I made plenty of food," Serena chimes in, pulling up another chair, but Luke doesn't budge.

"That's a very kind offer Serena, but I should be getting home. I wanted to say a quick hello to Ariana now that I'm home from my trip. It was nice meeting all of you," he waves and turns, high-tailing it out of here, but I'm right behind him. He opens the door, making his way into the hallway, but I cut him off before he can get in the elevator.

"Hey wait," I say grabbing his arm, "it's not what it looks like."

"Tell me how it's not what it looks like? It looks like the girl who made it very clear she didn't want me to go to dinners with other women waits for me to leave town for a few days to have a cozy double date with another guy. Is that not what is looks like?"

It's totally what it looks like, but he's not giving me a chance to explain myself.

"Luke, come on, you know I didn't set this up."

"How do I know that?" He gives me a smoldering glare, and not the hot and steamy kind; instead, it's the pissed off kind.

"Because you know me!"

"Not really." Luke spits the words out with a look of fire in his eyes.

"Not really?" I repeat his harsh words—I'm taken back that he'd say them. "I've shared more of myself with you than I have any other person and you want to tell me you don't really know me. Are you fucking kidding me?"

He looks at me with slightly softer eyes now, but he doesn't say a word. We are at a standoff in the middle of the cramped hallway. Now I'm the one giving the pissed off glare. How could he say that?

"If you would have just listened to me before jumping to conclusions, I could have told you I didn't even know about this dinner until 20 minutes before it happened. Serena invited her friend Jack over when you and I weren't speaking. Jack asked if he could bring a friend, and Serena said yes. She didn't want to tell him to uninvite his friend—we are just friends having dinner. Now stop being a little baby and let me do what I've wanted to since I saw you walk into that kitchen."

I run my hands up Luke's strong chest, pulling him by his coat jacket in for a hot, passionate kiss—a kiss I've wanted to give to him not just since he walked into the kitchen but since I knew he was leaving for a few days. We stand in the hallway kissing each other, letting our hands roam freely over one another's bodies. I kiss this man so fiercely like I am drowning and he is my air.

That is until we hear a tiny giggle; we both pull apart in a sheer panic.

My neighbor, Ashley, and her adorable little son, Joseph, have just got off the elevator. They need to pass us to get to their apartment. Ashley blushes, saying she's sorry, but Joseph seems to think he just caught the best show. He's laughing now as I hear her open their door, "Mommy, mommy, they were kissing. Ew!"

When we are alone in the hallway again, Luke laughs and I lean into his chest, laughing too. "I feel like we are teenagers just caught by our parents making out when we shouldn't have been," he says still laughing.

"Me too! Did your parents ever catch you? One time I got caught kissing a boy in his car in my parents' driveway, I was mortified," I say, still buried in Luke's chest, holding him tightly with my arms wrapped around his middle.

"No, my parents never caught me," he says in a serious tone, holding me to him a little tighter.

"Let me guess, you didn't make out with girls at your house? You did all the naughty stuff at theirs?" I tease him, looking up to read his expression.

"No—we didn't invite people over to our house when I was growing up. And making out with girls wasn't really a concern of mine."

"Oh come on, I can't believe that! A stud like you? I bet all the girls were all over you. Your parents didn't ask you why you didn't have girlfriends then?"

"No—my parents were dead."

I gasp, completely caught off guard. Why am I just finding out that the man who I … *who I what? Love?* Has no parents?

"Oh Luke, I'm so sorry," I say, trying to pull myself away from his chest to get a good look at him, but instead he pulls me tighter to him. He's holding on to me like he's afraid I could break away at any moment. I squeeze him tighter for reassurance that I'm not going anywhere.

"Don't feel pity for me, Ariana."

"I don't feel pity for you. That's not even close to the right word. I feel sorrow. What happened to you after your parents died?"

"I was in foster care," he says, squeezing me a little tighter. "My foster parents didn't give a shit about me. They took in foster kids so they could collect some checks but they didn't give us kids a penny. They'd leave us alone for days at a time, with no food, and sometimes our utilities would even turn off. That's when I started to steal from the diner."

It's hard to imagine this handsome man with his designer suits all polished and perfect living this life he's talking about. But my mind remembers the small scars on his face and hands. Who knows what's under those tattoos? My heart hurts for the man I see as so strong.

"Were you with Lisa and Eric?"

"No, we were all split up at that time, but that wasn't for long. I worked hard to get my family back together."

He doesn't say anymore, and I don't push him for details, knowing he didn't push me to tell him about why I wouldn't let him touch me until I was ready to talk.

We stand in the hallway just holding each other until Serena opens the door, throwing her head back to laugh at something funny Jack or Paul must have just said. Then she spots us and her mouth drops, literally drops open.

"Have you two been out here the whole time?" she asks us while the guys say their goodbyes and walk into the elevator.

"I guess we have."

She smiles at us then closes the door to give us some privacy.

Luke kisses the top of my head and pulls us apart. *How long have we been standing here in each other's arms?*

"I have to go now. I have an early morning ahead of me trying to catch up at work. I'll call you tomorrow. Want to have dinner?"

"Yes, I'd love that."

And just like that he finally goes into the elevator. Just a short time before he was trying to fly to get the hell away from me. He waves as the doors shut, closing him in, and I sink down to the floor to catch my breath.

What the hell just happened between us? How many more secrets does he have?

CHAPTER SEVENTEEN

Luke is waiting outside the hospital after my shift; of course, he's right on time. He drives the Jag up to the curb so I can dash inside and escape the snow and wind. The car feels nice and warm, like I've arrived on a tropical island, and in this moment I'm so glad I didn't have to walk or take freezing public transportation. This is the first winter where I didn't dread how I'd get home from work.

"You look happy," Luke says, interrupting my blissed out moment.

Leaning over to grab his face, I kiss his addictive lips. "I am! You know how cold it is? You just saved my ass from freezing off."

He laughs as he drives towards his place. "That would be a nightmare. I'll do anything to keep that ass warm."

"Anything you say?" Now I laugh and curl into the heated seat. "Even letting me select the music?"

Luke rolls his eyes and nods his head in the direction of the pretty intense looking car stereo system.

"Be my guest."

He's made it clear already I listen to "garbage" music, but I couldn't care less what he says as I take over the radio and play DJ. Luke laughs seeing the little dance party I'm having in my seat, and I laugh too seeing I'm amusing him.

I notice as he turns the steering wheel he drums his fingers along to the beat.

"Are you serious? You *like* this song!" I dance even harder.

"Calm down woman, just because a song has a catchy beat doesn't mean I like it."

He pulls the car into his private spot in the parking garage. We both climb out and dart to the elevator. Standing beside him as we ride up, I take in the distinct look of his profile next to me. His strong jawline, the way his suits lay on his muscular body, and even the faint scars on his tan hands and forehead—it's all breathtaking.

"You know what that stare of yours does to me. I don't think I'll be able to keep my hands off you if you don't knock it off," Luke growls, catching me checking out his delectable body.

I pull him by his suit jacket into me. "Don't keep your hands off me, please." I moan as I push my lips to his.

Luke leans into me until my back hits the wall of the elevator; then he starts unzipping my coat. His tongue darts inside my mouth as I suck on it. Wrapping my hands around the back of his head, I run my fingers through his hair. Pulling on his hair and sucking on his mouth, I can't help but feel my body heat up.

I unbutton his suit jacket and throw it on the floor when we hear a *ding* as the elevator door slides open. Damn, I accidently pout at my disappointment that our elevator make-out session has to come to an end so soon.

"Don't be disappointed," Luke whispers into my ear, taking my hand leading me out of the elevator, "I have something planned for you."

We head straight to the living room, the one with the floor-to-ceiling windows, where I notice a blanket laid out on the floor alongside a tray full of fruit and a pot of chocolate fondue.

"This is for me?" I ask, kicking off my shoes and taking a seat on the blanket, in awe of how ridiculously sweet this is from a man who doesn't scream 'sweet' at all.

Hot, sexy, insanely masculine—yes.

Luke mimics me kicking off his shoes and joins me on the blanket. He pours us both flutes of champagne and turns on the pot over the chafing stand. As the chocolate heats up, we catch each other up on how our days went. It makes me happy to have someone to talk to about what's going on in my life—even the little details that aren't all that important. I normally keep this crap to myself, not wanting to bother anyone else. Serena and Drake have way too much to deal with themselves.

"I think it's ready," Luke says, spearing a long-stemmed fork into a plump strawberry and then into the warm milk chocolate. "Open up," he says, airplaning the strawberry towards my mouth with his hand under it to catch dripping chocolate.

As the fruit nears my lips I open my mouth and bite into the strawberry causing juice to dribble down my chin. I don't have any time to clean myself up before Luke puts down his fork and leans in to trail his tongue along my chin where the juice is running. He makes his way to my mouth and plants a deep kiss. I moan, feeling my nipples straining against my scrub top in need. I want to rip these things off and ravish this man besides me. But I control myself. Chocolate first.

Pulling us apart to catch my breath I say, "It's your turn for some chocolate now."

Grabbing the fork I scan the fruit tray, deciding on a slice of banana. Dipping it into the chocolate, I swirl it around before turning back to Luke who's staring at me with a pair of dark hazel eyes, watching my every move. He parts his lips, swollen from all our kisses, as I bring the fondue closer. I put it in his mouth but not without smearing a small dab of chocolate next to his lips across his cheek.

"Oops," I tease, shrugging my shoulders, "let me get that for you." Leaning into him I ever so slowly lick the chocolate from his cheek to his lips. As if the tease didn't turn me on, Luke grabs the back of my head, pulling my mouth down into his. We are both hungry for much more than dessert.

We become a tangle of limbs as we fall back onto the carpeted floor, me straddling on top of him. When I manage to break free for air, I look down at this man laying beneath me staring up into my grey eyes so intensely. I want him inside of me now.

Pulling my shirt off over my head I unclasp my bra, revealing two very alert nipples. He licks his lips as he takes in my sight, slowly scanning my body. Luke dips a finger into the milk chocolate and then rolls my nipples between his index finger and his thumb, massaging me with the warm chocolate. Tilting my head back I moan as I circle my hips onto his—even through our pants, this feels divine as I rub my nub against his erect manhood.

Luke leans in to suck the chocolate away before squeezing my nipple between his teeth. When I don't think I can take much more before I orgasm, he pushes me to the side and quickly strips off my pants and underwear, losing his next. He lies back down on the floor and pulls my hips back on top of him.

"I want you to ride me," Luke commands in a raspy voice laced with sex and need.

This is the only position I've been in with the few other men I've had sex with. I had an unspoken rule—I had to be on top. I needed to be in control of what was happening. The first time I had sex after I was raped I was on the bottom and I started to have a panic attack. *Sexual trauma* is what my therapist called it. It took many years to work through that.

"Get out of that head of yours and just move. Let yourself control your pleasure. Your body knows what to do," Luke reassures me as he brings me back to the present moment.

Leaning down, I kiss from his earlobe to his chest. When I'm so desperate I don't think I can last much longer, I slide his cock into my wet sex. Luke and I both let out moans of absolute pleasure as I sink down on him, letting his manhood fill me up completely. I let my body adjust to him, and then slowly rock my hips and bounce myself up and down on top of him.

Luke takes my hands and places them on his strong chest. Leaning forward changes the angle of my body, causing his cock to slam up into me. My pussy tightens, making me feel dizzy with desire—I've only ever felt this the last time we had sex. I know now how people can get addicted to this.

Luke palms my right breast in his hand as the other finds its way to my clit and circles it with his thumb.

"Luke!" I gasp out in between breaths of pleasure. "Oh my god, please don't stop. Please." The way his thumb circles the wetness around my clit paired with his length sliding in and out of me—I know I'm on the verge of exploding.

"I love hearing you beg," Luke growls as he circles his finger faster and faster around my nub. Thrusting my hips to match his pace, I lock eyes as we both cling onto each other, me falling into this arms holding on for dear life as we ride out our orgasms as one.

Our breaths slow down and I sit myself up with him still inside of me. Looking down into Luke's eyes, I'm lucky to have someone like him show me what this is supposed to truly feel like.

This?

This as in sex … This as in making love … This as in being in love.

What the absolute fuck am I doing? I am a woman who loves her freedom, who vowed never to let a man stop her from doing anything she wants, who promised herself she'd never trust anyone because it only ends up in despair and heartbreak.

Heartbreak is inevitable when you are broken and when you are making love to a broken man. I don't know all of Luke's story. I won't push him to share before he is ready, but whatever it is, it haunts him.

I notice Luke staring up at the ceiling with what must be the same expression I have mirrored on my face: confusion, pain, worry, and love.

What a fucked up pair we are.

But damn, that was nice.

My hospital shifts seem to fly by lately now that Luke is in my life. I don't want to act all lollipops and sunshine because I hate those types of girls, but knowing someone is waiting to spend his or her time around you is a wonderful feeling. I have never had that before. After what happened with Allen, nothing was ever the same with my family. If I were to have turned invisible my parents would have been happy. I know they seemed relieved when I said I was going to Chicago for college—the looks on their faces were all I needed to know that I made the right decision to leave Florida.

"Are you going to pull your head out of your ass and do something around here?" Ben asks, snapping me out of LaLa Land as he shoves a medical chart into my chest.

Okay, he's right. I can't have Luke clouding up my brain when I'm trying to make a name for myself in this hospital. A good name, I don't ever want to be known as *that* resident: the one who cried on the operating room floor, the one who threw up at the sight of blood, the one that turned into a character from *The Walking Dead* because she just couldn't pull her shit together. I will never be that resident. Dear god, don't let me be that.

I flip the chart open and head to the computer station to see where I'm needed. Handing the chart over to Katie, she tells me to head to room 502 because there's a little boy who needs some stitches. Easy enough.

Before I swing open the door I hear hushed voices from the other side and then crying.

"But I don't want to say that," a little boy's voice pleads.

I have a feeling in the pit of my stomach that something wrong is going on behind this door, something I'll try to solve but that'll get me in trouble. No, I cannot do that. Again.

Pushing the door open, I throw a fake smile on my face that I quickly lose at the sight of this little boy. His chart tells me his name is Charlie and he's nine years old. He has red hair and a small patch of freckles line his cheeks—he's adorable. But if you weren't an ER resident, you'd never be able to see this adorable boy; you'd probably have to hold back tears. This little cutie has a deep gash down his cheek paired with cuts up and down his forearms.

"Hi Charlie, my name is Dr. Bellisano, but you can call me Ariana. How are you feeling?" I ask the little boy even though I should ask the woman sitting in the chair near the hospital bed. She's clutching her fingers tightly around her purse straps. Her knuckles look white. Is she afraid of something? Possibly what Charlie might slip up and tell me?

But Charlie doesn't say a word. Instead, he looks down at his feet, little feet much too short to come anywhere near the floor. They just dangle off the side of the bed swinging back and forth.

I get out some of my supplies to clean up his wounds. Once this blood is cleaned up, I'll need to decide if we should call in a plastic surgeon or if some stitches will work. I'll ask him one more time to tell me his side of the story before I have to ask his mom. This must be his mom—she's got matching red hair.

"You want to tell me what happened to get those cuts? I'd like to know before I clean you all up," I say, placing his tiny chin in my hands as I start cleaning up his face. He grimaces but doesn't say a peep. I've seen grown men cry when I've cleaned their open cuts and this little kid is acting like a champ.

He's done this before.

Finally I turn to his mom who looks frazzled beyond belief. Now that I'm staring at her, really staring at her, I notice she's got a few bruises on her arms too. She sees me eyeing her and pulls her shirtsleeves down to cover her arms.

Someone is abusing them.

"Would you tell me what happened?"

Letting out a shaky breath, Charlie's mom says, "He was playing outside and he fell out of his tree house into a pile of sticks and shrubs."

She doesn't even look convinced by her own statement.

"Playing outside … in the winter?"

I don't mean to grill her, but I want answers. To say she gave me a deer-in-headlights look would be an understatement. There's no way that a kid would be outside in Chicago this time of winter playing in a tree house that's covered in snow and ice. Unless he wasn't being watched?

And just like that she flips her shit. "What are you … the cops? Listen, my kid needs medical attention, not to be questioned. Can you fix him up or should I leave so this bullshit interrogation ends?"

I don't mutter another word to her but focus my full attention on Charlie. I go about my business getting him 'fixed up' and try to make small talk to get this kid to crack a smile at least. I'd hate to see him leave with this sad and scared look on his face.

"You like *The Avengers* Charlie?"

He looks up at me with wide green eyes—now I'm speaking his language.

"I love *The Avengers*!" he exclaims, and I hear the hospital gods sing. He spoke!

"Who's your favorite?"

Without even a second to think, he shouts, "Iron Man!" and then he lets me put in the final stitches before politely asking me who my favorite Avenger is in return.

"Hmm … that's a great question. I think my favorite is … Captain America because he's so cute," I joke.

Charlie's mom laughs from her corner of the room as Charlie makes a grossed out look on his face. "Ew! That's disgusting."

"Why is that disgusting?"

"Because girls are cute," he says as his little feet pick up speed swinging back and forth.

"Then what are boys?"

He pauses to think, "Boys are … awesome!"

Bless his heart.

"Well I think both boys *and* girls can be cute *and* awesome."

"Whatever you say lady."

Now it's my turn to laugh. I let Charlie know he's all set but that the physician overseeing my cases will need to come in and take a look at what I've done. As I'm heading out the door to get Dr. Horton, I stop Charlie's mom to whisper, "If someone is hurting you, you should call the police or reach out to an abuse hotline. Neither of you deserves this."

She doesn't say a word and just nods her head.

I find Dr. Horton near the computer stations and let him know about my most recent case. As much as it hurts to watch him do this, we call Child Protective Services because someone needs to interview this family. Becky, the CPS worker in the hospital, says she'll be right down.

A few minutes after we part ways I run into Dr. Horton in the hallway with a sad look on his face.

"Bellisano, no one was in that room when I went to check on them. The family left."

I probably scared her off with my talk about calling the police. I try to hold it together because I don't want to cry in front of one of my attending, so I dash into the nearest bathroom.

Why did I have to open my big mouth? I sent this scared mother and son back out into the world to get beat up again.

"Bellisano! Stop hiding in here, we've got cases to cover!" Ben shouts into the bathroom. Why does this guy always know where I am? It's like he has a tracker on me somewhere.

The rest of my shift goes by in a whirl of commotion. I'm back on top of my game after I convince myself that speaking up to the mother was the right thing. I hope. Ben doesn't need to tell me twice to pay attention, oh hell no. By the time I walk out through the big double doors I spot Luke waiting by his car yet again. He didn't even text me—he just showed up, and I am so grateful to see him.

I rush over and throw my arms around his neck. He stumbles back upon my sudden impact but quickly regains his footing, wrapping his arms around my waist to hold me tight.

"Boy am I glad to see you," I say, planting a deep kiss on his mouth.

"I could get used to this," Luke laughs, "but let's get in the car. It's freezing out here. It's in the single digits."

I let Luke know I need to go to my apartment for a change of clothes if he plans to keep me holed up at his penthouse again tonight. Not that I'm complaining. As he drives towards my place, I let out a sigh of relief and feel my body relax after holding all of my muscles so tense during this crazy shift. As much as I love it there, it feels great to be out of the hospital.

"Rough night?"

"I have a patient who's still on my mind. I hate when that happens. It's hard not to take them home with me."

"Want to talk about it?"

We are a block away from my apartment so I decide to make it quick.

"A little boy came in with his mom. There were clear signs they are getting abused—his face all cut up, her with visible bruises. But when I tried talking her into getting help, she basically told me to fuck off. We were going to have CPS talk to the family but when they went in the room … the family was gone." I sigh, feeling upset all over again. "What upsets me the most is knowing she won't get help when there is some out there, like the charity."

After I finish spitting out my story, I glance over to see Luke's hands clutching his steering wheel—he's got a death grip on the thing—and he seems to be holding his breath. He doesn't turn his head to look at me, instead keeping his eyes staring out at the road. They look like they've got fire inside of them. *Was he even listening to me?*

"Are you okay?" I reach over to lightly touch his bicep and he instantly relaxes. What was that about?

"Yeah, I'm sorry," he mumbles out too quickly, "I just got upset hearing what you dealt with today. That's terrible about that family. Was it just the mom and her boy that came in? No dad?"

"No dad," I answer.

181

He nods as he pulls into the parking garage connected to my building.

"Do you want me to go inside with you?" he asks. I feel like he's asking out of respect, but he still seems a bit off. I think he needs a minute.

"No, I'll be quick," I say, leaning over to kiss his cheek. Something tells me he needs an affectionate touch before I dash out of the car and up to my apartment.

I fly out of the elevator like a bat out of hell and crash into Serena and Jack. Serena's purse goes soaring. I stumble back into the wall, falling off balance, and then we both bust out laughing at each other.

"Whoa lady, are you being chased by a burglar? Slow your freaking roll," Serena laughs as Jack hands her the purse that went tumbling, looking at us like we are crazy.

"Yes, I'm sorry," I laugh, "I was just trying to hurry. Luke is waiting out in parking garage."

"Luke, the guy with a tight hold on you?" Jack jokes while Serena lightly nudges him.

Tight hold? What the hell is he talking about? Why is Serena nudging him to be quiet?

"What's the tight hold thing about?" I ask, sending glares to both of them, waiting for someone to explain the comment. They remain silent for much too long—I doubt if I even said it aloud. "Anyone? Bueller?"

"I'm sorry, I didn't mean to be rude," Jack says, shooting me an apologetic look. "I was making a bad joke about how you ditched our dinner pretty quickly after Luke showed up looking angry."

Wow. I didn't have that impression from our dinner night at all. I guess I can see where he's coming from because I did leave the dinner to stand in this very same hallway in Luke's arms for who knows how long. It blows my mind that while I was having a moment, I was being judged for the 'tight hold' my boyfriend has on me.

"Hey," Serena says touching my arm, "he didn't mean anything by it even though it was a pretty dumb thing to say." She turns to give Jack a smirk. "It's my fault. I didn't explain your situation with Luke very well when you went into the hallway that night. Let's all blame this on me." She tries laughing it off.

Explain my situation? I guess I have a situation now and I'm not talking about *The Jersey Shore* kind.

"Okay, no problem. I should head inside before Luke sends an emergency crew." I give them a tight-lipped smile just to end this conversation.

I push past them both and finally let myself breathe when I'm alone inside. I send Luke a quick text message letting him know I'll be right down, not overlooking the fact that he didn't text me to see what the holdup was. I bet he's still stewing inside his own head over who knows what because he didn't seem to want to open up about it. Now I've got a headache.

I pack a bag with the essentials and fly out the door. I find Luke in a much better mood. He even cracks a smile when I flop down inside. It's not my most graceful entrance, but I'm ready to get the hell away from this place.

"Serena just left, she gave me a little wave, but you don't look as happy. You alright?" It's cute he notices my mood is off, but I don't really want to get into it, especially because my mood change involves him.

"Yep, all good, let's get out of here," I say, trying to deflect the attention away from me. Two can play at the game of not giving all the details.

It feels like the ride to Luke's takes forever, but it couldn't have been more than a matter of minutes, as if traffic cleared the way for him tonight, which I'm grateful for. When we pull into Luke's spot, his eyes dart to two cars parked next to his that normally are not there. He stares at the cars and his shoulders tense.

"Are you okay? Do you know them?" I nod in the direction of the two luxury vehicles, just like his. One a black Mercedes, the other a white BMW—they could all be matching in their slick sexiness.

"My brother and sister are here, apparently," he says with clipped words.

"Oh, did you want to take me back to my apartment? I don't want to be in your way," I say, noticing how awkward the air between us got since seeing his family's cars. Why doesn't he want me to be around his family? I know he said he wanted better for me when Lisa caught us in a compromising position, but this is nothing like that. We have our clothes on for starters. Was that a lie when he said it?

"No, of course I don't want to take you back to your apartment," he says turning towards me, relaxing his shoulders and taking my face between his hands. He plants a kiss on my lips. "I'm glad you're here to meet them."

His words say one thing, but my gut is telling me he's full of shit. However, I'm not about to question him. He said he wants me to meet them both, so I let myself out of the car and follow behind him as we walk to the elevator.

"Is there anything you want me to know about your siblings before we meet?"

He shoots me an irritated glare I've never seen him direct towards me before. "No. You want a warning or something?"

Okay that didn't come out the way I meant.

"Don't couples normally give each other a heads-up before they meet the family? What to expect or something? I've never done this before. I'm sorry."

We are both tense, but before he can answer or acknowledge that I didn't mean to sound like a bitch, the elevator door opens and we hear laughter from the front room. I relax at the sound of Lisa—she was kind to me—but Luke doesn't look like he's any more comfortable.

"Hey guys!" Lisa shoots up from the couch to embrace us both in hugs. "It's so nice to see you again."

"It's nice to see you too!" I hug her back and I really mean it. It is nice to see a smiling face. My mind flashes back to her in the hospital and then flashes forward to what I see today—two completely different women..

"Hi," an attractive man about my age sticks out his hand towards me, "I'm Eric."

I extend my hand to take his strong grip. "Ariana, It's nice to meet you."

Staring between the three siblings I can't get over how much they look like one another. You'd never miss the fact that they are related. It makes me sad to know I don't have any family; just me, myself and I.

"Bro, you're terrible with your introductions," Eric says as he playfully punches Luke in the arm. Luke has been in a trance since we saw their cars.

"Sorry. This is Ariana," he says pointing to me.

"Dude, are you serious? I've already introduced myself. Are you okay?" Eric teases. It's kind of cute to see someone not affected by Luke's strong stance; Eric is not the least bit intimidated.

"Okay, this is super awkward," Lisa says, jumping to try to save this encounter, "want to help me get some drinks, Ariana?"

She doesn't wait for my answer but walks towards the kitchen. I follow right behind her like a lost puppy dog with her tail between her legs. *What is Luke's problem? He's not even trying to make me feel at ease with his family. Isn't that what boyfriends are supposed to do? And he yet again just introduced me by name to his brother—not giving me any kind of title. Why does that keep pissing me off?*

I don't think I can handle all of this tonight, not after the day I had at the hospital with the little boy. I'm suddenly very tired and want to just tuck my head under the covers.

"Hey, snap out of it," Lisa says, snapping her fingers in the air before returning to the iced tea pitcher she's stirring. "What's with you two tonight? You both seem off."

"I have no idea," I answer. I'm not sure if I can open up to Lisa but I really want someone to talk. "He started acting weird earlier when he picked me up from the hospital and his mood has not improved."

"Maybe he had a rough day at work or something? Let's take the iced tea in the room and see if we can salvage this situation," Lisa says, cracking a smile at me. I like her—she's trying to help me. And it's greatly appreciated right about now.

"Boys, drink up." Lisa puts down the tray with a pitcher and glasses.

Luke looks like a completely different person from just two minutes ago when I went into the kitchen. He's sitting on the couch opposite Eric and he's laughing at some crazy sounding story his brother is telling him. He appears relaxed and at ease. Luke makes eye contact with me, smiles, and then pats the spot next to him on the couch. *Who is this Luke imposter?*

I'm not about to question the change in front of his siblings. I take a seat right next to Luke and he puts his arm around me, pulling me in closer. Lisa sits down on the couch with Eric and we listen to him telling the rest of his story. Eric is really funny and animated, getting up and acting out his wild tale—it's hard to take your eyes away from him.

The rest of the night goes like this: Eric entertains us with stories about law school and the latest girls he's taking on dates. Just like his brother, he doesn't seem to have ever been tied down to one girl—maybe that will change? They don't talk about any family related things, instead staying in the present with recent stories. I don't push for any information about the parents that I know they no longer have. Staring from one beautiful face to the next, I can't help but to have so many questions swirling around in my head.

What happened to their parents?

What happened to them in foster care?

Who took care of these three children?

"You better get that girl of yours to bed—she looks like she's about to fall asleep right there. Which if I wasn't such a nice person, I'd be insulted she ignored my best story," Eric laughs.

I quickly come back to reality, realizing I was off in my own little world trying to figure them out. I guess I'll have to wait until Luke feels comfortable enough with me to let me into his world. *He's not ready now?* That hurts my heart a little bit. I wanted Luke to know all about the baggage I bring; however, he doesn't feel the same about his own demons.

Lisa and Eric hug us both goodbye and then it's eerily quiet in the penthouse without them. Luke takes my hand and we walk towards his bedroom together. I throw on the satin pajamas I brought as he strips down to his boxer briefs and we crawl under the covers. Both lying on our backs facing the white ceiling, neither of us has said a word since his siblings left. I really don't want to be the one to break the silence, I want him to say something ... anything, damn it. Clear up the confusion of this evening for me.

But I never know if he tries to as I drift to sleep where I have an unsettling dream about the little boy who came to the hospital with his mom tonight. In this dream, the little boy is being hit by an older man whose back is turned away from me. This happens right in front of me, but I cannot move to save him. I try to push forward, to run, to move my arms, anything, but I come up short. I'm frozen in place, forced to watch this beating.

Helpless.

CHAPTER EIGHTEEN

Waking up the next morning to an empty bed seems to be a pattern here. A pattern I'm quickly learning I'd like to change. I jump out of bed on a mission to find the guy who seems to be avoiding me. Searching all the rooms, I come up empty. What the hell is going on? It's not until I enter the kitchen that I see a green post-it note stuck to the fancy coffee maker—

> A,
>
> *I had to rush to the office for a work-related emergency. I'll call you tonight.*
> *L*

Okay, back it up ... no terms of endearment?

No apology?

No, nothing?

Ugh. Throwing the note into the trash feels just like the moment with his business card. I head back to the bedroom to pack up my stuff. I hit the Driver app on my phone and wait until I get a notification that someone is here to pick up me. I make it out of the elevator and through the front lobby before Ryan meets me just outside the front doors.

"Ariana, good morning miss! I'm here to take you back to your apartment," he says with his usual upbeat attitude. I surely don't want to drag him into whatever this is between Luke and me, but I really don't want anything from Luke right now, including a ride from his driver.

"Thank you so much Ryan, but I already have a ride," I say spotting the girl whose photo showed up on my app idling at the curb. I dash inside her car before Ryan can protest. I'm sure he'll let Luke know I blew him off by getting into a random car, but I could give two flying fucks what Luke thinks right now. Get me the hell away from here, pronto.

"Rough night?" Adele, the driver, asks as she looks through the rearview mirror at me in the back of her Ford Edge. Normally, I'd be insulted at a comment like this but she hit the nail on the head.

"You couldn't be more right." I give her my address and we take off. She doesn't ask me any more questions and I appreciate the silence.

I'm grateful Serena isn't home when I enter the apartment. I don't feel like answering any of her questions, which she'd have plenty of especially after our hallway exchange. I can't believe that was just last night—it feels like so much has happened in between the time I was last here. So much uncertainty.

But I can't let this day go to waste, and I certainly don't want to dwell over a guy. I am not a dweller. The last time I felt pity for myself and dwelled was when I was raped, when my choices were stripped from me just like my clothes. Fuck no that will not be the case over some man.

Come on Ariana, you don't need a man to make you happy.

Damn straight … or so I tell myself.

With this man, it just feels so different, or maybe *felt* is a better word? Am I romanticizing what I have with Luke when it's not even really like that between us? Did I make up all these feelings I thought we had for each other? When did I become this girl? Ugh, it makes me feel sick. I can't do this: sit and stew over questions I'll never get the answers to.

I practically bolt to the shower and jump in before the water even has a chance to warm up. I'm washing this experience away, and I'm going to go do something fun with my day. As I'm blow-drying my hair straight, I hear the doorbell ring. I clearly am not expecting anyone—maybe it's a delivery?

With my hair still half wet I walk to the front door and look through the peephole. Who I see shocks me.

Lisa.

What the hell is she doing there?

"I know you are on the other side of this door wondering what the hell I'm doing here. Let me in," she says, laughing and eyeing the peephole back at me. Do I want to let her in? "You have no choice."

What the hell. I know I was not saying all of that out loud. I swing the door open. "Are you a mind reader or something?"

"Nope, I'm just pretty good at reading people," she says, pushing past me into the apartment.

"Come in, make yourself at home," I say, indicating she's already doing that. "Do you want a cup of coffee or something? Water?"

"I'll take a water, thank you."

I head to the kitchen with her hot on my trail.

"Do you want to tell me what you are doing here?"

We both take seats at the kitchen table with our waters before she speaks. "I came to see how you're doing. Last night Eric and I caught Luke off guard by showing up unannounced. We're sorry about that. I know my brother, when something goes unplanned, he can be a bit … off. He likes to be in control of every situation. Last night he was not." She laughs as if what she's telling me is completely normal. "Are you okay?"

I take a swig of my water trying to stall before I answer her. This is so weird.

"Stop stalling," Lisa teases me.

"Okay, you're going to have to stop with the mind reading voodoo. You're creeping me out," I say. I take another sip of water to calm my nerves. "To be honest, I don't even know what to tell you. I was trying to put this all behind me before you showed up."

"Behind you? Why?" Her face goes from lighthearted to concerned in an instant.

"Behind me because I don't think I'm cut out to deal with … someone having to be in control or else they 'go off' … as you say. That makes me feel uneasy and uncertain."

She folds her hands on top of the table, very motherly, before saying, "I understand what you're saying. I really do. Maybe I misspoke. I don't want to see you give up on him before he lets you in; I just have this feeling that he will. I've never seen him look at another person like he looks at you. Maybe one other person, but it's not the same."

She must read the look of confusion mixed with jealously across my face. I thought he didn't have any other girlfriends before me?

"Calm down with that look," she says. "I meant he used to look at *our mother* with such admiration and love. I see that when he looks at you."

That's not what I was expecting to hear her say. I don't know the kind of relationship he had with either of his parents, but I feel a little better knowing it was a loving relationship with his mom.

"I'm sorry to hear about your parents."

"He told you about our parents?" Her jaw drops. She stares at me with a look of utter shock. Was I not supposed to say that?

"Uhh ... he just told me that they were dead and that you went to foster homes, no real details." I fumble over my words, not sure if I'm supposed to know this important detail in their lives.

Her jaw goes back to its rightful place but she keeps staring now, tilting her head to the side as if she's really taking me in. "See, I knew you were something special to him. We don't really talk about what happened to our parents; he let you into his world. It may seem small because he gave you very little information, but that means a lot coming from him. *Any* information at all about our parents is a big deal. He doesn't like to talk about them, ever." Lisa looks down at her hands, cupping her water.

It throws me for a loop that this woman who was so confident one minute ago is now avoiding eye contact with me completely. *What happened to their parents?*

"Do you not like talking about them either?" I ask my question carefully, trying not to pry too deeply into her life, but I mean *hello,* she came over unannounced. Wait, how does she even know where I live?

"Finally, you're wondering how I found out where you live? I asked Ryan."

"Dude, if you pull this mind reading shit with me one more time I'm going to punch you."

She tosses her head back in a fit of laugher. "I'm sorry! Anyway I should be going now considering I showed up when you were probably about to do something. Thank you for the water."

I see Lisa to the door, and as she's walking out she turns back towards me near the elevator and says, "Don't shut him out. He's stubborn and he might take more time than most men, but he's battling something fierce and I know you can help him. I just feel it."

And just like that she's in and out of my apartment causing a whirlwind in my mind in a matter of minutes.

It doesn't escape me she's the second person to utter words very similar to me. First the fairy tarot card reader and now Lisa … the mind reader. What's with these supernatural freaks? They can leave me the hell alone!

This day—as weird as it is—is not going to go to waste. I refuse to sit on my ass on my day off waiting for a man, any man, to "call me tonight" as his lame ass post-it note said. Bundled up in my winter jacket, I head over to the Art Institute of Chicago. I'm greeted by two giant lion statutes out front donning holiday wreaths around their green necks—a Chicago tradition.

Christmas is right around the corner. In the past I knew the date was near and would try to put the holiday out of my head—it only brings up pain from the past— but right now I don't feel anything about it.

I look towards those silly lions and smile. This time it's different. I finally let someone else in and now the weight of what happened to me isn't so heavy to carry around. Before telling Luke, it was like a noose around my neck; now maybe it can be a holiday wreath too.

Before getting hypothermia standing outside on a cold night, I head inside to browse around aimlessly. I walk from room to room, collection to collection, just taking it all in. I want something to jump out at me, as a sign or something, but how childish does that seem? *A sign, Ariana?* You are not supernatural; I should have brought Lisa.

Nothing 'speaks to me' and I find myself standing next to people staring at the same paintings or statues, hearing them "oh" and "ah," but I'm left wondering—what the hell do they see in this crap?

I'm just not in the mood tonight, feeling defeated that this trip really turned out to be a waste. I turn the corner to head towards the exit and I stop.

There's a photograph hanging on the wall in black and white. Three women hold flowers, looking as if they're picking off petal by petal like elementary school girls at recess. I step closer and see the words "He loves me, he loves me not" on the photograph and my heart stops. How beautiful, yet how heartbreaking all at once.

Why can't it be as easy as picking off petals? Why can't he just love me? Open up to me? Tell me what his battles are so I can slay them for him, or at least *with* him for god's sake. Why does he have to be so stubborn?

But no. If I played this little girl's game what would I end up with?

I look at my phone to see no missed calls or texts.

An empty flower.
He loves me not.

———

The night ends as weird as the day started. I come home to find Serena passed out on the couch covered in blankets and tissues. Spotting a thermometer on the coffee table and an empty cup with a teabag inside, I realize my roommate is as sick as a dog. I really want to be upset with her for the low blows I felt her and Jack were handing out to me in the hallway, but there's no way when I see her like this.

I hear her whimper as she rolls over, and I spot a tissue shoved up her nose. I want to laugh, I really do, but instead I go to the kitchen to make her a fresh cup of tea.

When I walk back into the room she's awake and sitting up now minus the snot trap.

"Here you go."

I hand her the hot mug and she smiles as she tries her hardest to breathe in the delicious scent of the peppermint tea with no luck.

"Thank you. I didn't hear you come in, have you been home long?" she manages to ask with a scratchy throat. I don't think in all the years we've been rooming together I've seen her sick. Hungover, hell yes. Sick, no.

"I just walked in minutes ago. What happened to you?" I ask, leaning over to put the back of my hand on her forehead confirming that she still has a fever. "You're burning up!"

She takes a sip of the tea and then pulls her blanket higher up around her. "I know but I'm so cold. I have the flu."

"Want me to draw you a bath or something?"

"No, but thanks girl. I'll just drink this tea and lay back down, try to sleep it off."

Even though I'm a freakin' doctor and deal with sick people all day long, I feel completely helpless in my own house. It's just different when it's someone you personally know, I guess.

"If you need me, I'll be in my room," I say as I move the tissue box closer to her.

"Thanks Ariana, and I'm sorry."

"Sorry ... for what?"

"For everything that was said the other day. I'm so ecstatic you found Luke and that you see something in each other. I haven't seen you this happy in the entire time I've known you. Don't let what Jack and I said get in your head—I know you, you'll think too much about it and that's my fault."

I don't have the heart to tell her that whatever I had with Luke is very questionable right now. She doesn't need to hear me vent when she's trying to fight off the flu, so I slip quietly into my room and grab my Kindle to get lost in a romance novel. At least someone's getting laid tonight—a *fictional* someone, but a someone nonetheless.

I hopelessly check my phone one last time for any sign of a call or text from Luke. I even desperately check my email. All coming up empty.

He said he'd call me tonight. That was a lie.

Whatever.

CHAPTER NINETEEN

Days like today remind me why I work. I hate having the day off. What the hell am I supposed to do with myself? Serena is still recovering, camped out on the couch. I haven't seen much of Drake since Luke's been in my life. And calling him right now would only result in his smug face telling me, "I told you so." No thanks.

That leaves … no one else.

I head to my bedroom and clear some space before throwing in a workout DVD into my DVD player. It's been a while since I've done a workout of any kind—unless you want to count sex with Luke. Okay, no, let's not count that. Let's get that out of my memory bank altogether.

I press *play* and let my mind focus on trying my damn hardest to copy the moves of the perky blonde lady on the screen shouting, "You're not even tired!" at me for the next 45 minutes. By the end of the Turbo Fire session I feel like I can't walk … or breathe … or even make it to the bathroom to take a shower. But somehow my wobbly legs carry me. I have a tug-of-war fight trying to wrestle my sweaty sports bra off and then jump in to let the cold water bring my body back down to a normal temperature.

When I hop out of the heavenly shower, I notice my phone is lit up—a text message.

I'd love to take you out to dinner to apologize for last night. Are you free?

Well, what the shit. Am I free? Just like that he wants to crawl his way back into my life with yet another apology. Actually, he's not crawling at all—he's waltzing in like it's no big deal. I shoot back a reply to get him out of my hair.

I'm not sure dinner is a good idea. I'm busy tonight.

I can't imagine him as the kind of guy glued to his phone, but he replies within seconds of my blow off message.

I understand. What about lunch?

Pushy much? I think so. Okay I said I was busy for dinner, so how the hell do I get out of lunch?

I don't think I'll be hungry at lunch. I ate a big breakfast. :/

I didn't even eat breakfast and I know that was the dumbest response I've ever typed up before in my life, but I don't care.

Ariana—What about coffee? Tea? Water? You want to sit and stare at each other? You don't even have to stare at me, just be near me. I don't care what we are doing or what time of day, I'd just like to see you.

Do I want to see him again? Yes, I guess I do. All the moping around I did yesterday proves that. But do I want him to know that? Ugh, no.

I guess lunch is fine.

I caved. Yes, I am that girl. Yes, I don't care right now what you think. I missed him and I want to talk to him about what the hell happened the other night.

I'm glad you changed your mind! :) Can you meet at my office around 11:30?

Who is this? I'm thrown by the fact that you—a tough manly tatted up CEO— just sent me a smiley face emoji. Did a 15-year-old girl hack your phone?

Do you want me to hold in my excitement? Fine. I knew you'd agree. Now get your hot ass to my office.

And just like that, my Luke is back! *My Luke?* I don't question my own inner stupidity. Instead, trying to channel my inner Serena, I put together a 'you made a big mistake, take a look at me now' outfit to hopefully wow this man.

Stepping out of my Driver ride to Vulcano Vodka Towers in a tight black pencil skirt and red blouse with matching red pumps makes me feel empowered and confident … until I approach the girl at the front desk on the lobby floor.

A Vulcano girl.

She's wearing a pair of gorgeous Christian Louboutins, an equally tight black pencil skirt, and a white blouse. And unlike my long light brown hair, she's a blonde. Let's not forget, she's the secretary. Does Luke have a type and is it this girl's look?

Focus Ariana—you aren't here to check out the secretary.

On the car ride over I gave myself this "mission" to keep from quickly falling for Luke's lame ass apology.

"Mission Possible: Don't be charmed by Luke's hot body, sexy smoldering stare, or knowing his rippling muscles are hiding tattoos no one else but me knows are there."

I step into the elevator with a pair of men in business suits and briefcases. Thank god, no more Vulcano girls.

"What floor?" one of the men asks, eyeing me up and down.

"33," I squeak out, feeling inadequate all of a sudden.

"33, huh?" the other man asks.

"What does that mean?" I finally find my voice.

This elevator has got to be the slowest moving elevator in the history of elevators. I think it's taking longer to get to Luke's office than it would to climb all the way to the top of the Willis Tower. And I feel uncomfortable with these guys.

"Mr. Vulcano's office is the only thing on floor 33. Are you prepared for that? He's a pretty intimidating guy," he says, giving me this stare yet again. "I know one intern left the building in tears after going to floor 33. Prepare yourself."

Oh, they think I'm an intern.

I don't know if I should find that cute or insulting. And what's with this story about Luke making someone cry?

The elevator stops on floor 25 and the two men get off, not before I can so graciously thank them for the warning about the intimidating Mr. Vulcano. The doors close and now alone I feel like I reach floor 33 in a matter of seconds. Is this some kind of magic time wrap contraption?

Stepping out of the elevator there's a long desk with yet another a drop dead gorgeous looking blonde woman behind it. I'd guess she's in her late 20s. With fair skin and green eyes, this woman could be a Disney princess. Instantly, I feel jealous that she gets to spend time every day with Luke. But before I can hate on her, she greets me with a kind smile.

"Hello! You must be Ariana. I'm Tracy, it's a pleasure to meet you," she says, standing up from her desk to shake my hand before walking me towards the double doors outside of Luke's office. "He's been waiting for you."

She opens the door gesturing in an elegant Vanna White motion for me to walk inside. I thank her and shut the door behind me, instantly spotting Luke.

He gets up from his grand looking desk and walks towards me. He stops when we're standing in front of one another, neither wanting to be the first to break the silence. I simply have no clue what to say.

"I'm glad you came," he says, reaching his hand out to tuck a piece of hair behind my ear that's escaped my long ponytail. "You look as stunning as ever." Before I have a chance to respond, his phone rings, he walks back around his desk, and we both spot Lisa's name on the caller ID. "I have to answer this."

"Of course," I say, taking a seat in a comfortable chair across from his desk.

"Hello," he answers and the tone of his raspy voice mixed with seeing him behind his desk does something to me. I feel a sense of arousal, a need. I know he's a powerful man—no one becomes the CEO of the most popular vodka brand in the world by sitting around on his ass—but seeing him right now in his element turns me on.

Lisa must be doing all the talking as he nods his head and murmurs, "yes ... okay ... I see."

Even though he's on the phone, his eyes haven't left my body. They scan from the top of my head to the hem of my skirt. The passion I feel for him intensifies with his smoldering glaze. With his eyes locked on mine, I take it upon myself to make him feel the way I do, to make him regret not calling me back, to make him see what he's missed out on.

I ever so slowly uncross my legs and slide my fingers down to the end of my skirt to hike it up just a little before crossing my legs again. His hazel eyes darken—he gets my message loud and clear—and just to make sure, I lick my lips and gently bite down on my bottom one.

"Lisa, get to the point," Luke shouts into the phone. "Okay I'll be right there."

Then he slams the phone down and stalks over to me like I'm his prey. He hovers over me with his arms on either side of the chair and he growls into my ear, "You want to put on a show Ariana? Are you trying to tease me? I'd love to see what else you can do."

He trails passionate kisses down my neck until I hear myself let out a moan, which causes him to instantly pull back. "I'm sorry to cut this short. We will finish where we left off, don't worry. I told Lisa I'd go down to this photo shoot we're doing for the new campaign to double check a few things. Do you mind joining me before we go to lunch?"

"Lisa works with you?"

"Yes, she's in charge of marketing and promotions."

I don't know why I never knew this before. There's still so much to this man and his family I know absolutely nothing about.

Trying to be agreeable I say, "I don't mind, let's go."

We hop into the town car with Ryan driving and travel just outside of downtown Chicago to what looks like an art district. Breathtaking graffiti covers businesses, statues, and murals all over this hidden gem of a block. The car pulls up in front of a warehouse and Ryan opens my door.

"This should only take a minute or two," Luke says, putting his hand on the small of my back leading me inside. The warehouse has many windows allowing light to shine through in contrast to the black and grey painted brick walls. In the center of a large empty room is a King-sized bed covered in white bedding and on a nightstand sits a single glass of vodka. Very classy, very sexy.

Lisa rushes up to us clearly frazzled. I don't think I've ever seen her looking this frantic—even when she came into the hospital.

"What's wrong?" Luke is the first to ask as she stops with a clipboard directly in front of us, looking like she's on the brink of tears. I immediately want to pull her into a big hug.

What the fuck? I've never wanted to pull anyone into a big hug before.

"Our female model is sick. She showed up and threw up like four times and we had to rush her to the hospital. I don't know what I'm going to do!"

"Lisa, it's not a big deal, can't we reschedule this with a new model or when this one is feeling better?"

She slumps her shoulders looking utterly defeated.

"I wish! This photo shoot was already pushed back once and now it's due to the publishers if we want it to be in print by the holidays. There's so much money riding in this."

I watch as Luke goes from concerned brother to instant dominating CEO. He scans the room and Lisa's clipboard looking for any sign of help.

"We can't do this photo shoot with just the male model?"

It's then I notice a rack of clothing to the side of the bed, and huddled around it is a man with a large camera draped around his neck beside an attractive looking man in a white robe.

"Ugh, god no. We need to have a female model. This shoot is all about romance, passion, intimacy," Lisa cries.

"Okay, let's go talk to Neil. He should be able to come up with something," Luke offers. Lisa rolls her eyes at her brother as they both head over to the photographer, who I learn is Neil. I stay back by the food table, not wanting to be anyone's way while they solve this dilemma. I have no advice to offer.

I grab a small bottle of water and turn around from the table as Neil rushes up to me while Lisa is right behind him. He grabs the water out of my hand and pulls me away from the table.

"Excuse me!" I say, not prepared to me manhandled today.

"Her!" Neil shouts towards Lisa, pointing at me frantically. Luke strolls over to us with a look of confusion on his face to match mine.

Lisa shakes her head in agreement. "Yes! Ariana is perfect. I'm an idiot for not thinking of this sooner."

"No." Luke's one word silences us all. Neil and Lisa turn towards him with jaws dropped.

"Luke, please, we need her help," Lisa pleads with her brother.

"My help? Is anyone going to let me in on what the hell is going on here?" I ask, pulling myself out of Neil's tight grasp. It's then that all three of them turn to face me with intent stares.

Neil reaches behind my head, yanks my ponytail holder out of my long hair, and says, "See!"

"Okay, enough touching!" I say, dodging him as I try to smooth down my crazy hair.

This entire situation is making me uncomfortable.

"Ariana, would you help us?" Lisa asks. She looks at me like my answer will change her whole world.

I still don't understand.

"Help you … what? You already sent the model to the doctor?"

"No, we don't need you as a doctor," she smiles at me a little too sweetly, "we need you as our … model. Please, please, please with a cherry on top."

I bust out laughing, looking around for someone to be filming.

"Is this some kind of hidden camera prank show? Is there where you tell me I just got punk'd?"

"Girl, we don't have time for games. Are you going to help us or not?" Neil asks with a hand on his hip and an intense gaze I feel deep in my bones. Damn, this guy is seriously bossy and I'm a little scared.

I look into Lisa's sad pleading eyes and then shock myself by making a decision 100-percent out of my comfort zone: "Fine, I'll try."

"Yay! Thank you so much," Lisa squeals while jumping up and down clapping her hands. For the love of god, I hope I didn't just make the biggest mistake ever.

I look towards Luke, who hasn't said much during this exchange except the word no. He's now staring over at the photo shoot set in silence. Lisa pulls me near a rack of women's clothing away from everyone else. She grabs the rack and rolls it off in another direction, and I follow quickly behind her.

We walk into a makeshift dressing room, complete with a vanity and lights. Lisa hands me a red pair of underwear and what has got to be the smallest lingerie I've ever seen.

"Put this on," she instructs, shoving the clothes at me and pointing towards a secluded room just past the vanity.

"Where's the rest of it?" I ask, holding up the underwear to inspect it.

"Rest of what?"

"The outfit I'm supposed to wear. You just gave me underwear."

She smiles like she's got a juicy secret. This must be a technique that runs in her family because I've seen the same grin plastered across her brother's face a time or two. And it's annoying.

"That's it," Lisa answers, pointing towards the clothes in my hand. "Now we don't have all day for you to get your panties up in a bunch, literally. Go, change, now." This time she shoves me into the room, closing the door behind me.

Just looking at these sexy clothes in my hands, I begin sweating. This can't be good. How the hell am I supposed to go through with this? I'm not a model. I'm not sexy. I'm not meant to be photographed for something like this. Oh my gosh, there will be other people watching out there.

Just as my hand reaches the door about to push it open and tell Lisa to hell with this ridiculous plan, I hear her say, "Stop second-guessing yourself. Cut the shit right this instant. You are a gorgeous woman; you will look stunning in that lingerie and you are doing this to help me. To help Luke, to help this brand. We need this photo shoot to happen. We need *you* Ariana."

There's a part of me that would feel horrible about letting someone down—especially Lisa or Luke. Before I can think about this any longer, I strip off my pencil skirt and blouse and replace my white cotton undies with this lacy pair of red bikinis. Once the matching red teddy is in place, I glance up to stare at myself in the full-length mirror.

Fair skin.

That's all I see.

"Come out of that room right now before I come in there," Lisa yells.

Stepping out of dressing room I look to the ground to avoid eye contact. I'm normally a pretty confident person—I know that I'm pretty in terms of general attraction, but this is so different for me.

"Holy shit!" Lisa exclaims.

I try pulling the teddy down to cover my bare legs but realize that only shows more of my C-cup cleavage that's being pushed up on full display.

"That bad?" Ugh, this was such a stupid idea. I'm going to ruin this for Luke and Lisa.

"Bad? You look incredible! Your legs look insanely hot and your boobs, girl, who knew you were hiding those under your scrubs?" She laughs as she continues hitting on me. "Here, put on this robe and sit down. I'll have hair and makeup in here in just a minute."

Hair and makeup go by in a blur; I wish I could have relaxed more to enjoy being pampered. It's not every day you are treated like a princess. The stylist, Kristine, is so kind, but I'm spitting out answers to her questions without really remembering what she's even asking me. I'm working through my nerves.

Luke hasn't appeared since I agreed to Lisa's hair-brained scheme, making me nervous that he doesn't think I can do this. He didn't say anything but his opposition when the idea was pitched. If the man I'm sleeping with doesn't have the faith that I can model half-naked … who else is going to believe in me? I'm praying to the Photoshop gods that they don't really need a model, just a body they can warp into anything … including a hot model. That's what I'm telling myself anyway.

"You're all set Ariana, you look beautiful!" Kristine encourages me while putting down her brush. She gives my long, curled, Old Hollywood-styled brunette locks a final spritz of hairspray. She spins my chair around and now it's my jaw that drops. Pinch me.

"Damn Kristine, the Pope should anoint you into the Sainthood—you've just performed a miracle," I say, staring at my reflection. The reflection I cannot believe belongs to me. To go along with my killer hair that I'll never be able to replicate, Kristine performed wizardry to give me a sultry yet romantic smoky eye and red lip.

"Okay you can head out towards the set. They're ready for you," Kristine says, egging me out of the comfort zone of this chair. I pull my silk robe a little tighter and head back towards where we came in just an hour ago. No one seems to notice I've left the dressing room, which I'm thankful for. I spot Neil and the male model—where are Lisa and Luke? With the two people I know nowhere to be found, I walk in the direction of Neil.

"I'm ready, let's get this over with," I say as I approach Neil.

He stops to stare at me and smiles an ear-to-ear grin. "Lose the robe and let's do this." I didn't think I'd ever hear anyone—let alone a photographer—say those words to me. "And while you're at it, perk up doll. This is an opportunity so many girls would die for. Don't be an ungrateful cow."

I should be seriously insulted, but instead I laugh. He's right. I know this is completely outside of what I'm comfortable with, but I shouldn't treat them like they're torturing me.

"Fair enough."

I do as he says, slowly removing the robe. The chilly air hits my barely covered skin, causing my body to break out in goose bumps. When I finally have myself as ready as I'll ever be, I put my robe on a nearby chair. The male model starts strutting towards me. He's wearing a pair of black designer boxer briefs … and that's it. He's all tan skin, dark thick hair, rippling muscles, flawless skin, and teeth entirely too white and too fake. I mean he's not my type whatsoever, but goddamn, I can see what others might see in him.

Now this is a model.

"Hey, I'm Colton," model man says, extending his hand towards me.

"Ariana, nice to meet you. I want to apologize in advance that I have no idea what I'm doing," I say, shaking his hand.

215

"Don't worry. This isn't mine or Neil's first rodeo. We'll help you. Thanks for stepping in; I wouldn't have been able to do this shoot if it had to be rescheduled. This is a big opportunity for me."

I instantly feel bad for judging him because he seems so nice and appreciative. Before we can get to know each other much longer, Neil is shouting for us to get on the set because he needs to do a couple test shots. Like a lost puppy, I follow Colton towards the bed and just stand there feeling like a complete idiot.

"Ariana, the point of today's shoot is seduction. We want this new drink to kick off the holiday campaign to bring in the New Year. You will be the temptress," he says, eyeing me like he's not quite sure he thinks I'm following. "But don't worry, Colton will quickly give in. The drink should be on display at all times. You'll both play around with it in your hands."

Drink, seduce, holidays, temptress. Okay, got it.

My nerves realize that this is about to happen.

"Fake it 'til you make it," Colton whispers into my ear; he must see pure panic on my face. Him being this close sets my nerves on edge. If him whispering to me is too much for me to handle, this is going to be so uncomfortable. I need to get my head in a good place.

"Can I have a second?" I spit the question out in sheer panic.

Neil gives me the most irritated look; he looks like he swallowed something sour. "Fine, two minutes. And don't make me come to get you."

"Thanks!" I say as I dash over to the food table to practice a breathing routine I learned in yoga. I don't really know what I'm doing, but I focus on my breaths … in, out, in, out.

You can do this.

You are helping people.

You are going to be fine. No one is going to hurt you or manipulate you.

You are giving these people permission to touch you.

Colton seems nice. This is his job.

Neil is a professional.

Breathe. Be confident. Breathe.

Okay, this is as good as it's ever going to get for me; the longer I stand over here, the longer this whole process takes.

"Ready," I say, walking towards Neil and Colton. I notice a few more people around, fixing lights, catering to Neil's commands, and pouring alcohol into a crisp clear glass. Yet no Lisa or Luke.

Why did they leave me in my time of need?

Okay that was dramatic. A photo shoot is not a 'time of need' but I sure as hell could use a friendly familiar face.

"I want you to stand close to the bed and put your hand on Colton's chest," Neil commands, his face disappearing behind the camera lens.

I walk over to Colton, repeating the "Fake it 'til you make" mantra to myself. Touching a strange man makes me feel just as uneasy as him touching me.

"These are just test shots, relax," Colton says as I near him. I really am appreciative of him. I could be paired up with an egotistical jerk treating me like I don't know anything, which I don't, but instead he's trying to help me.

I do as Neil says and place my shaky hand on Colton's broad chest.

"You're going to have to get closer to him, dear," Neil jokes from behind the camera. He's right; I'm standing at arm's length away. If I could be any farther from him I'd probably be in another room. I slowly inch my way closer but Colton takes matters into his own hands, pulling me into his chest. I'm standing so close to him that I can smell his strong cologne, placing my hand on his oily tanned muscular pecs.

"That's great Ariana, now look into Colton's eyes … bedroom eyes girl. Work it," Neil barks orders at me.

Bedroom eyes? What the fuck are those?

I stare up at Colton trying to give him a look. I hope the look says 'bedroom eyes' because I don't think I've ever given bedroom *anything* to anyone before.

"Great, great," Neil keeps encouraging us. Colton winks to let me know I'm not completely fucking this up.

Okay I can do this.

We do a few more test shots—me holding onto his bicep, Colton giving me the bedroom eyes, and both of us taking turns holding the glass of vodka. Neil calls for a quick break so he can review the photographs. His interns jump into motion, moving light fixtures and re-arranging sheets.

Taking that as a hint to move out of the way, I walk over to the food cart and stand awkwardly with Colton, sipping on a glass of water. There's no sign of Lisa or Luke. I glance over to the clock and realize that the test shots only took 15 minutes. Damn, in my head that took hours upon hours. I guess that's what happens when you are having an anxiety attack.

"Let's do this thing!" Neil calls us over and it's go time.

We take more shots like we did standing near the bed, looking into each other's eyes with our hands slightly on one another. It's nothing too threatening or uncomfortable for me. I should get an award for coming out of my shell and letting a complete stranger touch me. My therapist would freak out if she knew I was doing this.

I try my best to keep a lookout for Luke, but it's hard to do at the same time as giving 'bedroom eyes' to Colton.

"Okay Ariana, lay down on the bed. Colton is going to hover over you. We'll do a few shots like that and then he'll kiss you."

Kiss me?

"Oh honey, don't be a prude," Neil orders. I must have expressed my shock out loud. Where the hell is Luke? Will he care that I'm kissing this dude? I mean it's fake … *acting* … but still. Well I guess he has to know; this is his company's photo shoot and all.

I lay down on the bed, glancing at my wardrobe to make sure everything important is still tucked away; I don't need the cameras getting a glimpse of anything they shouldn't. I feel the bed dip low as Colton takes his place above me. Neil starts snapping away as he encourages us to keep looking at each other and touch one another.

"Flirt with him Ariana, show him how irresistible you are."

This is my nightmare. For a girl who has avoided these kinds of interactions with guys, I don't know how to do this whatsoever, but I keep on faking it.

"Okay, now kiss. I want to see steamy passion," Neil shouts.

Colton leans down to grab my face in his hands, planting a sloppy kiss on my lips. We miss each other's mouths and clumsily try to correct ourselves. My nerves are in my throat.

"Stop," a deep voice growls from behind us. Just like *that* everything freezes. Neil stops barking commands, Colton stands up, leaving me laying there feeling exposed, assistants stop doing whatever it was they were doing, and I swear time stands still. Everyone is silent and a little frightened.

I prop myself up on my elbows to see what the commotion is about to find Luke glaring at us. I've never seen him look this angry before. If smoke could come out of a person's ears like in the cartoons, that would be happening.

Lisa runs up beside him and pats his arm before whispering something in his ear. It looks like she's trying to calm him down, but whatever she says doesn't register with him. His eyes are locked on me. I glance down to see his fists are clenched tightly; he looks like he's ready to throw an uppercut at anyone who comes too close.

"This photo shoot is over," Luke demands through gritted teeth.

"No, please, for the love of god, Luke." Lisa throws her hands in the air clearly annoyed with her little brother. "We cannot reschedule. We've already gone over this."

"I don't give a shit about rescheduling. I said it's *done*."

Lisa takes a step back, looking like she's just been smacked. I don't know much about their brother-sister dynamic, but I'm going to guess by the look on her face Luke does not talk back to her often.

Neil calmly walks over to them, and I take my cue to slip on a robe and join in the conversation.

"Okay, let's fix this. Why do you want to cancel this shoot?" Neil asks gently, as if he's walking on eggshells. He seems to have lost the attitude. I don't blame the poor guy because these are his bosses.

"She's not going to be modeling," Luke spits out as he nods in my direction. Now I'm the one who feels like she's been smacked as my jaw drops in disbelief that he's just said that in front of a bunch of people. Way to knock my confidence to the ground. Luke thinks I'm good enough to fuck around with but apparently I'm not good enough to be a model for his stupid vodka company. I want to bolt out the door, but I remember that I'm half naked and have no ride.

Lisa is the first to speak up for me. "Luke, why can't Ariana model? She's doing great!"

"No."

And with one word he has me fighting back stupid tears that are making their way to my eyeballs. Goddamn it.

"Is there a different model you prefer? One that we could get here in under an hour?" Neil asks Luke.

"How the fuck do I know? Do you think I have a male model database?" Luke angrily asks.

"*Male* model?" Lisa, Neil, and I all say at the same time. "I thought you wanted Ariana replaced?" Lisa adds.

"Ariana is fine," Luke says without making eye contact with me, "but *he has* got to go."

"I don't understand what's going on here. You want to replace the only actual model we have in this shoot?" Neil seems perplexed.

"Can I talk to my brother for a minute in private?" Lisa asks. Neil and I start walking away to give them space but Lisa lets me know I can stay. I'm not sure I really want to hear this conversation, but I don't want to piss off one of the few people on my side, so I stay.

"Okay brother, what's your deal? Why do you want Colton gone?"

"He's being really helpful," I whisper. I suddenly feel extremely bad for Colton, who already told me he needs this photo shoot for his career.

"What did you just say?" Luke turns his body to face me. I don't know why I said it but he's pissed, really pissed. I pull my silk robe a little tighter to act as a shield against his rage.

"I said he's being really helpful. This is scary. I came out here all alone, you and Lisa nowhere to be found. Colton has been helping me feel slightly less of an asshole pretending to parade around like a model,"—I notice I'm rambling but the words just spill out—"which you clearly do not have faith that I can do. You haven't said one nice thing about me *helping* you since the idea was pitched. You don't think I'm pretty enough to model? Tell me."

Luke glares at me.

"What the fuck are you talking about? Of course I think you're pretty enough to be a model. You look fucking breathtaking out there. I want to fucking kill that guy for having his hands on you ... his lips."

"You're jealous?" Lisa squeaks out, looking a little too excited. Why is this a good thing that he's jealous? Is he really jealous? Of what? Jealousy is not a trait that should be rewarded. "I've got an idea then. If you don't want Ariana to pose with Colton, *you* be the model. We need to get this done," she says as she points her finger into his chest, clearly loving her own idea.

"I'm not going to be a model. You know better than to say something like that," he says.

"Why not?" Lisa asks.

I'm pretending I'm invisible during this whole conversation.

Luke gives his sister a death stare. "I don't put myself in the public."

My very limited Google searching of him does confirm this. I didn't find anything from him in a direct source—no interviews, no articles, no posed photo shoots. Everything was taken from the paparazzi—of course of him in his tailored business suits with random women on his arm. As for a bio, there's only a brief one put together by 'fans' but it has little information.

Luke is a Man of Mystery to the public eye. To all eyes, except mine. Do I want to share him with others? I squirm with my indecision and notice the conversation around me got suddenly quiet. Lisa and Luke are now staring at me.

"Are you okay?" Lisa asks. I fumble my words telling them I'm fine. Lisa believes my lie and turns to face Luke. "So are you going to do it or is Colton?"

"Fine," Luke says like an irritated child through gritted teeth.

"*Fine?*" Both Lisa and I repeat in utter shock.

"Don't make me change my mind and cancel this whole thing. I don't give a fuck right now about this photo shoot, but I don't want you to be upset," Luke says to his sister.

Lisa squeals and gives him a kiss on his cheek before sprinting off towards Neil to tell him the show will go on. Luke is whisked away to his own dressing room, as

I stuff snacks from the food table gracelessly into my mouth. Get me the fuck out of here.

A now fully clothed Colton is waking towards me and says, "Hey. So that was ... interesting."

"I'm so sorry they pulled you off the shoot. You were doing a great job and I really appreciate you trying to help me."

I've never talked to someone after they've gotten fired, especially when it's because of me.

"Don't worry, at least they paid me. I do wish I could have continued the shoot with you," he winks at me, making me feel a little uneasy. "Don't let yourself get controlled, okay?"

He doesn't give me time to respond. He just walks away and out the warehouse door.

Controlled—that's the second time someone has said something like this to me in regards to a situation with Luke. Controlled is not a word I want to be known for. Controlled makes me feel all kinds of things and they are not good emotions.

I don't have time to dwell over my feelings because Luke is walking out of his dressing room equally draped in a robe. We both head towards the set where Lisa and Neil are waiting for us.

"Let's do this thing boss man," Neil says, clearly excited about the turn of events. It must be a big deal to get to capture Luke for the first time. This is sure to take

Neil's career to unbelievable levels if these photos turn out any good.

I drop my robe feeling the same jitters as I did earlier. Neil nods his head for me to get on the bed, and I lay down where I left off before Luke interrupted.

All eyes dart to Luke as his hazels find my greys. He slowly unties the sash around his robe, dropping it to the floor. I hear a few of the female interns gasp; even Neil raises his eyebrows in complete surprise.

He's mesmerizing, there's no question about it. His tattoos are now on full display for the world to see along with his scars and ripped muscles. Luke has a refined confidence about him that turns the vibe in this room to extremely hot. Everyone looks like they like what they see, practically drooling over him.

There will be no more three-piece suits to hide behind—nothing left between us that is sacred. I break eye contact with him and instead stare at the ceiling trying to collect my thoughts.

That was a bad idea.

Luke is instantly on top of me, in the same position Colton left off, but it feels much more intimate, much more vulnerable. He hovers over me and leans down to whisper in my ear, "What's wrong?"

"I don't like that they can see you," I whisper back.

"See what?"

"See ... *you*. All of you, what you keep hidden and only share with me." The words come out in a breathy whisper. I'm holding back tears. I don't want to share him with whoever will see these photographs. Hopefully this campaign is not as big as Lisa is making it out to be. Maybe just a few people here and there.

Luke holds my face and whispers back, "Baby, they'll never see it all. No one will ever understand. No one but you."

And just like that everything and everyone around us disappear. Grabbing onto his tatted up biceps I pull him down into a deep, passionate kiss. He growls back into my mouth as our tongues twirl around each other. He rolls me over so now I'm the one straddling him. Our mouths devour one another. I kiss him with such force as I feel his hands move from my hair, down my back, until he cups my ass. I moan into his mouth and then trail kisses down his neck. It's just him and me.

That is until I hear someone clear his throat.

I pull away from Luke and shyly look around the room. We definitely have a captive audience—everyone is staring directly at us. It feels like the temperature is closer to a sauna in here, but I think that's my body heating up in embarrassment.

"I think we've got all the pictures we need! Great job everyone," Neil says dismissing his staff. I notice he sends a discreet wink my way. Ew. Luke and I peel ourselves off one another, put our robes back on, and walk back to our respective dressing rooms to reclaim our dignity.

We both walk out at roughly the same time colliding with a bright-eyed Lisa. "That was … something," she says. I don't know what's worse—the fact that I made out with my boyfriend in front of a bunch of strangers and a camera … or in front of his sister. Kill me now.

"I hope you're happy the photo shoot is done. Now if you'll excuse me I'm taking Ariana out to dinner," Luke says, taking my hand in his, escorting me past his sister.

"Have fun you two! Try to keep the PDA to a minimum if you're out at a family restaurant." Lisa says as she laughs and takes off to do whatever it is her job is.

We get into the back of the town car and I sit silently, not sure what to say to Luke after that entire experience. Luckily, he is the one to break the ice.

"Sorry that we had to miss lunch. I hope you're okay with dinner?"

And just like that I throw my head back and laugh, truly laugh.

"What's so funny?" He eyes me curiously.

"We just stripped naked for who knows how many people to see, rolled around on a bed making out, and you're worried I'm upset we missed lunch?"

This man is too much. He's perfect. And on that thought, I stop laughing. I can't fall back into believing he is perfect because as soon as I get attached, he can easily dismiss me again.

Don't forget he's done it before.

CHAPTER TWENTY

The week after the scandalous photo shoot flies by. I'm working in the emergency room from the time I wake up to the time my head hits the pillow. One night I even crashed in the staff room because I didn't think it was safe for me to walk back to the apartment—my eyes were closing while I was talking to my last patient.

But I can't let the rest of the staff see me as a slacker. I just can't. After hearing all that bullshit about Luke "controlling" me, I decided I had to remember who I was, who I'm trying so damn hard to be. I've made it this far on my medical journey that I need to pull my head out of my ass and focus. I am so close to the finish line that I can taste it.

Dr. Ariana Bellisano, keep your eye on your prize.

Luke has let me blow him off this past week without much complaining. He too is busy at work. Apparently, the holidays are a critical time to put your liquor brand out there. Who knew? I guess it makes sense though. You want to celebrate around your family and friends having a merry time, so you drink. You want to drown away your sorrows because you're alone or you hate said family and friends, so you drink.

I don't know why I never turned to drinking during the holidays. Maybe because when I started to hate them, I was too young to drink. The irony doesn't escape me—I wasn't too young to be sexually assaulted by a disgusting piece of shit man, but I was too young to drown my own sorrows in booze.

The time to think about this is not now though; Luke and I are finally getting a chance to go out to dinner and he'll be here any minute. I look in the mirror and marvel at the fact that I remembered how to do my own hair and makeup. There's no time for makeup when you're trying to save lives—or at least that's what I tell myself to excuse the fact that I am a hot mess most days. Okay, all days. But it does feel nice to dress up a little. I hear the doorbell ring, so I get one last look at my knee-length red dress that I paired with a black pair of tights and black stilettos and head towards the door.

"Well hello there stud," I say, swinging the door open to catch Jack in the hallway. Oops.

"Hello to you too Ariana," Jack says as he laughs back at me. Luke comes off the elevator right behind Jack and he catches my red face but doesn't question why the hell I am embarrassed. Serena runs up behind me and jumps into Jack's arms, planting a big smooch on his lips.

Leaving these two to make out in the hallway, I pull Luke's arm into the apartment so I can take the beautiful flowers he has for me and put them in a vase.

Alone in the kitchen away from the lovebirds, I put the long-stemmed red roses in a crystal vase, placing them in the center of our kitchen island.

"These are stunning. Thank you."

"I have something else for you. Well … something for both of us," Luke mischievously says. It's the way he says *both of us* that has me on edge.

"Oh yeah? What's that?"

He nods his head in the direction of the front door. "Are those two going to barge in here any minute? It's something you might want to open in private."

My face flushes and my body heats up, but my curiosity is at an all time high.

"Let's go to my bedroom," I say, yanking his arm yet again and dragging him as quickly as my feet will carry us to my room. Luke comes very willingly behind me. I shut the door and stare at him. Whatever I have to open, I have to do so in front of him.

What if it's something super weird? No, he wouldn't give me something weird. It has to be something sexual, right?

"Calm down. I can see the wheels turning in that brain of yours." Luke laughs, handing me a small black box with a red ribbon tied around it. It looks harmless enough.

I shake the little box and hold it to my ear, hearing something rattle inside. "Well, I know it can't be a puppy."

"I knew you were smart," Luke laughs, knowing I'm stalling on opening this thing.

I pull off the red ribbon and place it on my bed before opening the lid of the box. Inside I find a small pink vibrator. He got me a sex toy? I look up at him confused.

"It's a wearable vibrator that you can slip into your panties. I want you to wear it … tonight."

Still confused I ask a little embarrassed, "I can't keep it on all the time. Are you planning to tell me when I go to the bathroom to turn it on? This seems like a lot of work."

Luke pulls out his phone, "No darling, there's an app for that."

"Shut the fuck up. I've seen it all now!"

Luke throws his head back in a deep laugh. "Ariana, you will wear the vibrator and throughout the night I'll turn it on and off."

He makes this sound so easy.

I whisper, "But what if someone finds out?"

"This vibrator is very quiet. It's meant for this. Don't worry," Luke says, walking closer to me to brush a piece of hair back from my face, "and if someone were to find out, who cares. They'll know you're having the time of your life."

He kisses me and just barely teases my tongue with his before pulling away. "Go slip it in."

As I walk towards the bathroom, he smacks my ass. If I weren't so damn horny and confused, I'd turn right around and hit him in the face. Or somewhere equally important, like his dick.

Putting a little lube on the small pink vibrator makes it easier to slip it inside my pussy. Pulling up my panties part of the vibrator lays just on my clit with another inside my sex, pressing against my G-spot—it's dormant right now, but just the thought of what this toy can do makes me feel a little buzz.

Luke is at the front door holding my coat open for me. He's got a grin on his face—looking too eager for my liking. But seeing a boyish Luke makes me smile. I let him help me into my coat and then we head out the door.

Luke is driving us tonight as we slip into the Jag. As diva-ish as this is going to sound, I enjoy the time when we can sit side-by-side without Ryan carting us around. I love my quality time with Luke. He catches me smiling like a big clown and flashes his own grin at me right back. He is a swoon-worthy man.

We pull up outside The Fat Tomato and Luke hands the keys over to the valet. He's an eager looking teenager whose face lights up when he sees Luke's wheels. I can only imagine what kind of joy ride he'll be taking this bad boy for. I can only imagine what kind of joy ride Luke will be giving me later.

Okay that was the vibrator talking.

A hostess walks us over to a table near the window overlooking the Chicago skyline; it doesn't escape me that it's a quiet restaurant with a romantic vibe. Other couples sit near our table, making me nervous for what Luke could do with the little tease between my legs.

Luke pushes my chair in like a gentleman. And by the devilish look in his hazel eyes, this will be the last of his gentlemanly acts for this night.

"Can I start you off with a bottle of wine or maybe champagne?" a waiter asks as he fills our water glasses.

"Your best Vulcano Vodka creation," I reply, I'll need a stiff drink or five to get through tonight. Luke smiles at my order and agrees to the same.

When I believe we are both looking down at our menus, I suddenly feel a small pulse in my sex. I drop my menu to the floor and an alert waiter scoops it up for me. I take it with a shaky hand, trying to say thank you, but the words come out all messed up. The pulsing has not stopped; I look across the table and lock eyes with Luke.

"What's gotten into you?" he asks with a smirk.

"Well, we'll see if it's you or not who gets into me," I say, throwing out my threat with as much sarcasm as possible.

Luke laughs, putting his phone on top of the black tablecloth. It doesn't escape me that this everyday device holds all the power to my pulsing pussy. I want to grab the phone out of his damn hand, but that will cause an even bigger scene. And, to be honest, this is kind of hot. I've definitely never done anything like this before, and I want to see where it ends up.

The pulsing stops as our waiter appears with two martini glasses and an appetizer of Antipasto skewers, which he says are "on the house" from his manager. Turns out, the bartender spotted us at our table, alerting our waiter that the Vulcano Vodka drinks were going to Mr. Vulcano himself. The waiter is falling over himself trying to impress Luke.

When he finally leaves after taking our order, I notice Luke taking in a deep breath quickly to regain his composure. If you weren't reading into his emotions, you'd miss it.

"Everything okay?"

He looks at me surprised to see I noticed. "Yes, I don't do well with people fawning all over me. It's not necessary."

What so many people would kill for, Luke doesn't want.

"You come off like a Man of Mystery to most people. You seem to be very private. I'm surprised he recognized you," I say, thinking of what the girls at the hospital said when they saw him.

"You don't think I have a recognizable face?" He raises one eyebrow at me.

Did I offend him?

"Oh my gosh, I am so sorry!" I say, eating my words. My face flushes in embarrassment.

"Are you kidding me? You throw around so much sass and you think I was insulted by that?"

He laughs again, and immediately I feel a sense of relief.

"I wish I could punch you in the arm right now, but I don't think violence is welcome in a nice place like this," I say, and it doesn't escape me tonight I've wanted to inflict pain upon this man a few times already.

"Hit me baby. I like it rough."

I want to laugh at his cheesy pickup line, but I play along, licking my lips and locking eyes with him. "Bring it baby."

And just like that, he picks up his phone and taps the screen. Subtle vibrations rock through my body as I try hard to remain composed. I'm safe as there are no menus to throw around. Clenching my legs together, I try to focus on anything else besides what's happening between my eager thighs.

He taps his phone screen again and the frequency of the vibrations gets higher.

It's mind-blowing.

"Ariana, you look thirsty *sweetheart,*" Luke says, encouraging me to take a sip of my martini. Is he challenging me? Oh yes he is. Okay Mr. Vibrator Man, I can do this. And the vibration strength goes even higher.

Ariana, don't let him know he's affecting you.

Taking a deep breath in and out, I smile while reaching for my glass. My eyes across the table lock on Luke's, and I slowly bring the rim to my lips and toss a sip back with confidence. As I'm putting down the glass, that newfound confidence quickly leaves me as vibrations rock through my core. My hand shakes as I set the drink down on the table, trying not to spill any. I'd consider that a victory knowing what's happening in my now-soaked panties.

Just as the waiter shows up the vibrations stop, amen.

I dig into my lasagna and bring a cheesy bite to my mouth. I moan in pleasure at how absolutely delectable it tastes. Right now I'm grateful that this meal is warm and that I can eat it sitting down.

"Slow down, you're going to choke on your food," Luke warns as he slowly takes his fork full of New York Strip Steak to his lips. He knows I'm eyeing his sexy mouth. "My eyes are up here. What do you think, I'm a piece of meat?"

"You are a crazy man," I laugh as I slow down my eating pace. "I haven't sat down to eat a meal in days. I've been on the go at the hospital, forcing myself to cram food into my mouth while running around."

"You work too hard."

The irony of that sentence coming from him does not escape me. Luke loves to work, and he's always striving to improve his company.

"You do too."

"I guess that's one of the things I admire about you," Luke says.

"Just *one* of the things," I tease, trying to give him my best flirty eyes. "What are some of the other things?"

He puts down his fork and looks at me seriously. "You want to play this game? I didn't think you were the kind of girl who fishes for compliments."

Is he serious? Men are absolutely clueless.

"Of course, I want to hear compliments. *Everyone* loves to hear compliments once in a while—especially from their man. Why *you* don't want to hear the things I admire about you?"

He smiles at me. "I don't need to hear compliments. I guess words of affirmation aren't really my thing."

Not his thing? What the hell does that even mean?

"I'd think a man like you would like to have his ego stroked."

He throws his head back to laugh. "I'll give you something to stroke."

"I didn't know I was eating dinner with a sixteen-year-old horny boy. Next are you going to ask me to send you nudes?" I blush realizing I've already done that.

Change the topic quick, Ariana.

"Tell me more about what you'd like stroked." And that's the best I have. I'm going to stab my fork into my eye now.

"Let me see ... you can start with my cock."

And just like that he taps a button on his phone and the pulsing starts again. The vibrations are in just the right spot to shake my tender clit. I cross and uncross my legs beneath the table, trying to adjust the position of the vibrator to a less than pleasurable area but there's no moving it. It's stuck and it's giving my clit the ride of her life. I don't think I can do this much more; I may explode at this table in front of all these people.

"I, uh, I need to use the restroom." I toss my napkin on the table and stand up.

"Ariana, if you take out that vibrator, you will be punished."

"Excuse me sir. I didn't know I signed up for some BDSM stuff here. Maybe *I* want to be the dominant in this relationship?"

He gets in a good laugh before clicking his phone to increase the speed of the pulsing. I nearly fall over, stumbling into our table as I clench my legs tightly. I'm sweating here. My fall gains our table more attention from the fellow diners as all eyes flock to us. My face must be as red as my pasta sauce; I dash towards the ladies room trying to keep my head low.

Throwing the bathroom door open, I almost run straight into an older woman who gasps in shock at my high rate of speed. I apologize for nearly giving her a heart attack as I run into the nearest open stall where I take some deep breaths. The pulsing between my legs is still happening, and I shimmy my tight dress up my body with a plan to remove it.

But as my hand moves to my panties, I touch the vibrator applying a little pressure to where it's hitting my clit. I feel a tightness in my stomach and my legs are nearly at the point of collapsing but I hang on. I will not pull this out and get "punished."

But he didn't say anything about giving myself an orgasm. I shut my eyes and focus completely on the vibrator. I feel it change from pulsing to vibrating and I let out a quiet moan. Oh it's so nice. It's even nicer to know that Luke is on the other end, controlling my vibrations.

Closer and closer I get to pure ecstasy. I feel like my breath is shorting and just when I know I'm going to come, the vibrations stop.

No more. *Nada. Niente.* The fuck?

How did he know? I open my eyes and quickly scan the bathroom making sure he's not standing in here. Nope, it's empty.

Well now I'm pissed. I was so freaking close to enjoying myself in this stupid bathroom and now I have to go back out there to see his smug face, knowing he's a big tease.

I walk out of the stall with the vibrator still inside my panties and I'm pissed about that too. Taking a look in the mirror, I see my face flushed. My hair is sticking to my neck like I've just run a marathon, so I pull it up into a high ponytail. I reapply some lipstick and splash myself with a little water to cool off.

I'm going back out there and I'm not taking any more shit. It's game time. I strut my stuff all the way back to our table where I see our dinner plates cleared and a piece of strawberry cheesecake waiting for me.

Don't be tricked by the dessert, Ariana. Stand your ground.

But that cheesecake looks so damn good.

No, focus.

"Thank you for ordering me cheesecake," I say in the most monotone voice I can muster. There's no smile on my face; instead, I force a frown as I bring the delicious looking forkful of cake to my lips. This is going to be a challenge.

"You're very welcome sweetheart. You were in the restroom for a long time. Is everything okay?"

I finish chewing what turns out to be the best cheesecake I've ever eaten—which I will not be telling this big jerk.

"Do you always ask your dates about their bathroom habits? Do you want a play-by-play?"

He laughs at my ridiculousness, and I can see by the smirk reaching his eyes that he's on to my sassy attitude.

"Can I get you two anything else tonight?" Our waiter swoops in, breaking the tension coming off my body and clearing my dessert plate away. I inhaled that cheesecake like it was my job. I'm going to need to throw in an extra workout DVD tomorrow to make up for this dinner ... okay and the last week that I haven't worked out either.

"No I believe we are all set. Thank you for your excellent service," Luke says, picking up the black bill holder. Our waiter's face lights up at the compliment, which must mean a lot coming from a guy like Luke, who he was trying to impress all night.

When the waiter is out of hearing distance I say, "I thought you didn't do compliments. That was kind of you to make the waiter's night."

"It was nothing," Luke says, brushing off the entire exchange as he helps me into my coat.

Back in the car I feel like we're racing towards Luke's penthouse. I don't know what the hell he's in a hurry for—he wasn't the one left hot and bothered in a restaurant bathroom. He's also not the one with a sex toy still inside of him.

"I didn't know this was a racing Jaguar." Luke looks over at me with a serious expression, clearly missing my lame attempt at a joke. "Why are you driving so fast?"

And then he surprises me. "I started something in that restaurant that I plan to finish thoroughly."

"Are you talking about …?"

Before I can even finish my thought, he says, "You. I saw how you came out of that bathroom."

"*Came* out of the bathroom? That's a joke, I didn't *come* at all," I say with a laugh.

He gives me a devilish expression, "I could tell you were angry. I didn't want you to be upset. I just wanted to get you ready. That was a mistake. I'll be righting this situation soon."

"So you won't be punishing me?"

"You can still get on the punishment list in between right now and when I'm sinking my cock deep inside you."

Well alright then. I squeeze my thighs together at his delicious threat. We drive back to his apartment in silence as I try to think of what him punishing me would really consist of—maybe I want to try that? I'll keep that thought to myself for now until I'm a little more comfortable with everything.

As soon as he pulls his car into the reserved parking spot we are both dashing out of the doors and rushing towards the private elevator. We fly into his penthouse and practically throw ourselves into his master bedroom.

"Wait, give me a minute," Luke says, as he goes into the bathroom leaving me high and dry yet again. If he didn't give that little "thoroughly finish" speech in the car I would seriously have a complex about his feelings for me. "Okay, get in here."

"I've already been teased in a bathroom once tonight. If you do this again, I'm going to cut off your balls and I will not surgically put them back on."

I hear him chuckle as I push open the door. The hue from the vanilla candles he's lit covering the countertops gives the otherwise dim bathroom a glow.

Through the glass double door shower I see Luke standing inside waiting for me just how I like him. Completely naked. I frantically strip off my clothes—leaving the vibrator inside for him to give me permission to remove. The temperature must be hot as the room is filling with steam. I pull open the door and step inside.

"Hi," I say coyly. Suddenly the sassy attitude has left as quickly as she came.

"Hi to you too," he says, stepping closer, reaching for my hip to pull me the rest of the way towards him. "I see you've been a good girl and left in your toy."

I let the *good girl* comment slide because I like where this is going. He slides his hand down my stomach and cups my sex before gently pulling the vibrator out of me. I feel like a part of me is missing and I want that part to be filled by his cock … now.

Luke places the vibrator to the side. I stare into his hazel eyes and lick my lips waiting for what he's promised. And I don't have to wait long at all; he's on me in a second. His tongue dips into my willing mouth as we explore our dripping wet bodies with our roaming hands. Running my hands up his broad chest and around the back of his neck, I pull him in as close to me as I can get. His hard cock presses into my belly. Taking my eager hands down to meet his waiting manhood, but before I can stroke it, he pulls away from me.

"You've had a long night. You first darling."

And just like that he backs me up against the shower wall and kneels down in front of me. The sight of him with water droplets covering his muscles could make me orgasm if I stared long enough.

He doesn't give me that option.

Luke reaches up to massage my breast before pressing his lips to trail kisses up my inner thighs. Sensations of arousal roll through my body. Heaven. Luke removes his mouth from my legs to rub his thumb over my sensitive spot as my back arches off the wall. "Yes, Luke."

I hear myself pant out, sounding so desperate, but I'm not the slightest bit ashamed. Before I have the chance to keep begging, Luke puts his mouth on my pussy and sucks, and then he sticks out his tongue, twirling it around and around and around my clit. Pressure builds again, just like when I was in the bathroom earlier. But this time it's much different.

This time it's not a machine rocking through my body. It's Luke—the man of my dreams—hitting every nerve in just the way he can. Grinding my hips into his mouth, it's a magnificent sight to see him between my thighs as he nibbles away where I need him the most.

Luke picks up one of my legs and drapes it over his shoulder to change our angle. And just like that I'm hypersensitive and tingling with absolute desire.

"You look ravishing. I love the look on your face, knowing how much you want this," Luke growls before he tastes my entrance with such force I need to hold on to his head for balance.

"I'm going to come if you don't stop."

He stops just long enough to say, "I want you to come baby," before he gets back to sucking, nipping, and lapping.

"I want to come with you inside of me," I plead. Luke stops and stands back up. I grab his face, forcing it close to mine to kiss him. Tasting myself on his tongue and it drives me wild. I've never imagined wanting a man to do what Luke does to me, but now I know I never want him to stop. Ever.

With both of my feet back on the floor, I steady myself by pulling him closer to me by his rock hard ass. He kisses me while his cock presses eagerly against my stomach. I grind myself against it as best as I can because of our height difference, and it feels like a torture.

"Stop teasing me," I moan, closing my eyes to take in the sensations of all the feelings ... hot water spraying against my body, his muscles wrapped around me, my throbbing clit, my want, my need.

He doesn't make me beg again when he asks me to turn around and spread my legs. My eyes go wide at the idea of what he plans to do. What could he need back there?

Luke senses my shock and reassures me, "No, not that ... yet. I would never do anything like that without talking about it first."

I trust him when he says that. Turning around like he asked, I widen my stance, wiggling my butt out to give him a little show. He gently slaps my ass and we both laugh at our playfulness.

"This ass should be illegal, it's too perfect," he growls into my ear before grabbing a handful of one of my butt cheeks. The fact that he likes what he sees turns me on even more.

"Ready?" he asks from behind me as one of his hands grips my hip and the other guides his cock towards my entrance.

"Yes," I pant.

I stand on my tiptoes so he can slide his cock inside and then I adjust to find just the right angle for this doggy style to work. Luke pumps himself in and out while I hold on to the wall in front of me, rocking back into him as much as I can. His cock is hitting me inside in just the right way that I see stars.

Luke lets out a growl as he grips my hips so tight as he fucks me. I can't take much more—my arms shake from basically holding up my body that's quickly giving out on me.

"Ariana," he commands just as we both bliss out on each other.

I can't help but smile as I think about how upset I was earlier in that bathroom to be greatly surprised in this one.

Luke and I stumble to his cozy bed and curl up together. It feels so heavenly to have someone next to me. But as I lay here my mind drifts to worry. I can't help be on edge wondering if I'll wake up to find him still there. I have yet to experience that.

CHAPTER TWENTY-ONE

Waking up without Luke yet again instantly pisses me off. I roll over to grab my phone to see it's only 9 a.m. on a Saturday—it's not even like I sleep in late! But before I can pout for too long, Luke is walking into the bedroom in sweaty gym clothes again. Okay, if this is how I'm going to see him first thing in the morning, I'm not going to bitch about him leaving the bed. He looks damn good.

"Want to grab some breakfast?" Luke asks as he strips off his sweaty shirt. It's not until he waves his hand in front of my face that I realize I was just staring at his chest and tattoos without answering.

I laugh in embarrassment. "Yes, breakfast, let's do that."

"Give me a few minutes to take a quick shower."

I stand up and search around for my clothes. I should really leave some clothes here so that I don't have to do a 'walk of shame' to the breakfast place.

Wait. I want to leave some clothes here?

The thought makes me extremely uncomfortable. I don't know if that's because I don't want to be the girl who needs to leave stuff at a man's house or because I'm terrified Luke would laugh in my face if I ask him.

"What's the matter?" Luke asks, walking out of the bathroom completely naked as he heads towards his walk-in closet.

"Nothing," I quickly reply, dismissing the whole idea. I think we're a long way off from leaving clothes at each other's place—that should be a conversation for another day. He doesn't push me to answer and I appreciate that.

When we are both dressed, we head out the door. I'm happy to see my walk of shame isn't very far. Directly across the street from his penthouse is the Stone Vana Hotel, which I hear has a killer restaurant with a brunch menu worthy of taking food pictures of. That's what I need right now. Not food pictures, but food worthy of them.

"Can I get you something to drink?" a cute waitress asks, approaching our table. "Luke?"

Luke peers up from his menu and he smiles at whoever this waitress is he knows. "Chelsea, it's good to see you. How are you?"

She fiddles with her ticket pad, looking a bit nervous to be talking to Luke. "I'm doing great, thank you. I can't wait to start on Monday."

Start what on Monday?

I want to ask, but I'm the third wheel in this conversation. It's then I take a good look at this Chelsea … a leggy blonde with curves in all the right places.

"I'm so sorry, you guys came here to eat, I shouldn't bore you. Can I get you something to drink?" Chelsea asks now with a regained confidence that she clearly did not have two seconds ago.

"We'll each take a coffee," Luke answers.

Chelsea turns around, strutting away from our table with her hips swaying in all the right ways. I watch as men and women turn their necks to watch her.

"Who was that?" I ask with a little edge in my voice.

"That was Chelsea," Luke says without even looking up from his menu. Is this really all he's going to give me? Why doesn't he understand when a hot blonde is chatting him up he needs to tell me a little more about her?

"I got that much. You want to tell me anything else about her? Maybe why you didn't introduce me?"

I put my menu down on the table to hopefully signal that I want to have a chat about what's happening here. Luke looks up from his menu but doesn't put it with mine on the table. Apparently, my hint was not taken.

"She's my new intern. She starts on Monday."

He's going to be working with her?

He's going to be her boss. Her hot dreamy boss.
How often are they going to be working together?
How close does he get with his interns?
Are all of his interns this pretty?
Am I losing my shit for no reason?

My mind is going crazy and Luke is not even paying attention. Before I can ask any questions, Chelsea is back at our table with two cups of coffee and smiling from ear-to-ear.

"Thank you Chelsea. It's nice to meet you, I'm Ariana, Luke's *girlfriend*," I say, taking the cup from her. And just as the words leave my mouth I want to punch myself in the face for saying them. I can't believe I pulled the 'I'm the girlfriend' card in front of another woman. Gross. *I hate myself right now.*

Luke looks over at me with a smirk but doesn't say anything about my obnoxious comment.

"Nice to meet you, Ariana," Chelsea's perky voice takes on a clipped tone. "Are you guys ready to order?" The perky voice is back and just like the waitress at the last hotel bar, she turns her body towards Luke.

Before I explode or run out of here, I give myself a much-needed pep talk.

You go home with him.

You fuck him.

You know what he's rocking under the dress shirt he's wearing right now.

You spend time with him.

Why am I giving myself a pep talk?

Because your man should be reassuring you that his new hot intern doesn't mean anything to him.

Oh yeah, that's a good point. But he's clearly not doing that.

We place our orders and Chelsea's hips don't lie yet again as she walks towards the kitchen. I sip my coffee and immediately want to scream out because I just burnt the crap out of my tongue, but I refuse to look like a damn fool at this place again. Can this brunch be over with already?

"What are your plans for the rest of the day?" Luke asks before sipping on his own coffee.

"That's what you want to talk about?" I ask in shock, a mix of surprise and annoyance. He doesn't want to tease me about making myself look like a crazy girlfriend or give me any further details about his intern?

"Did you have something else in mind?"

Well, looks like he doesn't want to address what just happened. And I'm kind of okay with it, considering I looked like an ass.

"Nope. I have a midnight shift tonight at the hospital. I'm filling in for another resident. This girl takes off so many days; I highly doubt she'll land any kind of job after this is over. I'm surprised they haven't terminated her residency but I guess they need all hands on deck."

Luke takes in every word as I speak about what I love the most—the hospital—and it makes me happy he pays attention.

"Do you plan to shop your resume around to any other hospitals after you graduate?"

I sit my cup down in its saucer and realize I haven't thought about it. I have been so focused on proving myself at St. Francis and getting a job there that I haven't thought about if they say no.

"Well now I feel like an idiot. I haven't thought about it."

Luke reaches across the table to take my hand into his—a public display of affection that just weeks ago I would have punched him in the face for trying.

"You're not an idiot. You are one of the smartest people I know," Luke says with such confidence that if he weren't talking about me I'd believe him. "You don't have to, but I think you are valuable and you'll want to see what other hospitals would be willing to offer you. You don't know how much you're worth until ask around."

"I'm glad my boyfriend is so smart," I say while giving his hand a little squeeze. And to break up our adorable love fest, Chelsea is back at our table with our meals.

"Luke, is there anything I should do to prepare for Monday?" she asks a little too eagerly. And did she unbutton one of the buttons on her blouse? I feel like she didn't have that much cleavage when she brought over our coffees. This girl is definitely trying to threaten me and I don't like it one bit.

"Your first day will be pretty easy—get to know the staff and my schedule. You'll mainly be working with my assistant, Callie, most days."

Her face falls and I snicker on the inside.

"I'm sure I can find a way to be a big help to you too! Just wait, you'll see I can prove myself," she says before hurrying over to another customer who is waving his hand at her.

I raise my eyebrows up at Luke and laugh but don't say another word about the subject. The intern to the assistant—this changes how I feel. We eat our delicious meals in peace. Chelsea tries to linger a little too long at our table while dropping off our check, but Luke stands up and excuses us.

"See you Monday!" she shouts as we walk to the door to leave. Eager—I'll give her that because I see myself in her. However, I know we have very different motives for why we work hard. And for that I can't say that I admire her eagerness.

CHAPTER TWENTY-TWO

A few days have passed without any hiccups in our relationship. Things are also going smoothly at the emergency room. Well, as smooth as broken bones, allergic reactions, amputations, and whatever else people get themselves into can be.

After a fairly easy shift, I notice a text message from Luke waiting for me—

Party tonight. Wear a hot dress—the one waiting at your doorstep. Pick you up at 9.

What's this about? Party? A hot dress waiting at my house?

This doesn't sound like the kind of dates I go on, but I'm excited for the thrill of the unknown. It's also the thrill of having someone else plan it for me. I hurry my ass home because I need to catch some sleep before tonight's party.

Sleeping is the most amazing thing that's ever happened to me. But waking up, that's a bitch. I hate every minute of rolling over to shut off the alarm clock screaming at me from my phone. I flip it over seeing that it's 7 p.m. I guess it's time to get out of this bed and ready for the mysterious party Luke is taking me to.

I wonder what kind of party it is. Probably something for rich people … I can expect fancy, stuffy, and boring.

Grabbing the big purple box waiting in the hallway, I drop it on my bed and lift the lid. I didn't even have the energy to open it earlier. My tiredness hit me like a ton of bricks the minute I stepped outside the hospital. But now that I'm well rested, I'm eager to bust this baby open.

Underneath the red tissue paper I find a surprise. We definitely can't be going to a fancy rich people party … unless he wants me to stand out from the crowd? I pull out a tight, short black leather dress. Also waiting for me in the box: a sexy pair of silver studded Christian Louboutin stilettos. It's like I've died and gone to fashion heaven. If Serena were home, she'd lose her mind right now.

But I don't have time to sit around and drool. It's time to get ready!

Shower.

Shave.

Pluck.

Smoky eye.

Blowout.

And just in time because the doorbell is ringing. I slip on the shoes and carefully trot my way to the front door. These bad boys are tall! Let's hope I don't break my neck tonight—I really don't want to go to the hospital. With just a twisted ankle, they'd probably ask me to help out if I was in the building.

Pulling the door open, I need to catch my breath. Luke looks drop dead sexy. He stands in front of me in black dress pants and a black dress shirt. To match my shoes, he wears a silver studded belt. I want to claw off his clothes and lick every inch of his body.

What the hell has gotten into me?

I don't think any man has ever gotten a reaction like this out of me. No, I *know* no one ever has.

"That dress looks spectacular on you," Luke says, pulling me in for a kiss.

"Thank you for getting it for me," I say, doing a little twirl to show off the outfit. I laugh at my ridiculousness and catch Luke smiling at me, which makes me blush a little.

"Let's go," I say, grabbing his arm and heading towards the elevator. I'm eager to see where we are going.

Ryan stands at the curb waiting for us. Inside the car, Luke wraps his arm around my body. I'm cuddled into his side and I feel safe. And I love it. I put my hand on his thigh, which feels rock hard.

The ride is taking a little longer than our normal drives in the city. Peeking out the window I notice we're heading out of the downtown area. I get more comfortable in my seat, deciding I'm going to try something new for me.

Fun in a car.

I'm quickly interrupted by Luke's phone going off. He looks at the screen and then makes an annoyed face. "I'm sorry, I have to take this real quick for business."

I don't mind his phone call, but I don't want my fun idea to go to waste.

Let's see how focused this CEO can be.

I trail my fingertips up and down his thigh, getting closer and closer to what I feel straining against his dress pants.

Luke grabs my wrist while muttering into his phone something about spreadsheets and the Food and Drug Administration. He locks eyes with me as if to warn me to knock it off. With his hazel eyes still on me, I take my time teasing him by licking my lips and slowly biting my lower one.

He lets go of my hand and shakes his head as if he's amused by all of this.

Instead of light strokes on his thigh, I increase the pressure while leaning in to kiss up and down his neck. I moan into the ear free of the phone and then suck on his earlobe. His breathing grows heavier as he answers whatever he's being asked.

Reaching towards his studded belt, I undo it and then bring down his zipper. Slipping my hand inside his boxers briefs, I feel his erect manhood. Rubbing my thumb back and forth over his tip, I watch his cock drip his liquid.

This will get his attention—taking my finger I bring it to my lips before sucking on it. Moaning, I arch my head back, turned on knowing he's turned on.

"This call is over," Luke says and clicks the 'end call' button. "Ariana, I don't know if this is a game you want to be playing."

"Is that some kind of threat?" I ask, seeing the need in his eyes. I know he wants to play whatever game he thinks this is. And so do I. I growl into his neck before I bite down. I hear him hiss. "I know you want this too," I say.

"I want anything you want to give."

"Well then I have a present for you," I say with a wink before leaning over his manhood and taking him deep into my mouth.

"Oh fuck," Luke hisses as he fists his hand through my hair.

Bobbing my head up and down, I deep throat him. When I think he's about to hit his breaking point, I change up my technique. Holding his shaft in my hand,

I slip the tip of his cock in and out of my mouth while sucking on it. His grip on my hair tightens just a little and I know he's enjoying my present.

"Ariana, if you don't stop I'm going to come."

Why would I stop? That's exactly what I want him to do.

Cupping one of his balls with my hand, I take his length deep into my mouth and let my tongue go wild. Luke pulls my long brown hair as he explodes into my mouth. When he's finished, I swallow and return to my rightful seat as I wink at him.

"You think that's it?" Luke asks, turning to face me as he pats his lap. "We aren't finished darling. I want to return the gift."

I laugh! There's no way he could be ready for round two. And it's as if he could read my mind and takes the challenge.

Luke reaches up my black dress to slip off my panties before pulling me into his lap. Straddling him, I rub my clit up and down against his wet cock. Feeling him between my thighs pressing against my pussy, I can't help but want to surrender myself to him. I position my pussy over his cock and slowly sink down on top of him. We both let out moans.

Luke cups my ass as I bounce up and down while I devour his mouth with my own. Pumping my hips, going faster and faster, I know I'm on the brink of coming. Both of us are shaking as he emits a low growl and I wrap my hands around his neck.

"Fuck," I hiss out in absolute pleasure. Collapsing into his chest, still straddling his cock, I let out a slow breath. Fun in a car *is* really fun.

I hear a ding before Ryan's voice fills the backseat of the car. There must be some kind of intercom back here. "We're here, Mr. Vulcano."

"Mr. Vulcano," I whisper into his ear, "I don't know where we are, but the ride was sure worth it."

The girl at the desk checking the partygoers in hands us both a pair of red headphones. This place is so out of character for both Luke and I—I shoot him a 'what the hell?' look as we stand in a group of people huddled together waiting to get into another room.

Luke quietly says to me, "This is a club that wants to stock our liquor. I wasn't sure because this is a pretty rare concept. Normally we go for high-end, but I think this might be something special. We are here to check out the atmosphere."

"What is this place?"

And before he can answer, a tall, lean looking man in a tight black T-shirt steps up on a platform with a microphone and yells, "Welcome to What A Night Pop-Up Party, bitches! Get ready to rave out with your cock out."

Is this guy serious? I laugh out of confusion when Luke takes my hand in his and squeezes.

"Alright bitches, get those headphones ready! We're opening the doors in 3 … 2 … 1."

And that's when the crowd goes crazy! Everyone rushes to put headphones on. Luke and I send each other curious glances, but we join the group putting the giant headphones on and plugging them into our phones like directed. The doors open to a giant dark room with neon strobe lights. Then with the app the club had us download, techno music starts streaming through my headphones.

Just like that the entire club dances like there's no tomorrow. Bodies grinding together, hands in the air, sweat flying, smiles all around, drinks flowing—this place is hot.

I lift my headphones off my ear and I'm startled by how quiet it is in the building. All the noise is happening inside our own heads. What a crazy experience. I look at Luke as he's eyeing the bar and realize I'm going to do yet another thing I'm not used to. I grab his arm and pull us out in the middle of the dance floor. And yet again, Luke surprises me—this guy can move!

We must be out on the dance floor for at least an hour with the music pumping through our ears, immersing ourselves in the crowd of ravers also having a great time.

"Let's get some water," I mouth to Luke. He leads us towards the bar. While waiting for my water and Luke's drink, I spot a man walking up to us. He is not wearing headphones and when Luke spots him, he takes his off. I follow suit. If Luke can hear, I can too.

"Mr. Vulcano, it's a pleasure to meet you. I'm Andy," he says extending his hand for a shake. Andy sticks out from the rest of the super young looking staff as the only middle-aged person in the room. I assume he must be the man in charge. And by the way he's falling all over Luke, I think my assumption is correct.

Luke puts his hand on my lower back and says, "Andy, I'd like you to meet my girlfriend, Ariana."

It's one word. A simple word. But it brings me absolute happiness.

Ladies and gentlemen, he said I'm his girlfriend.

"It's nice to meet you. You are quite the beauty," Andy says with a warm smile lighting up his brown eyes. "Can you hang out a minute while I go talk business with your boyfriend? I promise I won't steal him for long," Andy asks. Luke looks at me with an expression of reassurance, and I tell them to have fun.

With the men in Andy's office, I'm left to people watch at yet another bar; I don't mind at all. My eyes scan the room and then they stop on a set of familiar ones looking back at me.

"Ariana!" Drake screams from across the room with his headphones on. It sounds even louder to me as I have yet to put my headphones back on. I laugh at how loud he sounds as he approaches me with some of the frat guys and a few girls I don't recognize.

Drake takes off his headphones. "You're the last person I thought I'd see here. How'd you find out about this place?"

"I'm going to pretend you didn't just call me a loser," I say, laughing and punching him in the bicep.

Trey stops a shot girl and passes drinks off her tray to all of us. Tonight has been an awesome night—from the beautiful outfit, to this cool club, to Luke introducing me to someone as his girlfriend. That deserves a toast!

I grab my shot and hold it in the air with the rest of the group. The boys start chanting some ridiculous fraternity chant and then we all toss back our shots. Some pretty blonde girl who looks like a real life Barbie approaches Drake, but he blows her off to turn to face me.

"Ari," Drake slurs into my ear as he drapes his arm around my shoulders, "I am so glad to see you here. I've missed you."

Holding up the weight of Drake, I realize just how drunk he is. Even at his worst, I don't think I've seen him like this. I turn towards the bar with him glued to me as I ask for more waters. He's going to regret this hangover in the morning. Of course, I'm the party mom making everyone hydrate.

"You're a good friend, you know that," Drake slurs as he takes the water. Some enters his mouth, but most ends up on the floor or down the front of his dress shirt.

And just as I'm about to turn to ask for some napkins … it happens.

Drake plants a sloppy kiss on my lips. It happens so fast, I don't even have the time to push him off me or knee him in the balls—both of which I would have contemplated. As fast as the kiss happened, Drake is being thrown off me.

I can only spot a muscular back in a black dress shirt starting to pound into Drake's face. But Drake regains some kind of strength, lurching in Luke's direction. Luke stumbles but comes back strong and throws a right hook that connects with a loud pop on Drake's jaw. Trey appears out of nowhere, jumping in-between the two guys, shouting for them to knock it the fuck off, but he has no luck.

"Stop it! Stop it!" I scream, pushing myself closer. A mob of people have surrounded the two guys and I just can't get close enough. I'm throwing elbows and trying to tunnel my way through, but they are so far out of reach.

This needs to end. Someone is going to get seriously hurt.

Just as I think that, I get a good look at them both on the ground pummeling into each other—both of them are covered in blood. And it looks like someone lost a tooth.

It's then the crowd parts like the Red Sea as I spot Andy strutting over calmly with two huge bouncers. The two big bald-headed man jump right into the action—they both grab a guy and pull them apart. They make it look like it's no big deal.

"Are you okay?" Andy asks Luke as I rush up to them. When the fighting stops, people move back away from the drama. Luke doesn't say a single word—his eyes locked on Drake look full of rage. Drake has the same dead stare back at him. They aren't done. "Take them out. Make sure they get into separate cars safely," Andy says to his bouncers.

We are escorted out of the club. Ryan is standing outside by the town car when he sees us hurry out of the bar. He doesn't say a word about our sudden urgency to get into the car—he jumps into action and drives us away from this insane experience.

"I'm sorry about all of that," I say, not really sure what else can be said about what just took place. My heart rate is still racing.

"Your friend is a jackass. I don't want you to see him anymore," Luke growls. I take in a look at his face: he's bleeding from his temple and his knuckles are all messed up, but other than that he looks okay. It definitely wasn't *his* tooth that was knocked out. Poor Drake.

"I agree that my friend was acting like a jackass tonight, but normally he isn't like that," I say. Drake is normally such a chill guy and nothing gets under his skin. He was clearly drunk; he didn't know what he was doing. I could have handled myself in pushing him off me.

"Are you defending him?" Luke's hands clinch into fists resting on top of his thighs.

"Well no, I mean, yes. I guess? What happened back there? You immediately reacted by throwing a punch. We could have talked it through."

It concerns me that Luke was quick to throw a punch. If it was a stranger all over me, then okay fine, hit him. But this was Drake, my friend. My drunken friend who normally treats me like a sister. He didn't know what he was doing.

Luke hasn't said a word in response to me questioning his actions. Instead, he turns away from me to face the car's divider in silence, looking deep in thought. He's clearly not in the moment.

"Did I say something wrong?" I ask, placing my hand on Luke's bicep, giving it a reassuring squeeze. I don't want to fight and I don't want him to think I'm siding with Drake. I think they both acted stupidly. "I'm going to clean up your cuts when we get back to your place."

Luke hits a button and the divider between us and Ryan slides down. "Ryan, take us back to Ariana's apartment."

"Wait, what? Why are we going back to my apartment?" I ask confused. We don't normally spend the evening at my place, always his. I grab my phone from my purse getting a text message ready. "I should let Serena know we are coming back just in case she's there with Jack doing something we shouldn't walk in on," I laugh. I've walked in on a few too many things I'd rather not when it comes to Serena.

"No, I'm not coming to the apartment with you. I think we should end this."

"Why? I understand getting into a fight with Drake is probably not the highlight of our evening, but that doesn't mean that you and I need to spend the night alone. This date doesn't need to end."

We are pulling up in front of my apartment quicker than I expected and Ryan puts the car in park.

"I'm sorry but this is not going to work out. We shouldn't see each other anymore."

Whoa! I thought he didn't want to end this date, not our relationship.

"Luke, what the hell are you talking about?" I reach for his hand to take into mine but he pulls it back quickly, rejecting me. "Please, tell me what just happened? None of this makes any sense."

Luke reaches across me to open my car door as Ryan waits just outside of it. I'm getting kicked out of his car—and it appears his life.

"Luke, you don't have to do this," I beg. It's like the words are coming out of my mouth without any thought. I can't decide if this is happening in slow motion or hyper speed.

"Ariana, go."

Just like that I take one last look at his busted face before rushing out of the car into my empty apartment, where I spend the night crying in confusion.

What the fuck happened tonight?

CHAPTER TWENTY-THREE

Two weeks have gone by with no word from Luke. I miss him.

I'm still confused.

I randomly burst into tears when I'm alone.

Everything reminds me of him. Even the hospital.

Christmas comes and goes. I spend the evening alone, lying to Serena that I have plans while she goes to be with her family.

I throw myself into my work. Luckily, the end of my residency is right around the corner.

I want to know what caused Luke to get so angry and kick me out of his car—but I don't think I ever will. I've sent a few text messages and made a few phone calls. No answer. I will not beg someone to talk to me, to respect me enough to give me closure. I know how to be alone and I can slip back into the mode if I choose.

I guess that's what I'll do.

I've done this since I was a teenager.

I never needed anyone.

I am better off alone.

Fuck this.

This was the longest shift in my entire residency. I was all over the place! Just when I thought I was done with my shift, there was a shooting. Not just any shooting. This one broke out in our parking lot between two families feuding. It's stuff like this you think can't be real until you work here.

There doesn't seem to be any Drivers nearby so I decide the cold yet fresh air may do me good on this dark night. I start the journey through the downtown streets towards my apartment. Instead, I end up mindlessly walking until I find myself entering Molly Diner's. Luckily, it's 24 hours because it's two in the morning as I shuffle myself towards the booth I sat in not too long ago with Luke.

I pick up the pink menu and scan the list of options, but when Kathy walks to my table it's like I didn't read a single word. I put the menu down and look up to meet her kind, warm eyes.

"Want can I get you, kid?"

"I'd love a coke and a cheeseburger," I say.

She writes my order down on her pad. "You want some French fries?"

"You know it!"

She winks at me before walking to the table across from mine to get their orders too. The crowd right now is quite a mix—between teenagers binging after a night of drinking, night shift truck drivers, and a few sketchy individuals that I couldn't guess their stories if I tried. But maybe they are looking back at me the same way? I think my scrubs give me away though.

Kathy is back at my table setting down the glass of coke. "Aren't you Luke's friend?"

And there is it. I was sure she didn't recognize me because I made it this far.

"Yeah, but I don't think you'll see us in here together anymore."

"And why's that?"

Normally I'm not the kind of girl who offers up information about my life to anyone—let anyone a stranger. But the way Kathy asks makes me feel like she truly cares, not like she's prodding for gossip.

"I don't really know to be honest. Things were going pretty good." I look down at my hands now clenched on top of the table. "Until they weren't. He ended things and we haven't spoke since."

She shakes her head and lets out a small sigh. "Luke is a lot work."

"You're telling me," I mumble under my breath. Kathy chuckles hearing my whispers.

"I can see that you know he's a lot of work." She laugh before taking a more serious tone. "To me that means you've gotten close to him. He doesn't let many people close—really he doesn't let *anyone* close."

I nod my head in agreement and she leaves me alone for the rest of my meal. With warm food in my belly, I continue my cold walk back to my apartment. It's when I turn the corner that this walk suddenly proves to be the worst idea I've ever had. Staring me straight in the face is a giant billboard of Luke and me … nearly naked. Oh my god. I want to be embarrassed or even sad, but I can't. The photo is absolutely breathtaking. The overwhelming part is the sheer size—you cannot miss our billboard. A freakin' billboard hanging off a downtown building right in the middle of all the city's action.

Showcased in black and white, Luke is laying on top of me on the bed with his forearms on either side of my face. He's staring down at me in what looks like awe—the same look is reflected on my face back up at him. If you saw this picture, you'd think these two people were in love.

Our lower bodies are tangled in the sheet and Luke's arms cover my naughty parts … but Luke's tattoo sleeves are on full display. And just like in that moment, it pisses me off that they are no longer our secret. But right now, I'm happy to see them one more time.

I don't know how long I stand on that corner and stare up at the billboard. It's like time stands still.

"Hey lady! Get out of the way!" an obnoxious man shouts as he bumps into me and snaps me out of my daze.

"I'm sorry," I mutter back towards him even though normally I'd get tell him to fuck off.

"Wait. Isn't that you?" he asks, pointing from the billboard to me.

"No, you're mistaken," is all I say before continuing the walk I started hours ago.

CHAPTER TWENTY-FOUR

S lumped over on the couch, with takeout Lebanese food probably stuck to my face, and another episode of *Keeping Up With The Kardashians* playing on the TV, I can't even count the amount of times Netflix has asked me if I'm still watching the show.

Yes, Netflix. Mind your own damn business.

"Girl, you can't live your life like this. This is kind of gross," Serena says, reaching for my takeout container. A sound that can only be described as an evil growl comes out of my mouth.

"Put that back down, now." I didn't tell Serena about the billboard or how I stood and stared at it for much too long. I know people will recognize us, but I'm not ready to talk.

Serena looks at me trying to decide if I'm a threat or not—you know because of the growling and all. She walks away with the container, apparently deciding I'm not.

"You can't keep going on like this. He's not worth it."

"That's not what I'm doing. I just need a break to relax, okay?" I'm not even convinced by my own lame ass lie.

"Clean yourself up. We are going out tonight. If you try to fight me on this, I will drag you out by your hair," Serena commands before going into her bedroom.

Ugh. I know she's serious about the 'pulling you out by your hair' threat because I've seen her do that to another friend back in our college days. Damn it.

Maybe you need this.

Before I question the sudden positive thought, I head to the bathroom to shower. When was the last time I showered? Who knows. Okay, maybe when Serena called me gross she was right. I take a long shower and play some girl power anthems while getting ready. If I'm going out tonight and I have to stand next to Serena, I need to be presentable.

When I feel adequate enough, I find my friend waiting in the living room. And for the first time in history, she's there before me.

"I didn't want you to use me taking too long as an excuse not to go," Serena says as she jumps up from the couch, handing me a clutch as we walk out the door. Luckily, she's called us a Driver who's already idling at the curb. I don't ask where we are going, but I know Serena will not disappoint. I also assume we aren't going out alone—Serena travels with a crew unless she's with Jack. The minivan makes two stops to pick up Serena's wolf pack and then pulls up at the hottest nightclub in Chicago—Crave.

We pile out of the van in a flurry of long legs, big hair, and tight dresses. Serena walks us towards the bouncer, past the long line of people waiting. I try hard not to look at their faces—I can only imagine the glares—as I stick by Serena's side. She drops her name to the lady with a clipboard next to the bouncer as he moves the rope and lets us pass.

"Let's do this thing, ladies!" Serena shouts before strutting towards the bar.

Stephanie, Tonya, and Cristal excitedly head towards the bar with me slowly dragging ass behind. I don't know if I'm ready to let go and 'do this thing' with the ladies but I'm here so what the hell.

Yet another pep talk time …

You need this.

You need to let go.

You are uptight.

You deserve to have fun.

You didn't do anything wrong. *That you can figure out.*

"Tequila shots!" Serena turns from the bar pointing towards a line of shots waiting for us. My stomach is already nervous, but I down the shot with the rest of the girls, ready to move past whatever depression I've been sinking into.

Shots down.

Round two down.

Then it's time to hit the dance floor. We move to the center of the room and stick together. The alcohol moves through my body and I feel good. Swaying my hips and tossing my hair back and forth with my hands in the hair—I let loose. Hands roam over my body and I look down to realize … they aren't mine. I'm not the type of girl who lets a guy paw all over her in a club but fuck it.

I push my hips back and rock into this dude's erection. Ew. Okay, be a grown up. I turn around to make this a little less awkward and notice this guy is hot. Tall, dark, and handsome kind of hot. He smiles at me before gripping onto my hips to continue the dance.

The other ladies have also partnered up with random guys. A shot girl walks around with a tray of shots that I take one off and immediately down. Looking at the hot guy dancing with me I conclude I'm feeling zero emotions. Absolutely no emotions whatsoever.

"You're beautiful," hot guy shouts into my ear over the loud music.

"Was that an accent I hear?" I shout. Good looks and an accent—this should be any girl's dream. I wish I had feelings right now because my lady parts would be singing.

"Scottish," hot Scottish guy says pulling me closer to him by my hips. He presses his lips to mine and my brain says to punch him but my body doesn't give a shit. I kiss him back. I kiss him back hard holding onto his biceps. He's sloppy with his tongue but I'm drunk enough not to care at all.

We continue to be all over each other in the middle of the dance floor for the next few songs and then I feel someone's hand on my lower back. I jerk out of Scottish guy's arms and turn around ready to fight. That's when I see a surprised looking Serena.

"Hey, calm down," Serena shouts towards me, "it's time to go."

"Already? But I don't wanna," I say pouting and holding on to her, praying I don't fall over.

Scottish guy is within grasp as well, eyeing me like a piranha.

"The bar is closing girl." Serena turns us towards the door. "Say goodbye to your friend and let's go."

I wave goodbye to Scottish guy who looks annoyed that he's going home alone. Before I can give him a chance to say something to me, Serena and I walk arm-in-arm out of the club.

I don't remember the Driver ride back towards the apartment but somehow I'm getting into my bed while Serena is pulling the covers up for me.

"Goodnight my sweet friend. I'm glad you came out with us. Proud of you," she says before she presses a kiss to my forehead and I slip into a knocked out sleep.

I dream of hurt little boys, loud yelling, being rejected, and then the familiar dream with Allen makes it way back in. I haven't dreamed of what happened to me since I told Luke about it.

I wake up screaming.

CHAPTER TWENTY-FIVE

Making my rounds the next day with a killer hangover is probably one of the dumbest things I've ever done. I am chugging water whenever I get the chance to rid the alcohol from my bloodstream. Passing by the staff room, I want to curl up on the couch to get some much-needed sleep, but I spot the chief rounding the corner.

Pretend you didn't get drunk last night.

"Your mother is on the phone," Chief Pitters says to someone behind me as she walks towards me in the hallway. Instead of being nosy and turning around to look, I walk right past her without batting an eye. "Ariana, hello," I hear her say in an annoyed tone.

I turn around. "Chief, what's up?"

"I said your mother is on the phone. Sounds urgent," she says in her straight to the point way. This lady has delivered the worst news to many people within her career that she is numb to emotional reactions.

"My mother? Are you sure you have the right person?"

"Are you or are you not Dr. Ariana Bellisano?" She sasses me. "Go pick up the nearest phone, she's on line three."

I walk away from the chief in utter disbelief. My feet carry me to a phone in the staff room and somehow I answer line three without realizing how I even got here. I haven't spoken to my mom since I moved out of the house after graduating high school. Why the hell is she calling me? Is this some kind of prank?

"Hello," I say, unsure of who is really on the other end of the line.

"Ariana," I hear my mother's voice say with zero emotion, "hello?"

"Hello, yes I'm here."

I can't believe I'm on the phone with my mom.

"Your father is in the hospital. He's had a heart attack. Come home if you want to see him. It's not looking good."

My stomach drops.

"When did this happen? What are his physicians saying? Should I call the hospital?" A million questions run through my head, and I seem to spit out as many as I can in a frantic exchange with my mother.

"Ariana, I don't have all day to answer questions. I need to get back into your father's room. I will email you the information about the hospital. Get yourself on a plane here."

Did my mom just say she'll email me important information about my father's health instead of just talking to me? Wow. I remember why it was so easy not to miss them. It's all business, no compassion in her voice.

"Okay. Do you know my email?" I ask. This is so weird. I didn't even know my mother knew how to email.

"No."

Pulling teeth would be easier than having this conversation. I give her my email address and she quickly says goodbye. I pull the phone away from my face with a shaky hand, realizing I've had a death grip on it the entire time.

My father had a heart attack.

It's not looking good.

I walk around the hospital aimlessly looking for the chief. I find her in the cafeteria sitting alone reading, so I take a seat across from her.

"Ariana, everything okay?" Chief Pitters asks, putting her book down.

"My dad had a heart attack and my mom thinks I need to go right away," I say the words in a panic. "Can you have someone cover my shifts for the next few days? I would really appreciate it. I mean if you can't let me that would be okay, I can stay but …"

"Of course! Ariana, go be with your family. Take the time you need," the chief says in a surprisingly caring tone.

That was way easier than I thought. I've never taken a day off work before, and now it's for my parents who I haven't spoken to in nearly eight years.

"I can finish tonight's shift though," I say standing up.

The chief shocks me by saying, "No. Go home. You won't be able to concentrate here tonight."

She's right. Since the minute I found out it was my own mother on the phone, I started shaking. My heart is racing, my blood pressure must be through the roof, and somehow I walked into the staff room to put on my jacket.

Now what do I do? Cab. I need a ride. I hit the Driver app on my phone seeing Ali is five minutes away in a Chevy Malibu. I hit the "Pick Me Up" button and walk towards the parking lot to meet her. I can't wait to just sit down and collect my thoughts.

Just as the wind hits my face while walking into the chaotic parking lot, I see the Malibu pull up. I get into the car and tell Ali my address. She doesn't push me with any questions beyond the general 'how are you?' garbage. My bad mood must be loud and clear, which I'd normally try to hide, but right now I can't focus on making nice. Luckily, the ride is short.

The apartment is empty when I walk in. I head straight to the liquor cabinet to pour myself a stiff drink before plopping down on the couch.

How did it feel talking to mom? Nerve-wracking.

Do I care that dad had a heart attack? Yes.

Why? He's my dad. He could die; mom said things don't look good. The last time I saw him, I hated him. Okay, that's not true. I felt indifferent to my parents at that point. They broke my heart when I was 14, and then I was extremely angry for a few years until one day I woke up and I was over it. Over them. We coexisted in the house basically keeping out of each other's way, not speaking at all. And we were all okay with it. I didn't want to speak to people who didn't believe me, want to help me, or stick by my side. No thank you.

But no one was about to die during that time.

It's not until Serena wraps her arms around me that I realize I'm still on the bathroom floor sobbing hysterically—who knows how long I've been down here. She doesn't ask me any questions, just cradles me close to her chest like a baby. And it's just what I need.

CHAPTER TWENTY-SIX

My bags are packed and I'm slumped over in my airplane seat on a red-eye to Florida. After picking myself up off the bathroom floor, Serena helped me find the earliest flight. I'm coming mommy dearest.

Chicago to Orlando—about three hours.

Headphones in and sleep mask on. I look like your average 'don't talk to me' passenger on the flight. Drifting off to sleep I'm awoken by the flight attendant. Looking around the plane I see everyone else is gone. I slept through the entire flight and de-boarding process. That's a first.

I find the baggage claim and see the last lonely bag slowly making its way around the carousel. It's a sad sight really. I glance over and see a set of parents eagerly excited to welcome their daughter home. She's about my age. Her parents are smiling so wide I think they are about to break their faces. She's engulfed into a huge group hug.

A part of me wants to make a bitter comment about how nauseating that must be. But to be honest, I'm bitter because I'm jealous. I don't think anyone has ever looked as happy to see me a day in my life. I like to think that when I was a child my parents were happy about my existence, but truthfully, I don't remember them ever being warm and welcoming.

I know not to look around for mom. I head out of the airport and straight to the taxi cab line outside.

"One?" A small man asks waving me forward in the line.

"Is the lonest number …" I reply.

"What?" He looks truly confused.

"Sorry—yes one."

"Number four."

And just like that I'm in a yellow taxi rushing through the Orlando streets on the way to my parents' home. My parents. I don't even feel comfortable enough to call it 'my' home, like so many people I know do when referencing their childhood homes.

We pull up to the house about twenty minutes later. All the lights are off. Mom knew what time I was getting in; I guess I'll see her tomorrow? I tip the driver and head inside, wheeling my luggage behind me. Yet another sad sight. I will not let this experience slip me back into becoming the shell of a person I was when I lived here. I fought so hard not to be her anymore.

I'm half-surprised to see that my key still fits in the lock and opens the front door. Normally an alarm would go off but mom must have disabled it for tonight—at least she did that for me. I'm going to guess she didn't want to be bothered by me setting it off this late. I hit the flashlight button on my phone and head straight to my old room upstairs trying to be as quiet as possible. It's a blast from the past when I open the door.

Nothing has changed since I moved out. It's nauseating. It's not because my parents are trying to hold on to my memories—they just don't want to sort through my belongings. I change into a pair of pajamas and crawl under the purple covers of my twin bed and drift to sleep for the second time tonight.

Cabinets slamming around startle me awake. I open my eyes nearly having a panic attack upon seeing where I am.

How the fuck did I get here?

It's then the blur of last night's flight comes back to me and I take in a good look at the bedroom I'm sleeping in. Purple walls donning Backstreet Boys posters—I'm stuck in my 14-year-old life. I lived here until I was 18, but after my parents made it clear they didn't believe me, I didn't make this place any more of a 'home' than I needed to four years prior.

I wonder what the homes Luke lived in looked like. I can't believe I just thought about Luke. I've been so good with not giving him much space in my mind.

You're under a lot of stress.

The cabinets have not stopped slamming, which was a trick my mom used to pull when she wanted to wake my dad up.

I stumble down the stairs to face whatever mood my mother is in. In the daylight I see most of the house has been completely remodeled. It's all upgraded—granite, hard wood, marble, mud room, you name it. It's nice to see their lives are going well.

I stop dead in my tracks when I see my mom in the kitchen. She has her back to me, giving me a second to collect my scrambling thoughts. I feel like a child again. Why is this happening to me? I am a grown up—I am a doctor; I can surely handle this woman I spent years ignoring.

"Good morning mom," I manage to say as I take a seat at the kitchen table. She turns around from the coffee pot and I see the stress on her normally primp and proper face. "How's dad?"

She places a cup of coffee in front of me and takes a seat. If it wasn't this early in the morning, I would be utterly shocked that she gave me something.

"After his heart attack they noticed a few heart complications and want to monitor him. I usually go to the hospital when visiting hours start, which is in about an hour. Get ready."

Just like that she excuses herself from the table, leaving me alone in the kitchen. After news like this, I've seen hundreds—maybe even thousands—of families rally around each other to console one another in their time of need. I guess we are not going to be doing that in this house.

Facing mom was one thing. Dad is going to be an entirely different battle. When I get back to my room to pick out some kind of outfit for the day, I see a missed text message on my phone—

Are you there? Girl, at least send your friend a text! xox Serena

For the first time since I've landed in Orlando, I smile.

Sorry! I'm here, sleeping in my old room. How weird! Haven't seen my dad yet, going in about an hour. I'll text you later!

Mom doesn't take shit from anyone and she's definitely not going to wait around for me if I'm late. I don't feel like taking another cab so I jump in the shower at lightning speed and head downstairs to wait for her. Of course, she's already there, this time looking like your regular Stepford Wife. We get in the car and drive in complete silence to the hospital.

I should be used to this—the whole not-talking-to-my-parents thing—but for some reason it makes me sad.

They should have been in your life to protect you.

I hear Luke's voice cloud my thoughts, remembering what he said when I told him about being raped. Glancing over at my mom I take in her stoic profile. She should have protected me, but she didn't—can I just forgive her now and let it all go? But that's a whole other issue that I won't be getting an answer for today.

We pull into the hospital parking lot and my mom navigates the beige colored hallways like she's the president of the hospital. As we walk through the lobby, several nurses and physicians stop to say hello or wave at her as we make our way to the Cardiac ICU. She completely transforms in front of other people—long gone is the face of the woman who sat in the car not speaking a word to her daughter after years. Instead, she's the bubbly woman who people see as a saint.

The thought of forgiveness slips away a bit.

"This is his room," she says as we come to a stop before a door. "Don't alarm him," she utters in a tight-lipped smile. Goodbye saint.

"Mom, I'm a doctor. I know how to talk to a heart attack patient."

She rolls her eyes at me like she couldn't care less what I just said and pushes the door open.

Just like the moment in the kitchen with mom, I freeze staring at my dad lying in this bed. Mom gives me a little push from behind and I walk into the room. Usually looking like a modern day John Wayne, my dad intimidates even the manliest of men with his stature; however, now he looks like a shadow of that man.

Planting a fake smile on my face I say, "Hi dad."

Part of me feels bad for how fake I'm being. Just days before getting this news, these two people meant absolutely nothing to me.

"Ariana, you're here," dad says, looking weak and surprised.

"How are you feeling?" I take a seat in the chair at the foot of his bed.

"Like absolute shit," he says with a half-ass smile. It's weird to hear my dad swear. My parents usually act so proper. I've never heard either of them 'lower themselves'—as they'd think—to say a 'bad' word.

"You look good," I lie, trying to console him.

He laughs. "That's a terrible lie but I appreciate it. Enough about me. How are you?"

I'm thrown a little by the question since my mom has yet to ask me anything about how I'm doing. I turn around and realize my mom didn't follow me into the room.

"Looking for your mother? She's probably off telling some doctor or another how they should be doing their job."

First swearing, then asking me about myself, and now poking fun at mom. What did this heart attack do to my dad? He's a changed man and it's freaking me the fuck out.

"I can only imagine the kind of hell she's giving them," I say, laughing and feeling thankful that I am not on this hospital staff.

"How's your residency?" dad asks before taking a sip of water from the plastic cup on his tray.

"My residency? How did you know about that?"

Dad puts down his empty cup before saying, "You think because you're in Chicago, I don't have ways to keep track of you?"

"I didn't think you'd want to even if you could."

The words slip out and I immediately wish I could take them back. It's not that they aren't true; it's just that I don't feel like adding anything else to his list of worries right now.

"That's a fair statement. Things aren't the best with us, haven't been in awhile, have they?"

I'm utterly in shock. Our conversation is cut short when mom and a nurse walk into the room, mom shouting at her for the type of care he's receiving. Or as mom thinks the lack of care. The nurse rolls her eyes like she's had enough of my mom's drama, but she picks up the chart.

"How are you feeling today, Mr. Bellisano?"

"How do you think he's feeling? A heart attack then catheterization, yet he's still having an elevated heart rate. Something is wrong. Why can't you explain this?"

Mom doesn't hold back a thing.

"Could I look at his chart?" I speak up.

"Who are you?" The nurse asks, giving me an up and down look.

I extend my hand. "Hi, I'm Dr. Ariana Bellisano, Mr. Bellisano's daughter."

She gives me a pointed glare. "I'll have to check with Mr. Bellisano's physician to see if he cares if you look over his charts."

"Okay, you do that. And keep me posted."

My dad laughs and my mom looks surprised yet proud that I stuck up for dad. Oh for the love of god, I'm becoming rude just like her.

The uptight nurse takes the chart and leaves the room in a dramatic show. What a diva. I make a mental note to never act like that in the hospital, or in life really.

Dad drifts off to sleep with mom, and I sit down and read the magazines on the table. It's comfortable yet awkward at the same time. I should be able to just sit and relax with my parents. But I don't really know these people even though they have major titles in my life: mom, dad.

An hour passes before the door swings open and an middle-aged gentlemen in blue scrubs strolls into the room holding my dad's chart, looking like he doesn't have a care in the world.

"You must be the daughter," he says, eyeing me up and down.

"You must be the physician who guards the charts?" I return the eye glare. Two can play at that game.

He laughs and the ice seems to be broken between us. The nurse returns and stands at his side. She doesn't seem as sassy anymore.

"Here you go," the physician—I see with the last name "Dixon" on the badge clipped to his scrub top—says before handing over the medical chart. The nurse looks a little taken back at his instant trust but doesn't question him.

I flip the folder open and read every word carefully, over and over.

After he was brought in for a heart attack, he had an invasive procedure testing for heart disease. It looks like things went smoothly in clearing his blockage but dad is still feeling extremely weak. Slight discomfort is normal, but dad looks rough. What could be wrong with him?

"That's what we are trying to figure out," Dr. Dixon says.

I guess I was rambling that information out loud.

"Can you run another test?"

"Are you questioning the results?" The nurse decides at this moment she's going to speak up, but the physician gives me a reassuring look, not even glancing her way.

"We certainly could do another test. I want to do another procedure. However, the staff let me know your father's insurance will not cover that."

At this point my mom, who I'm surprised remained silent this far, speaks up. "This is about money? Give him the test again. We'll pay."

Dr. Dixon turns to the nurse, "Let the team know that Mr. Bellisano will be down for another procedure this afternoon."

The nurse's face says she wants to fight him on this, to fight us for questioning her, but she does as she's told and leaves the room.

I look over towards the hospital bed and dad is now awake from his nap. I'm not sure if he saw the entire exchange, but he gives me a small smile.

Is that the look of pride? I'd have no clue what that would look like.

My emotions are all over the place right now. I take a seat and pick up my magazine again. I read the same stupid article about some Real Housewife going to jail over and over again, yet I've never really looked at the words.

"You have anyone special in your life Ari?" dad asks as mom puts down her magazine to listen.

Why do they care?

I should tell them the truth about how I couldn't even let men touch me, even in a friendly way, until just recently. Until Luke. But I can't seem to bring any of that up right now.

Luke, Luke, Luke.

I've been doing so great not giving him space in my mind ... until this goddamn trip. Why does he keep coming up in everything that I'm doing? My brain should be busy doing other things, like worrying about my dad.

"No, no one special."

"You should really think about settling down because you aren't getting any younger," mom chimes in with her stellar words of wisdom.

"I've been focused on my residency. No time for dating," I say, laughing off her bitchy comment and pretending that it doesn't get to me.

Why does it get to me?

Just months ago I would have laughed at a comment like that because a relationship wouldn't mean anything to me, so who cares how old I am. I wanted a career as a doctor and that was it. Nothing more, nothing less.

I never wanted a husband.

I never wanted children.

I never wanted love.

But I think all that changed within these past few months because of Luke.

"Don't pressure her, Diane. I'm sure if someone worthy of her comes into her life, she'll settle down and let us know."

I pass off a small smile to try to end this conversation, a conversation I don't think my parents truly deserve the right to know anything about.

Yes, I thought I found a man worthy of settling down with. I thought we were having a great time together. I thought wrong. Luke so easily pushed me out of his life … his car … without so much as an explanation. I don't want to go through that again.

A different nurse walks into the room with a smile on her face, pushing in a gurney.

"Gabe, you ready to go for a ride?" She laughs towards my dad. Instantly, I feel at ease for the first time since I got the call about his heart attack. All it took was a kind face.

"Let's rock and roll, young lady," dad says before we help him out of the bed and onto the gurney. He huffs and puffs that he doesn't need our help but I see the struggle in his face. He's in pain.

Dad is wheeled out of the room and I give him a little wave goodbye before he rounds the corner with the nurse. I'm suddenly very tired.

I've seen many heart attack patients leave the hospital with a couple medications and a list of lifestyle changes. But dad's heart attack is serious. Potentially deadly. For the first time since I was 14 I am talking to my dad … and I could lose him. I get up from the chair next to my mom and pace the room. I can't sit still—I need to do something.

"We need to stay strong," mom says. Looking over at her I notice she's drying her tears. I didn't even see her start to cry with all my pacing. "He's going to pull through this."

Hearing her say that makes me feel a little better. As a doctor, I know she's just guessing to make herself feel better; she has no real knowledge of the procedure, but I don't care. My mom says he's going to pull through— he better.

But they've lied to me before.

I can't think like that right now. I shouldn't think about the reality of my relationship with my parents at a time like this. At a time when dad could die and we spent years upon years completely shutting each other out, can I forgive them? If we are going to be honest, I forgave them years ago. I just thought I didn't need them in my life whatsoever so I got along fine without them. And up until right now, that was true.

"I'm going to the cafeteria to get something to eat," mom says as she stands smoothing her black skirt. I don't want mom to be alone so I follow behind, even though I can't tell if she wants me to join her. She's extremely hard to read.

We walk down a few floors to the now busy cafeteria. I glance at my phone to see it's dinnertime. I grab a Caesar salad and bottle of water before joining mom at a small table.

"It shouldn't be much longer until someone comes to tell us he's okay." I try to say it as strong as she would, but I hear my voice waver with my delivery. She doesn't say anything more.

We sit in silence for what feels like eternity, but it can only be minutes, as we eat our salads until mom says, "Thank you for asking them to look into this further."

Looking up from my salad I see she's still eyeing hers. She doesn't meet my eyes, but I think she just said the nicest thing she's ever said to me.

"No problem," I try not to make this a big deal.

We keep eating until mom's phone goes off. She snatches it up in an instant, "Hello?"

I see the worry back in her eyes as she listens to the person on the other end until she ends the call. She doesn't say a word, but she's only on the line a few seconds.

"Mom?"

"Dr. Dixon wants to speak to us in dad's room."

"That's all he said?"

"That's it. Why didn't he say everything went well or mention the surgery at all?" Mom looks at me with pleading eyes; I've never seen her look so worried, so childlike.

I shrug my shoulders and say, "I don't know. Let's go."

Usually they don't say anything over the phone when … it's bad news. My stomach drops. I don't want to jump ahead of myself. We walk side-by-side to the elevator and cram ourselves inside with another family. They seem extremely happy and when they get off on the maternity ward floor I know why.

They're welcoming a new member of their family.

I feel a tear slip from my eye, but I wipe it off before it's noticeable.

Dr. Dixon is in the hallway outside of dad's room talking to a nurse we haven't seen before. When he spots us his face is neutral, not giving anything away. I pity him for what I know he's about to do.

"Mrs. and Miss Bellisano," he says as he nods his head at us, "we tried everything that we could. Your husband went into cardiac arrest during his procedure. His heart stopped and we could not revive him. I'm so sorry."

"No!" mom screams before cupping her hands over her face to sob. She makes a noise I've never heard before, a primal animal noise. The sound you'd make when your true love is ripped away from your life. The tears don't stop.

"I'm sorry, let the staff know if there is anything you need," Dr. Dixon says again before leaving us to grieve alone.

I haven't spoken to my dad in years … and now I'll never be able to again.

I'll never hear his voice.

I'll never get to ask him a question. To answer one of his.

I'll never get to hug him.

I'll never get to have a family dinner.

Or lunch. Or breakfast.

Or goddamn anything.

I look at my mom who continues to sob; she's the only family I have left. Wrapping my arms around her, I let her sob into my embrace. The tears don't seem to leave my eyes.

Shock. Numb.

The door swings open and we pull apart from our embrace. The bitchy nurse from earlier stares at us a little stunned. "I'm so sorry, I didn't know anyone was in here."

She leaves the room as quickly as she threw herself into it.

Mom pulls her shoulders back and holds her head high despite her puffy eyes and says, "Come on, we need to make arrangements."

If I didn't work in a hospital myself, I would be thrown by how quickly she's tried to change her feelings. But it's quite normal to go through many stages of shock, denial, and grief.

We walk down the hall back to the elevator of doom when another nurse stops us. I'm standing here, but I have absolutely no idea what she's saying to mom. My head spins in a million different directions.

The elevator dings and for some reason I glance in its direction. Luke.

The man who left me is here, in this very hospital, walking out of the elevator towards me.

I run. No, I sprint down the hall and throw myself into his open arms. It's then I finally cry. The tears fall from my eyes like a waterfall as I collapse into his strong arms. He holds me tight and keeps me upright in his embrace.

"I'm so sorry, Ariana," he whispers into my ear.

My sobs subside when I realize I'm standing in the middle of a hospital causing a scene. I pull myself out of his grasp and wipe at my eyes, mimicking what I just saw my mom do just minutes ago.

Mom. I turn around and see she's walking towards us.

"No one special, huh? I see the last thing you said to your dad was a lie," she says as she brushes past us and steps into the elevator. Staring straight into her cold eyes as the doors close in front of her face, I can't believe she just said that to me.

But what she said was the truth.

"Hey," Luke says as he grabs my arm, forcing me to look at him. "Breathe. In, out." He kisses my forehead before taking my hand in his, guiding us towards the elevator. I melt into his side, letting him put me in a red Prius rental car. If I wasn't feeling like a crazy person I'd make a joke about the fact that this manly man CEO is driving a tiny hybrid, but I don't even have it in me.

I've got nothing left in me.

CHAPTER TWENTY-SEVEN

In silence we drive until we reach a Marriott not too far from the hospital, and Luke parks the car. Everything else is a blur—how I got up the stairs, into the room, and inside a shower with the hottest water streaming across my body. Looking down at my hands holding a bar of orange soap, I watch it slip from my hands to crash on the ground.

"Fuck ... fuck, fuck, fuck, fuck!" I scream, slamming my fist into the wall. I can't tell the difference between my own tears and the water from the showerhead. Neither stops flowing down my face. Just as my legs feel like giving out in utter defeat, I'm caught.

Luke stands in the shower in all his clothes to hold me up. Now I know it's tears streaming as I sob.

"I can't do this. I'm not strong enough for this," I cry out.

Luke scoops me up and carries me to the bed. I stare at the ugly white stucco ceiling trying to catch my breath. I think I'm hyperventilating. No, I'm a doctor; I *know* I'm hyperventilating. I hear the water shut off before Luke comes out of the bathroom holding a fluffy white towel. He gently rubs the towel over my wet body, drying me off. He's gentle and patient. Tears must be trickling down my face again because Luke takes an extra second to wipe my cheeks.

"How did you know I was here?" I ask, my voice hoarse from all the crying.

Luke lays next to me on the bed, still in his wet clothes. He stares up at the ceiling too. "I went to your apartment to see you and Serena told me."

"Why did you go to my apartment? You made it clear you didn't want me in your life anymore."

He's silent for a minute too long, but I don't have the energy to fight with him or plead my case—my case for wanting a fucking explanation for why he threw me out of his car and cut off all connection without a single word. The first time I decided to trust a man since I was raped and he leaves me. I already felt unworthy; this was just a confirmation.

"I'd like to tell you about what happened to my parents, if that's okay with you."

"Oh, now you want to open up and share with me? On the same day my dad died." As soon as the bitchy words leave my lips I wish I could take them back. They are poisonous and I don't mean them. I do want to know what happened to his parents.

"I've never told this to anyone before," Luke says, ignoring my asshole remark.

He lost his parents when he was 14 and he's never spoken about it? I thought I was depressing, since I only told a few close friends part of my story. But telling absolutely no one is worse. How lonely. His heart must be heavy, carrying around whatever he's about to share with me.

"Tell me, please." I can't bring myself to look at him yet, but I do want to hear what he's been through. I've wanted this for so long—I'll take it however it comes.

He takes a deep breath. "My dad used to beat the shit out of my mom."

He pauses and I let out a small gasp. Trying to stay quiet, I keep all the questions swirling around in my head to myself … for now. Suddenly, I have a flashback to when he reacted in the car to the little boy and his mom who I knew were getting abused. That could have been him. Little Luke.

"My dad was an alcoholic. He'd come home and blame my mom for everything wrong in his life. That's how it all started. A drunken punch here, a slap across the face there.

"Then as I got older, it got much worse. He started accusing her of having affairs with random men we'd never heard of, and she'd reassure him each time she had no idea what he was talking about. He was an extremely nasty, jealous man."

"Did he hit you too?" I know the answer—I've seen his scars but I need to know for sure. The thought of someone laying a hand on young Luke makes my blood boil.

He chuckles at my concern. "We all got hit, except for Lisa, until one day he lost it on her too."

A man who hits his kids and his wife is the ultimate coward. He's supposed to protect them.

Luke takes a few minutes to collect his thoughts. "Two days before my fifteenth birthday, my dad came home and interrupted what would have been a nice family dinner. Mom had all three of us kids at the table talking about our days and dad stumbles in. A big fight broke out and then dad left the room. I thought it was over with and he'd go sleep it off somewhere. I was so fucking wrong. Dad came back into the kitchen holding a nine millimeter."

I gasp in shock and slip my hand into Luke's.

"Mom makes us kids go to our rooms, which isn't anything out of the usual. She could calm him down much better if we weren't around bickering at him. Just the sight of us—me especially—would enrage him. So, we all went into Lisa's room and then I heard a blood curdling scream."

Luke grips my hand a little tighter. I'm not even sure he's aware he's doing it.

"I run out of my bedroom and into the kitchen. Dad has his disgusting hands wrapped around my mom's throat; he is choking her to death. I see her face turning purple. I run at them, knocking my dad over and I beat the shit out of him. I pretty much space out from that moment until I hear the first shot. Everything snaps into focus and is crystal clear after that."

My heart is breaking for where this story is going—for this young boy and his beautiful siblings who have been nothing but kind to me. I roll over onto my side to stare at Luke's profile; he's still looking at the ceiling with no emotion reflected in his hazel eyes. I can see he just wants to get this off his chest. It's a story I can't believe he's never told to another soul.

"He shot her." A tear slides down Luke's cheek; he wipes it away just as fast as it falls. "He shot her in the head right there in front of me. I watched her instantly take her last breath," Luke pauses, "and then he turned the gun on himself and took his own life. That fucking bastard. That fucking coward. Out of rage and jealousy he took the one person who truly loved us away. His cowardice took away our angel."

"Oh my god. Luke," is all I can say as I cuddle up next to him embracing him in the biggest hug I can give. I kiss his cheek and squeeze him tight to me.

He has battles too.

"You are nothing like your father."

He finally turns to me and it's then I see the pain in his eyes. "You're wrong. You don't see it, I'm *just* like him."

"What are you talking about? You have one of the biggest hearts out of everyone I know. You wouldn't hurt anyone."

"No, Ariana. At the club when I saw Drake kissing you I became a different person. I saw red. I wanted to murder him for putting his hands on you. And I wanted to scream at you for letting another man touch you. I was engulfed in jealousy. Don't you see? I'm just fucking like him. I can't be with anyone because you never know what I could do."

I curl myself into Luke's side, laying my head on his chest to listen to his heart's fast beat.

"Luke, you are nothing like your father. Absolutely nothing like him. I don't know how to say that any other way."

I wish I could make him see himself how I do.

"You don't know that. You don't really know me."

"How can you say that? Yes, I *do* know that and yes I do know you." I sit myself upright to stare at Luke. I really look at him and marvel at his handsomeness. Placing my hand on his strong chest I feel a tiny scar, which has a completely different meaning for me now.

He's a fighter. Something extremely tragic, that many people would use as an excuse to give up on life, hasn't broken him down. Luke has done just the opposite. To anyone meeting Luke today, you'd see a man who is thriving as the CEO of the largest vodka company in the world.

"You are an amazing man. Just the way you act with your brother and sister is something to admire. You protect them, take care of them, honor them, and you love them. It's obvious; your heart is full of love. Don't compare yourself to someone like ... that."

"Someone like *that* is in my DNA. That jealousy runs in my blood." Luke rubs at his eyes with his fists before sitting up next to me. "You can believe what you want, but I know the truth about myself."

"Well, I know what I know."

He smirks and says, "You're goddamn stubborn."

"Damn straight. That seems to be the only thing you're right about." I lean in, kissing him.

I've missed this. I've missed him. I want to talk about everything that's happened—all the stupid things I did to distract myself from missing him—in the time we've been apart, but right now my brain doesn't care about all of that.

All I want to do is kiss him. Luke kisses me but I can tell he's holding back. "Are you sure you're okay? Today has got to be a tough day for you," he says, pulling back to stare at me. "We can wait."

"No, I don't want to wait." I pull him towards me by his shirt. "Please. I really need you right now."

And that's all it takes; he kisses me back. It's no holding back. I slowly bite his bottom lip as my hand trails up from his chest to wrap around his head. As I run my fingers through his thick hair, he moans into my mouth.

His fingers move to the towel he wrapped me up in earlier, which he's now slowly undoing. I feel a breeze as the towel drops to the bed, leaving me exposed. I'm not cold for long—my body heats up as Luke leans in to suck on my nipple. He rolls his tongue around it before squeezing it between his teeth. He moves from one to the other, taking his time to give both equal attention. Dropping my hands to the bed I cling to the sheets; this is absolutely delightful.

"Lean back Ariana," Luke commands. As I lean back, lowering my head on the pillow, he lowers himself down my body to hover his face between my thighs. "The view from here is nice."

I laugh, watching him check out my breasts. I never thought I'd be the woman who cares what a man thinks about her, but I truly find it sexy that he finds me sexy. I don't have much time to think about that though, as Luke dips his head down to run his tongue back and forth across my sensitive bud. My body quivers as he twirls his skillful tongue around and around. He alternates between licks and sucks in just the right way to send electric waves through my body.

Then an intense ravenous desire rips through me, urging me to return the favor and give him this pleasure.

"Luke, stop," I moan. Luke looks up at me to make sure everything is okay. I have him pushed back on the bed with me straddling his hips in what seems like a flash.

"How the hell did you just maneuver that?" he laughs at my ninja-like skills.

Kissing him from his chest to his erect manhood, which I lick after happily greeting it. Slipping his cock in between my breasts, I rub it up and down until I see a dribble of pre-ejaculation come out of the tip. I lean down to suck him into my mouth while Luke hisses out in pleasure.

I deep throat his cock while my hands massage his heavy balls. Hearing a low growl from Luke encourages me to keep going. I bob my head up and down as I continue twirling my tongue around his cock.

He must be getting close to climax—he's got to be— but before I can confirm that, he pulls his cock out of my wanting mouth and flips me over on the bed. I'm laying on my side as he maneuvers his body in-between my legs. One of my legs is under his body and the other draped over his torso; he slowly teases my wet clit by rubbing his cock up and down it.

Fuck, that's divine. I claw my nails into his bicep and start rocking myself into his cock.

Put it in already, man.

He reads my mind. For a split second everything stands still. His hazel eyes reflect the understanding that must shine from my greys.

I take his cock into my hand and slide it gently into my sex.

"I love you," Luke says with his eyes still on me.

He loves me. This man is the only man who has ever shown me true love and I love him back. Hell yes I do.

"I love you too," I whisper before leaning in to kiss him, which takes him deeper inside my body. He must hit something magical inside because I moan out.

"Oh you like that?" Gone is the loving look in Luke's eyes, replaced with the naughty confident one.

"I *love* that too," I wink before trying to grind on him, but in this position he's going to be the one who has to work. He holds on to my leg for support before he rocks his hips into me over and over again.

"Oh my god. Don't ever stop doing that," I whimper out, feeling sweat pool over my body. I squeeze Luke's bicep even harder before I slam my eyes shut as an orgasm rocks through my core. Luke pumps inside of me a few more times before he stops to pull me close to his shaking chest.

I let him hold me in his arms, post-orgasmic bliss, for what feels like eternity before nervously asking, "Where do we go from here?"

An overwhelming need to help him fight his battles is coursing through my bones. I don't want him to ever dismiss me again, especially now that I know the reason. He needs to see he is nothing like the man who he hates so much. His father is not in him.

"Where do you want to go from here?"

Pulling apart so I can look him in the eye I say, "I don't want to ever leave your side. Don't push me away again; I don't think I can handle that. And if you do, then do it for good because I'm too weak to be broken."

Luke lets out a sigh and says, "I'm sorry I left you broken."

I run my fingers through his hair and then tug on it a little. "I was so mad at you for kicking me out of your life with no explanation ... during what is normally a time of the year when I go completely numb."

Luke rolls over so we are both now facing each other propped up on our elbows. "It took everything in me not to drive over to your apartment on Christmas Eve. To do that every single day. I'm still not sure this," he moves his other hand between us, "is a good idea. We don't know how I'll react if I'm put in a jealous situation again."

"I'm going to ask you something that's important to me and I don't want you to judge the idea. Okay?"

"Should I be nervous?" He laughs.

"Would you be willing to go to therapy? I think that talking to someone can help you grieve and heal properly from what happened in your life."

"Ariana—" He tries interrupting me, but I'm on a roll and don't think I'd be able to finish my train of thought if I don't just spit it all out right now.

"Listen Luke. I know that therapy sounds terrifying. *Trust me.* I was terrified before I went too. I didn't go to therapy until I found the Stand Up Against Abuse charity—*years* after I was raped. I had pushed so much down and dealt with it in completely unhealthy ways.

And you know what? Therapy didn't cure me. Clearly I was a pretty fucked up person when you met me. I wouldn't even let you touch me...."

"You aren't fucked up." He picks my chin up and leans in to place a soft kiss on my lips.

"How can you be sure? When you left I started to slip back into the shell of the person I used to be. I'm still not cool with certain people touching me—that has to mean something."

"There are no guarantees that you won't slip back. But for what it's worth, I think you're incredible."

"Luke, I think the same of you." It's then the conversation we've been having about me hits him in the way I was praying it would. I see the confusion mixed with hope reflected in his deep eyes. "Just like there are no guarantees that *I* won't slip back or slip up, there's no guarantee that *you* are or are not like your father. Can't we just live our lives one day at a time? And you know what would make those days better? If we spent them together."

He doesn't say a word about my little speech; instead, he takes me in a deep kiss. We lay on top of the covers making out for what feels like hours, like a pair of carefree teenagers. A pair of normal teenagers—something neither one of us was allowed to be.

One a rape victim.

One an orphan.

Both with severe trust issues.

Yet both protectors.

CHAPTER TWENTY-EIGHT

The black pantsuit I squeeze myself into is not my style whatsoever, but it was the only all black thing I could find at the local mall. I didn't bring clothes for a funeral. Was I naïve enough to believe my dad would be okay? Why didn't I think about him dying before it was too late?

After the night at the hotel with Luke, I went back home to find my mom cleaning the house like a madwoman. Everything smelled like PineSol, and if I thought the cabinets were slamming yesterday, it is nothing like the show she was putting on now.

Doors, drawers, cabinets, you name it, she's slamming it.

I don't blame her.

She just lost her one true love.

When I thought Luke kicked me out of his life, I felt like someone reached into my chest, pulled out my heart, stomped on it, and then ripped it in half. I can't even begin to imagine the immense amount of pain someone would feel when the person they've been with since they were 19 years old dies.

Death.

She'll never be able to see him again. And neither will I.

I'm glad I came when mom called so I could have a few last words with dad. However, it does weigh on my heart that I hadn't spoken to him in years. But how was I to know? I hated my parents, and I was not in the best place to have any conversations with them if they acted like they did when I went away to college: happy I was leaving.

Mom still treats me the same as she did then: happy to have minimal interactions with me. This hurts me too. I try to stay out of her way the best I can because she won't speak to me. She brushes past me, mumbles rude comments under her breath about me being a liar, and makes me feel like I was the one who had something to do with this—as crazy as that sounds.

Standing in the stuffy funeral home now in the suit that's cutting off my circulation, I want to bolt. Family was allowed to be here early to have a private viewing. Mom and I are the only ones here; our immediate family is quite small. Both sets of my grandparents are dead. My parents are only children. Mom and I, that's it.

It's a million degrees in here; a bead of sweat rolls down my forehead.

"Here, dab your face. You need to look presentable," mom commands as she hands me a delicate white hand-kerchief. I hold it in my hand and examine it—people still have these? "Well use it already."

Damn, she's in a hurry. I blot the handkerchief on my forehead and hand it back to mom.

"Excuse me ladies," an older gentleman says after he clears his throat and walks into the room to greet us. "My name is Arthur Estep, I am very sorry for your loss."

"Thank you," I say, feeling self-conscious about every move I make. I don't know how to do this—deal with death. I'm much more comfortable on the other end of things—saving lives.

"If you'd like to take a seat, we are moments away from bringing in the casket."

And just like that mom drops in the nearest chair. She just plops down. I'm surprised she made it to the chair in the first place. Her face looks as white as a ghost and she's holding that handkerchief over her mouth as if at any moment she may throw up.

Before I can take a seat next to her, double doors open and two teenage boys wheel in the casket, placing it at the front of the room. They open the lid and my mom lets out a scream before throwing herself on the floor in hysterical sobs.

I have never seen my mother act dramatic or cause a scene. Normally, she's a cut-you-with-her-sly-words and evil glare kind of woman. Quiet, reserved, no true emotions, yet menacing.

"Why ... why ... why," mom mutters before she pounds her fists into the carpet. I stare at her during what feels like a private moment, having no idea how to console her. The teenage boys look at me as if I should do something for my own mother, but little do they know I haven't spoken to this woman in years.

And she was never there to console you. She left you alone as a little girl.

I let out a sigh and adjust my uncomfortable outfit before sitting on the floor to wrap my arms around her. Mom curls into my lap and continues to weep, muttering words I can't really hear but what sound like blaming my dad for leaving her.

Who knows how long we sit there with mom in my arms. When we hear a throat clearing sound yet again, we look up to see Mr. Estep standing in the room. This poor guy has a rough job. "Ladies, I'm sorry to interrupt. The family time is now over and in just a few minutes we are supposed to open the doors for visitation to the public. Would you like me to stall a few more minutes?"

I nod yes in his direction and he silently slips out of the room. If other people are here, then it's been two hours of me holding mom while she cries. I haven't shed a tear since the day of his death when I lost my mind with Luke.

My emotions are so conflicted; I'm having a hard time processing everything to be honest. Part of me wants to mourn the loss of my father, yet another part has no idea who this man was, and the last part hates the memories she has. What the hell am I to do?

A slight knock alerts us that the doors will be opening as mom slides herself out of my lap and dries her eyes. She smooths the hair on her head and double checks that her perfect tight hair bun is still in place. Other than her puffy red eyes, she doesn't look like a woman who spent two hours on the floor in hysteria.

The few members of our extremely extended family show up along with my parents' colleagues, church members, classmates, politicians, you name it. As I look around the room I see many people who filled the halls of our family home for parties upon parties. Everyone stops to pass along heartfelt condolences to my mother and me before branching off around the room to share stories in remembrance of my dad.

Gabe Bellisano, beloved by all.

I don't know what to think. Their stories sound like they are mourning a wonderful, kind-hearted man who would do anything for anyone.

Yet why did he let his 14-year-old daughter suffer in silence for something so horrific that happened under his roof with one of his friends? How can I stand here and listen to these stories? I can't.

When no one is looking, I run out of our viewing room and push through the front doors of the funeral home towards the packed parking lot. The humid Florida air hits me in the face as it steals my breath away.

I'm suffocating. Sitting down on the curb I try steadying my uneven breathing—that's when I feel his presence.

"You okay?" Luke asks as he plants himself down on the curb right next to me. He looks out of place on the ground in his impeccable black suit and designer dress shoes.

"What an awful day," I vent, looking into his caring hazel eyes.

Luke opens his arm up for me to cuddle into him and I do. Sinking into his tight hold, I instantly relax, letting go of the intense need to hold everything together while my mom crumbles and puts on a show. But with Luke, I am safe in his grasp knowing he'll protect me and carry this emotional burden for us.

And it feels so damn good giving that power to someone else.

"Look who the cat dragged in," says a voice that sends chills down my spine, "Ariana."

I bolt up from Luke's grasp seeing Sarah walking towards us.

"Sarah, nice to see you." I don't really know how to address her or why I said it was nice to see her. That's a lie.

"Is it? You did a good thing when you left Florida after your ridiculous rumors," she says looking me up and down. "But I'm not here to talk about any of that. I didn't even think you'd show. I'm here for your father. He was a good man."

And just like that she pushes, literally shoves, into my arm to move past me to go inside and join the rest of the mourners. Standing at the curb I'm in shock and disbelief.

"What the fuck was that about? Who was that awful woman?" Luke asks, reminding me he's here. For the first time ever I forgot he was standing near. I'm shaking when Luke grabs on to my upper arms to steady me.

"That was Sarah," I pause, looking at the ground while I try to collect my scrambling thoughts. "Allen's wife."

Yes, Allen has a wife. A woman I was able to forget until this very moment. Oh my god, is Allen coming here too? Looking up from the ground I meet Luke's eyes as all the color drains from my face.

Running inside to the nearest bathroom just in time, I lean over the toilet as my breakfast leaves my body. When I know I'm finished, I look into the mirror to see red blotches all over my face matching my red eyes. Trying my best to clean up my appearance before facing the crowd outside, I'm dreading every minute of this.

Why can't I be back in Chicago?

Why can't I be making my rounds at the hospital doing something to help other people?

Why can't I be in bed with Luke making love?

Why can't I be anywhere but here?

Opening the bathroom door, I spot mom and Luke going into a room tucked to the side of the main viewing room. Following behind them I hurry to not miss a word of whatever is about to happen.

"Why is someone like that even here?" Luke asks mom while I slip into the room. His body language screams rage.

"Ariana," mom says as she notices me walk up behind Luke. "It's adorable you found someone passionate, but he shouldn't be fighting your little battles. This was a family issue and it's been handled."

"What is happening right now?" I ask, looking between Luke and mom. I'm completely taken aback by this conversation.

"Your boyfriend is trying to confront me about Sarah being here at your father's viewing. He wants me to ask her to leave. Let's remember what this day is about," mom says as she walks towards the door as if this conversation is already over. "Your father, not *you*."

"Excuse me," Luke says as he blocks mom's way to the door. She stands back looking shocked. I highly doubt anyone has ever gotten in her way before. "Yes this day is about your husband. Your family. Ariana is your family too. Why can't you do anything for her? For once."

"What do you know about what I've done for her?"

"You haven't done anything a parent should do. You should listen to your kid, believe her, trust her, and protect her. As a parent you should do anything to give your child a good life."

Luke delivers the words with such conviction that it seems as if he's fighting for himself too. And I don't blame him. He has no one to unleash his hurt on. His father took away his opportunity when he took his own life.

"I did protect her!" mom screams out, looking as if she is at her breaking point.

"How?" I finally speak up. "How did you protect me? You made me feel as if I was wrong, basically blaming me for what happened. I had no idea what was going on. I heard you and dad talking behind my back, calling me a liar."

Mom's eyes widen at my confession.

"We didn't call you a liar."

"What? Are you crazy? Hell yes you did," I say, gaining more confidence. I know what I heard and she will not convince me otherwise.

Mom puts her head in her hands and lets out a strangled cry. "We didn't know what to do with you."

My head jerks back as if I was slapped across the face.

"*Do with me?* What do you mean?"

"Ariana, I've never met anyone who was," she pauses as if the next word is going to disgust her, "raped before. Let alone my own daughter. Your father either. We didn't know what we were supposed to do to help you. We just wanted it all to go away."

"Including me," I say as a tear slides down my blotchy cheek. Damnit, I don't want her to see me like this. It's now my turn to leave but Luke blocks me as well. I look up at him in confusion. Why isn't he letting me leave?

"Say what you need to say to her," he whispers into my ear.

He's right. Instead of running away, I turn to face my mother, maybe for the last time after this conversation.

"No, not including you. It just, it just happened that way," she says as she looks up at me with pleading eyes, yet I don't hear her say an apology.

"Is Allen going to be at here?"

"Of course not. Allen is not allowed within 50 miles of you."

She must read the confusion across my face. What is she talking about?

"Since you were a minor, we were able to file a Personal Protection order against Allen ourselves. As a judge with an order against him, Allen lost his job and moved out of state. He's practicing in Georgia. I have not a clue how he was able to maneuver that. Something shady I'm sure." Mom says this as if it's the most common thing.

"I had no idea."

"Ariana, we might not have been there for you to have someone to talk to ... but we didn't leave you in harm's way. We confronted Allen and Sarah about what happened. I mean, you are our daughter."

There's a knock at the door as Mr. Estep pops his head into the room. "I'm sorry to yet again interrupt, but the prayer will start in 10 minutes. You'll want to take your seats at the front."

Mom gives me a once over; she's making sure I'm presentable to go back out there.

"I'll save your seat," she says before slipping out of the room.

"Oh my god," I whisper before walking into Luke's open arms. He holds me tight to his chest and, yet again, I relax into his warm embrace. This is becoming a pattern with us, but I can't say I'm mad about it.

"That was ... intense. You okay?" Luke asks.

"I didn't expect that conversation to happen today. I was a little nervous when I saw you walking in here with my mom." I pull apart just enough to be able to look up at his handsome face. "Thank you for speaking up for me. I don't think anyone has ever done that for me in my entire life. *Ever.*"

"Oh Ariana," he kisses the top of my head, "I'd fight all your battles for you if you want, but I know you're stubborn and you won't let me take them all."

I laugh into his chest because he's so right. I am not the girl who would let anyone take on *all* her battles, but I'd let someone share some of the burden.

And I would do the same for him.

CHAPTER TWENTY-NINE

Back at home in Chicago I'm thrown into the jungle of the emergency room and I love every minute of it. This is where I belong.

"Get back to work," Ben shouts, walking past me in the staff room. I'm about to say something smartass back when I spot him wink at me before leaving. He's been much nicer to me since Luke helped his cousin land a killer internship, but deep down he's still an asshole. And you know what? I wouldn't change him; he keeps me on my toes.

I grab my raincoat, walking towards the front door. I've been here 10 hours and can't wait to see something other than these white walls.

"Your man hunk waiting on you?" Katie asks as I rush past the computer station to avoid her grilling me with inappropriate questions.

"Girl, you're crazy!" I shout, running through the automatic double doors where my man hunk is, like always, waiting for me with a smile on his face in yet another finely tailored suit.

I want to rip that thing off. Now.

Underneath that grey suit I want to see those tattoos wrapped around my body. It's been a few weeks since we've truly been with each other in that passionate way in which our relationship started.

Luke's trying to be a gentleman by giving me the space to deal with the death of my dad and the news that my parents did try to help me. And I so appreciate him for that. Sometimes my emotions are under control and I feel like I've moved past the idea that I'll never see my dad again. And other times I burst out into sobs in the middle of the day.

Grief, anger, sadness, letting go, forgiveness—it's all a cluster of emotions I'm trying to let myself feel what I need to feel. But fuck, sometimes it's just too much.

Mixed in with the feelings about dad, I find myself thinking more about what happened to me as child and what mom said. It's upsetting to know she didn't know how to handle me yet they did try in the slightest way to protect me. I'll ever look back and think they handled it correctly, but forgiveness is the only thing I can do.

"My gorgeous girl," Luke says, kissing me on the cheek. I move the kiss to his lips where I force my tongue into his mouth. "What's this all about?"

"Can't a girl just want to French kiss her man?" I ask before getting back to my kiss. I open the car door to the Jag to get out of the pouring rain but then I hear screaming.

"Help! Help!" A little voice comes rushing towards us in a panic.

Luke and I turn towards the plea for help. Running towards us are two little boys.

"What's the matter?" I watch Luke take on the role of protector in just a second as he bends down closer to the boys.

"There's, there's," the one little boy, who I'd guess is about eight, rambles his words together, "there's barking from the dumpster!"

"Come on!" the second little boy pulls on the bottom of my raincoat, tugging me towards the alley next to the hospital.

Luke and I look at each other and then towards the boys as we follow behind them. I have no idea what we are walking into but whatever it is we need to help them.

Approaching the dumpster, that's when we barely hear it: barking. Luke lifts the lid and we all step back as the smell of rotten trash hits our nostrils.

"Ew! That's disgusting!" one of the little boys screams as he plugs his nose. He's right about that. If green smoke could seep out of this trash, it would be happening right now.

While the boys and I are plugging our noses, Luke is taking off his jacket and handing it to me.

"Luke, what the hell are you going to do?"

He doesn't answer me with words; instead, Luke hops right into the dumpster. He moves the trash around as the barking gets a little bit louder. Then Luke dives under the trash and it's like he's disappeared.

"Oh my god! The trash ate him!" The little boys are now shouting frantically until we see an arm lift through the trash—in it a tiny dirty puppy—followed by a filthy Luke.

"Can someone help me here?" Luke asks, handing the puppy towards us.

Grabbing the tiny puppy from him, I cuddle it to my chest—dirt, trash, and all. His barks have changed to little moans. Luke jumps out of the dumpster and the little boys laugh. He's a sight for sore eyes! His expensive suit smells like death and is covered head-to-toe in trash. Luke sees the boys laughing at how ridiculous he looks and he busts out in a deep belly laugh too.

"We should get this little guy to a vet," I say, busting the laughter bubble.

"Do you guys know who this puppy belongs to?" Luke asks the boys.

"No clue," one boy says.

"We just heard the barking," the other boy chimes in.

"Do you boys mind if we keep this puppy?" Luke asks.

"No," they both say as I lower the puppy in my arms so they can pet him a few times before we get out of here.

"You boys did a great job by coming to find us for help," Luke encourages them. "Where are your parents?"

And as if on cue, a curly-haired redhead sticks her head out of one of the windows above the alley and shouts, "Frankie! Mikey! Get your butts up those stairs this instant. Did you finish your homework?"

Frankie and Mikey look at each other in panic before quickly saying goodbye to us and dashing up the fire escape stairs.

"I know a vet. Let's go," Luke says as he guides us back to the car while I wrap the little puppy up in my scrub shirt to keep him warm.

On the way out of the city, Luke calls a veterinarian. It's definitely after hours but, like he said, he 'knows a vet.' As we are pulling into the parking lot, lights turn on inside and a woman in a white lab coat stands at the door waiting for us. Luke tells me her name is Vivian and she's his former business partner's sister.

"Luke, how can I help?" Vivian asks, holding the door open and ushering us inside.

"Vivian, thank you for this. We found this puppy in a dumpster," Luke says as I unwrap the puppy from the little blanket I made out of my scrubs. The pup makes a little moan and Vivian jumps into action.

"Follow me," she says as we enter an exam room. "I'd like to take this little guy in the back for a bath and examination. Is that okay?"

"Yes," Luke and I both say in unison.

Vivian takes the puppy from my arms and leaves us behind in the exam room to wait. My arms feel empty without the warm little body to cuddle close to me. I feel like I'm missing something I've known my entire life— but it's only been 30 minutes.

"I'm really proud of you for what you did. You jumped into action so fast," I say facing Luke who is sitting down on a long bench in the room. He gives me a smirk and shrugs his shoulders. Is he ... blushing?

"It's no big deal, Ariana."

It's then I take a look at him and realize he's still in the dirty dumpster clothes. Upon noticing the clothes, the smell hits my nose. If he didn't just save a puppy, I would definitely toss my cookies. But somehow his act of kindness masks the trash smell.

Vivian opens the door and in her arms is a playful, adorable, clean puppy. If we weren't the only people in this animal hospital at this time of night I would not believe she brought back the same puppy.

She sits down a King Charles Spaniel on the exam table and the little guy runs with his white and brown fur flopping in my direction. My heart stops. I'm in love.

"Don't you look so cute," I coo at him as I pet behind his ears before he rolls over for me to rub his belly.

"This little guy is about two months old. Once clean, I got a good look at him and he doesn't seem to be hurt. The noises he was making were out of starvation. I don't know when the last time this little guy ate. His belly should be as full as it could get for tonight," Vivian says before petting him on the head. He sticks out his tongue to lick her hand. "Have you guys ever had a dog before?"

I can only imagine the deer in headlights look both Luke and I are giving her.

"Oh um, we aren't, we haven't," I mumble, not knowing how to address this dog. Is it really *our* dog? Would Luke even want to have a dog with me?

"This is our first dog," Luke exclaims quickly.

Our dog.

"I thought so," Vivian says as she winks at us before taking out a packet and putting it on the exam table next to the puppy. "Here are some of the basic things you'll need to know with your first puppy. I'd like to get an appointment set up to get him up-to-date on his shots. We aren't able to do that tonight."

"Whatever he needs," Luke tells her.

"I'll have one of the techs call you in the morning. For tonight you are good to go. I put together a little goodie bag with some essentials—puppy food at least," Vivian says, handing us the packet along with a bag full of dog things, much more than just food.

"Thank you so much!" I rush around the table to embrace her in a hug. When I pull myself back I can't help but laugh. I've never been so thankful to hug someone … ever.

A few months ago I wouldn't even let someone touch me. Now I'm the one embracing someone.

Luke, puppy, and I get into the car and drive back to the penthouse. It's a quiet ride home as the puppy falls asleep in my arms and I just stare at him as if it's the most precious thing I've ever seen.

When we get inside, Luke immediately showers off all the mysterious pieces of garbage. Puppy and I couldn't be happier to have him clean and no longer smelling like absolute death.

Luke sets a bowl of water on the floor and then collects entirely too many blankets to create a huge bed for the pooch in his bedroom.

"We are going to need to give him a name," Luke says as he looks up at me from the floor.

I sit the puppy down in the center of the mound of blankets, and he instantly looks even smaller.

"What about ... King?" I ask, proud of my suggestion—a play on words for his breed.

"Oh come on, we can do better than that," Luke teases me as he strokes the puppy's head. "What about ... Oscar?"

Oscar? Why would he pick that? Then it hits me. "Oscar the Grouch, who lives in the trash can!" I bust out laughing; that is an adorable suggestion from such a hard ass man with his tattoos.

Joining my boys on the floor makes me feel so at peace. "Okay little Oscar, welcome to our ..."

I stop myself before I say the word that was about to spill out.

"Welcome to our ...?" Luke asks, raising his eyebrows at me, egging me on to finish my thought. Now I'm nervous.

"Family?" I ask, the word with an anxious question mark at the end.

"Welcome to our family!" Luke exclaims, picking up Oscar and giving him a kiss, before pulling me into his side and doing the same to me. Looking up to see a smile on his face the confusion I was feeling just a minute before fades away.

"Let's leave him here and get in bed," Luke says as we hear Oscar let out a snore.

We slip into the bed as quietly as possible, as if a sleeping baby is in the room, and cuddle into one another. Finally ... I'm in Luke's arms.

"Have you ever had a puppy before?" I whisper to Luke, trying not to wake our baby.

"No, my dad wouldn't let us have a dog even though we begged for one. My sister would have done anything for a puppy; she's obsessed with animals. She's the girl who would feed the stray cats and once a possum until we told her to knock that off because they are gross. Did you have a dog?"

"My mom had a dog she'd carry around in her purse." I roll my eyes remembering Princess FeFe. "That dog was a demon and only loved mom. No one could even go by her without her trying to snap at us. She lived to be 15. So ... no I didn't personally have a dog," I laugh.

When Oscar is non-stop snoring we feel safe to turn our cuddling into the hot and steamy lovemaking I've missed so very much.

What a night this has been.

⊱━⋆⋅⋆━⊰

What the hell.

I don't want to open my eyes, but I know it's the morning by the orange light shining into the room. Then it happens ... something licks my face. Luke? I'd do so many things with my lovely Luke but this is something I'm not into. Face licking? It just seems ... unhygienic and sloppy.

I hear a little noise, barely even a bark, forcing me to open my eyes finding a brown puppy pair staring straight back at me. Last night's dog rescuing experience flashes through my memories. Lying on my chest is little Oscar nuzzling into me. How the heck did he get up here? Bless his heart. I laugh at how stinkin' adorable this is when I hear Luke laugh too. He walks into the room wearing his gym shorts and no shirt as he carries a tray with breakfast foods over to me.

"Now that's a sight I didn't think I'd ever see," Luke chuckles while placing the tray on the bed for me.

"Me holding an adorable puppy?" I scoop Oscar up to smooch his little puppy face.

"Well, yes, that's true. I also meant seeing a woman sleeping in my bed and knowing we have a puppy,"

Luke says as he smiles. He takes Oscar from my arms so I can enjoy the delicious breakfast spread he has for me: scrambled eggs, whole wheat toast with peanut butter, and a fruit plate.

But first, coffee! Sipping on my java, I grin in delight realizing it's just the way I like it. Luke remembered! I don't know if it's this adorable puppy now cuddled into Luke or the fact this powerful CEO, who came from an extremely tragic past, remembers a tiny detail many would forget ... but my heart would smile right now if it could.

After finishing this meal, I curl myself into Luke's side with Oscar in his lap. We sit in the stillness of each other's presence. Then I grasp what this ... dare I say ... *family* truly is.

A family of rescues.

A rape victim, an orphan, and a dog literally thrown away ... now loving, tending to, caring for, and protecting one another. I guess that makes each one of us *rescuers* as well. It feels good to be saved and protected ... for once. The power of salvation makes me feel alive.

Squeezing my arms around Luke's chest, he pulls me closer to him. Oscar has drifted back into sleep and we quickly join him.

It's been the laziest Sunday of my life. I love it. We woke up around ten and haven't stopped playing with Oscar in the living room, which Luke turned into a giant playroom. I can't believe I'm not freaking out because I didn't pick up a shift at the hospital. Instead, I'm relaxing with my guys in a gorgeous penthouse overlooking the Chicago skyline.

Luke throws a tennis ball back and forth as Oscar runs after it with his cute floppy tail wagging behind him. It touches my heart to watch Luke care for this little pup. He's scrappy in his efforts to bring the ball back to Luke. In Oscar I see a fighter and in Luke I see love. It's the same love reflected in his eyes when he's with Lisa and Eric. Pure love. I want to be a little jealous of that look but I can't be. One day he'll look at me like that … I hope. I know Lisa says he gives me that look now but I don't believe her.

A knock at the door interrupts playtime as Oscar dashes toward the loud noise, letting out his little barks as if to protect us from whoever is here. Luke follows behind the white and brown blur of fur; he scoops up the puppy to stop him from running out the door as he opens it.

"Oh my god!" I hear Lisa shrill, "Who is this little cutie pie?" Luke's sister walks into the living room with Oscar in her tight embrace as he plants kisses all over her face. Luke heads into the kitchen for who knows what. "Ariana, hello! Does this sweet guy have something to do with you?"

"No, it was all Luke," I say as she takes a seat on the couch next to me. "He jumped into a dumpster to rescue him."

Her face drops as if I've said the wildest thing she's ever heard.

"Shut up. He did? Don't tell me he was wearing one of his super expensive suits?"

I bust out laughing because yet again she sees the truth without me giving her any details. She takes my laughter as the answer before joining me in a fit of giggles.

"What's so funny, ladies?" Luke asks, entering the room with an armful of dog treats.

"Just heard you jumped in a pile of garbage to save this little guy," she coos, lifting Oscar into the air before planting smooches all over him. This little puppy seems like he's in absolute heaven and nothing makes me happier.

Luke steals Oscar right out of his sister's arms to give him treats as he attempts to teach him how to do tricks. Not that he needed any help securing himself as the favorite—he just made it clear to all of us that he's eyeing the spot.

"So … a puppy. What's next?" Lisa asks winking at her brother.

Where's she going with this? We just got back to an okay place—please don't make him run away.

Luke takes his eyes away from Oscar for one moment to give us a completely blank stare. "What do you mean … *next?*"

I can't tell if he's saying the word like it's poison in his mouth or if he's really confused as to what the hell could be next after a couple gets a puppy. Do I even want this conversation to be happening? Do I want 'what's next' for us?

"You're so clueless my dear brother. They say a puppy is a good test for a *baby*."

Luke's face turns ghostly pale.

"A baby? Ariana doesn't want to have a baby. She's just starting her career as a doctor." Luke says the statement with such assurance even I believe what he said.

Hell yeah I'm a doctor. I have lives to save. I won't have any damn time to have a baby. And if I did have a baby I wouldn't have any time to take care of it.

But ... a baby.

A cute little baby.

A cute little baby that will be the perfect mix of Luke and me.

My heart is swooning, but I have no time to add in my thoughts because Lisa pounces in support of this baby dream.

"So what? You don't think there are doctors out there taking care of families? You don't think any are married? I mean come on," Lisa scoffs at her brother.

Luke is silent. He's giving up the battle but Lisa won't let it go.

"Maybe we should just ask her," Lisa says, turning to face me straight on. "Ariana, what do you think? Do you want to have a baby?"

It's so quiet in the apartment you could hear a pin drop. Even Oscar is looking at me, waiting for me to answer. If I answer, that changes everything. I have no clue if I want to have a baby. Up until these last few months I didn't want to share any part of my life with another person. I wanted to work and that's it. That's as far as my plans for the future went because I was so closed off by my past to even entertain the idea of allowing anyone in.

Then everything changed in my entire life.

Luke broke down walls I never thought would fall.

I found out my parents—even though they didn't do anything to soothe my worries—tried in their own fucked up way to fix a horrific situation.

My father took his last breath.

My family tree is ending.

Do I want to create a family with Luke?

"I don't know," I say.

Luke and Lisa both look at me with stares as if to say 'that's all you can come up with?'—but for completely different reasons. Luke's look is out of shock that we are even talking about this and for the fact that I didn't come right out and say 'no.' Lisa's is for the fact that as a woman I'm not fighting for my precious baby.

Great, now the baby has become 'mine.'

Oscar jumps out of Luke's lap and dashes towards the kitchen in a panic. All three of us jump up too and follow behind him. He's crying so loudly and looking around frantically.

"He has to use the bathroom!" I shout at Luke who picks up Oscar and dashes towards the balcony. But he's just a moment too late. Luke turns around and his blue shirt is covered in dog pee—poor little Oscar is looking up at him with apologetic puppy dog eyes.

"First garbage, now piss. You are really pushing me to my limits little guy," Luke laughs as he puts Oscar down and then strips off his shirt. It's a sight I'll never get tired of: Luke's rock hard muscles covered in badass tattoos.

"Did you get more ink from the last time I saw you?" Lisa asks.

"Maybe," Luke laughs as he leaves the room to get rid of the dirty shirt.

I didn't know Luke wasn't done getting tattoos. I didn't even realize there was any empty space on his arms.

"I'll let it go that you didn't tell the truth about the baby question," Lisa smirks at me, "but we can revisit that topic at another time. Let's move on to something more recent ... have you seen your billboard?"

I completely forgot about the billboard. I never mentioned it to Luke to get his thoughts. Has he seen it? That's a dumb question—he must have seen it; it's for his company.

"Yes, I've seen it alright."

"That's all you're going to give me? You are the worst at answering questions today," Lisa says playfully shoving my arm.

"Hey! Keep your hands off my girlfriend," Luke says, reentering the room in a clean shirt. "What the hell are you guys talking about now? I seem to miss all the good stuff."

"We were just talking about your billboard," Lisa exclaims.

"Oh shit. Ariana, we never talked about the billboard. Have you seen it? Are you okay with it? I mean it was a little…"

Lisa interrupts him to shout, "Passionate! Beautiful! Sexy! That is the most talked about advertisement we have ever done as a company and it's been all the rage online. We even got a call from a fashion house in Italy to ask about our models."

I start playing tug-of-war with Oscar to avoid this conversation as much as possible. Yes, I agree it was passionate and beautiful, but I'm still not sure I'm fully okay with the world seeing us that way. So intimate. So in the moment. So raw. How stupid were we to forget that there were fucking cameras there.

"I hope you told them to fuck off," Luke says.

"Yes, I told them our models were exclusive to Vulcano Vodka," she says, winking, "but that made you two an even hotter commodity. We get calls daily. I think we'll have to make an automated message to field all the calls … unless you two decide you want to change your careers?"

"Ha-ha. You should change yours to comedian," I tease. If I changed my career to model I'd stress every day about everything—from the outfit choices to where I'll be touched and by whom. No thank you.

"Alright you two lovebirds, I'm outta here," Lisa says. Luke follows to let her out, but not before I catch her trying to sneak Oscar into her giant black Chanel bag.

"Put that dog back!" I say, laughing at this ridiculous sight before my eyes.

"Whatever. I had to try," she says, putting Oscar back on the ground. "I'll be back for you baby boo."

"If I catch you stealing that dog," I throw an evil glare her way, "you can read my mind so you already know what I'd do to you."

Lisa laughs and Luke looks majorly confused.

"Read her mind?" he asks to no one in particular. Good thing because we both ignore him.

Life with a puppy sure is fun … and extremely stressful. Luke and I have made an unspoken pact between us that we want to give this little pup the best life imaginable. This means daily walks around the dog parks, constant trips to the balcony as we potty train, cleaning up accidents when we don't quite make it, playing tug-of-war, going to puppy obedience classes, and staying up-to-date with all his vet visits.

Oscar even eats better than us with his all-natural food and treats. But I wouldn't have it any other way; he won over my heart the minute my eyes locked onto his when Luke handed him to me from that dumpster.

"You plan to do your rounds, *resident?*" Ben asks, walking up behind me as I pretend to read the medical chart I've been holding for the last five minutes, looking at the same words over and over again. "I'm not going to overlook that you've been holding that same chart for ever now."

He's right. I've been all about Oscar since the minute we've got him and I need to pay attention better at the hospital. I only have two weeks left of my residency and then it's all over.

What the fuck am I going to do if I don't get a job right away?

Don't think like that. What you think about you attract.

Where the fuck did that thought come from? Serena needs to stop playing those Law of Attraction podcasts before bed because she's seriously messing with my mojo.

"All available hands on deck!" Chief Pitters shouts as a slew of stretchers roll through the automatic doors of the E.R. "We've got a drive-by and at least ten bodies on their way in."

And just like that, for the next few hours, there are no thoughts of Oscar or Luke. It's all about checking vitals, giving stitches, removing a bullet from a thigh, and talking to nervous parents. The drive-by consisted of ten gang members who all happen to be teenagers. When you see 14, 15, or even 16 year olds in hospital beds you forget they are gang members and see them for the scared kids they become.

In a moment of calm after the crazy storm, I find myself in a packed staff room.

"This night was insane," Rachel, a fellow resident, says before plopping down on a couch. This lumpy green couch looks like it's been here since the hospital came about many, many years ago, but it's extremely comfortable and we all gravitate towards it. If this couch could talk it would have some wild stories I'm sure.

I wonder if anyone has had sex on it?

Oh hell no. Get that thought out of my mind right now.

"Residents. Who is graduating this semester?" Dr. Horton asks.

All four of our hands shoot up in the air as if we've been electrocuted. You'd be an idiot if you didn't let the rest of the staff know that you are soon to be out the doors—so they can vouch for why you deserve to work there.

"Anyone planning to apply here?" nurse Katie asks before she slowly eyes all of us.

No one comes right out and says 'yes'—instead we nod and make weird noises. They must feel like they are suddenly in the hot seat, like I do.

"Alright guys. It's been a great evening but I'm outta here," I laugh, throwing up a peace sign as I quickly walk to the door before anyone can ask me to stay. I've already been here two hours longer than scheduled, but there wasn't a chance in hell that I was going to leave when the team needed me.

Walking towards the curb I smile seeing my man waiting for me. It's comforting knowing he'll be there— even when he has to wait much longer than expected. I kiss him before jumping into the backseat where I'm greeted by a happy Oscar.

"He fell asleep waiting for you. He's going to be full of energy now," Luke says, laughing as he takes the seat beside me. With Ryan behind the wheel we head home.

Home.

We haven't had a conversation about *his* place becoming *our* place but I haven't slept a night in my apartment since Oscar joined our family—nearly two weeks. I want to bring up the topic, but I'm nervous he doesn't think officially moving in together is a good idea. He'll have some kind of logical reasoning why I should continue to have my own place. The whole thing will be embarrassing and make me feel terrible. I'm not ready for that.

Let's get through the residency first.

I can continue to live in Serena's apartment for at least another year because that's how much time she has before she completes her master's. Unless she wants to move in with Jack. I never thought about that. Serena could be having the same kind of battle about moving in with her man that I'm having. Well, hers would be different. At least she knows how Jack feels about her and their relationship. Jack surely didn't call everything off to then show up when she was having an extremely low moment in her life to tell her the saddest story ever. I need to talk to Serena, stat.

As a couple, Luke and I have worked through so much but there's still more to be dealt with. I know why Luke ended our relationship the night he fought with Drake. And him showing up when my dad died made everything so much easier to handle than if I were alone. But I don't believe Luke is convinced he's not just like his father. I know wholeheartedly he's not like that vile man, but I'm not sure my belief in him is what he needs to feel secure.

Could another moment come when he's confronted with jealously and he explodes? Does pure rage boil deep within his blood waiting for a chance to come out?

"You okay?" Luke asks, taking my hand in his before bringing it to his lips to place a kiss.

"Yes," the answer leaves my mouth entirely too fast for either one of us to believe it's the truth. Luke raises his eyebrow at Oscar as if to question my lie. "Yes, I'm okay."

Relaxing into the seat, I realize I was basically on the edge in a state of panic for most of this ride. The change in my body language must be the answer Luke needs as he drops the topic. Little Oscar is back to wagging his tail after falling asleep during the ride yet again.

I can't get over how much puppies sleep. I wish I had their life.

CHAPTER THIRTY

My residency is complete. I can't believe it. Those four long years passed by in a blink of an eye.

Tonight, Serena and Luke are taking me out to dinner to celebrate my accomplishment. My cheering squad. I wouldn't have made it to this point without their support.

Standing in front of my bedroom mirror, I study my navy blue dress and stilettos Serena convinced me to wear. She says tonight is a night to get dolled up—I'm not going to fight her on it because this outfit is screaming 'hot librarian' and I hope Luke likes it too.

There are a few minutes before Luke gets here and I take time to reflect on how far I've come in life.

Growing up as a little girl at the beach, making sand castles with dad while mom sunned herself on her beach towel nearby.

Singing in the elementary choir while my parents watched me.

To the Christmas that changed my world.

Instead of seeing that traumatic night as a heavy black cloud looming in my past, I see it for the first time with a new set of eyes. Not the eyes of a victim but the eyes of a guardian angel floating above, looking down on a little girl who did nothing wrong but is seeing the ugly truth that is the world. Feeling a strong sense to make that little girl proud and to guard her fiercely— that's what I've done all these years. I kept her guarded for so long but I went too far. Guarding her from friend-ships, life experiences, and even relationships with good, kind men—I did that too. Until one man bravely fought his way through my thick barrier making his way into my heart.

Luke.

From the moment I ran out of the hotel bar after watching a waitress throw herself at him. To letting him touch me. To the most romantic date I've ever been on at the Willis Tower, where we shared our first kiss. Then opening up about the truth I kept locked away.

It feels like a lifetime ago—in reality it was just months. The flashback quickly comes to an end when there's a knock at the door. Time to party! In the living room I find Luke and Serena with flowers and balloons.

"Congratulations Dr. Bellisano!" Serena shouts before throwing her arms around me into a giant bear hug, a hug so big she lifts me off the floor.

"Are you crazy? Put me down!" I try to shout, but I laugh at how ridiculous we must look. My tall model-looking friend lifting me into the air like a powerlifter.

"Are you kidding me? I am not crazy. I'm so proud of you!" Serena exclaims. When she finally puts me down, I lock eyes with Luke who smiles so wide I know without him even saying it, he's proud too.

"I'd love to play doctor with you," Luke whispers into my ear as he hugs me. "I'm proud of you but not surprised one bit. You are the hardest working person I know."

Coming from a man who I would say is the hardest working person I know, this is a huge compliment.

"Ariana." I turn from Luke's embrace towards a voice I never expected to be walking through the front door of our apartment.

"Mom," I gasp in shock.

"Ariana, congratulations on your graduation," mom says as she hands me a white envelope that I fumble with before putting onto the counter. It's extremely awkward for me to open gifts in front of other people, and mom would say it's rude if I did.

"Thanks," I mumble clearly confused by her presence.

How the hell did she know I finished up my residency? I surely didn't tell her; I didn't want to bother her especially with how we ended things after dad's funeral.

I flew back to Chicago and we haven't spoken to each other since.

"Thank you for inviting me," she says towards Luke, as we both glance at him.

Luke invited her? And, more importantly, she showed up? Why?

"Of course," Luke nods in her direction. It's not a warm 'of course' but more of a pleasantry to keep the peace.

"Hi, I'm Serena. Your daughter's best friend," Serena says, extending her hand towards my mom. "It's nice to meet you."

Mom shakes her hand, looking Serena up and down, before smiling to greet her, "I'm Diane Bellisano. Nice to meet you too."

Nice to meet her too? This woman knows how to smile? How the hell did an alien get inside of my mom's body and make her way to my celebration dinner?

Looks like mom approves of Serena, which makes me happy I guess. As I stand looking at my boyfriend and best friend, I feel how protective I am of them. These are my people. My world. My everything. I want everyone to see what I see in them—the love and happiness they bring into my life. Truly, I'd do anything for these two.

"Let's go, we have reservations," Serena herds us out of the door like cattle.

The Chop House is a few blocks from our apartment so there's no point in using the Driver app. We hit the streets and walk.

Luke slips his arm through mine with mom and Serena in front of us making small talk like old pals. I remind myself to thank Serena later for keeping my mom occupied. She knows we have an extremely rocky relationship and it can be hard to talk to her at times.

Do other people ever feel that way with their mothers? I sure hope so.

Looking down at the handsome hand intertwined in mine, I understand it's easy to bitch about my mom and our relationship but I bet Luke would do anything to trade places with me.

To have a mom in his life.

He's an orphan.

No parents to show up at his special events, no one to cheer him on, no shoulders to lean on, no one to be proud of him for all his success, no one to watch how he treats the people he loves. No nothing. The impact of that hasn't hit me until this very moment.

I gasp for air, feeling like I'm suddenly suffocating.

How selfish am I? At least I have one parent in my life I can complain about; he has none. And he didn't lose a parent to a sudden health issue, like dad's heart attack. He lost his parents because one acted like a coward and took the life of the other away from him. Suicide didn't take away Luke's dad's pain; it just passed it along for his children to carry.

His kindhearted, hardworking children who make everyone around them feel special. They carry the weight of their father's horrific act, leaving them alone in the aftermath of the chaos. Three kids turned in to invisible fosters who needed to fight for themselves.

Luke doesn't need to tell me with words how much his mom meant to him. His love is displayed on his arms in his tattoos. His angel. Her name is on his arm and her portrait. His arms are reflections of the love he has for his family and the struggles he's worked through to get to where he is today.

A beautiful tribute for the woman he lost.

And the woman who is here for him? Me. I am vowing to myself to be that person for him—the one to show up at his events, his shoulder to lean on, the person to brag about all his success, and the one to love him.

Squeezing his hand a little tighter I look up to meet his hazel eyes. He cocks his head to the side as if to silently ask me what's going on.

"I love you," I whisper. "And I'm proud of you. And even though I'll never have the honor of knowing her, I *know* your mom would be proud of the man you are."

Luke looks at me with wide eyes, and for just a moment I'm nervous that I overstepped my boundaries with him. We haven't spoken about his parents after the day he confessed their fates to me.

Then Luke smiles, "Thank you for saying that, Ariana. I love you too."

Luke leans in to cup my chin in his hand before planting a sweet kiss on my lips.

Hearing a little gasp, I turn towards my mom and Serena—who are both staring intently at us with their jaws dropped. Caught up in my own head with worries of Luke, I completely forgot they were with us or where we were walking. Clearly, they saw the entire lovey dovey exchange or else Serena wouldn't have that goofy look on her face.

"Vulcano," the hostess shouts before scooping up four menus, "your table is ready." She saves the day, amen. Serena is going to have plenty of questions for me later. Questions I don't know how to answer. You know, the girly kind:

When did you know you loved him?
Have you told him this before?
How big is his penis?
When are you getting engaged?
When are you moving out?
Can I be your maid of honor?

This all freaks me out. My hands are clammy—thank god we pulled our hands apart or else Luke's would be drenched from mine. He'd definitely know something is up with me.

Luke pulls out my chair and I take a seat. I watch as he does the same for all the ladies.

"Well, well, well … what a gentleman you've got here," Serena teases me with a wink.

Luckily, the focus on our relationship dies down as my mom begins to grill all three of us with questions about our careers—or for me, my hopes for one now that I'm no longer a resident. Any day now I'd love to get the call that I've earned the role of attending.

Our dinner goes by smoothly with easy flowing conversation and delectable foods. We avoid the tough topics and I appreciate that. Even with all the laughs, mom stays her stiff and proper self, but I won't complain because she's here and we are all together.

My family.

After dinner we hit the streets again to head back to our apartment for dessert. Apparently, my roommate whipped something up for all of us. I don't think I've had a day this great in so long.

"Oh. My. God!" mom shrieks, stopping dead in her tracks on a busy Chicago sidewalk. We all come to a screeching halt.

"Are you okay?" I ask, grabbing her arm. She doesn't seem to be having some kind of medical emergency. I'm utterly confused what the hell is going on until I follow her eyes to see she's staring at …

Our billboard.

Luke and I in a naked embrace for all of Chicago to see. Oh my god is right. I never thought my mom would see this, and even if she did, I never thought I'd have to talk to her about it. Let alone be standing right next to her when she discovered it.

"Ariana, how could you?" she asks as she gives me the most evil, disgusted look imaginable. "I can't believe you'd do something like this. It's pornographic. You put yourself out there for the entire world to see you like this. I'm disappointed."

All I can do is stand in silence not knowing what the hell to say. My heart is racing a million miles per minute.

"I think it's hot and done very tastefully!" Serena exclaims, looping her arm through mine and continuing to walk as if it's no big deal. As if that's the end of this discussion. And this is why I love her. With my arm locked in Serena's, we stroll back to the apartment and I don't look back. Poor Luke, I left him to deal with my mom, but I hear them chatting on in small talk behind me. I don't think she scolded him for the billboard; apparently the disappointment is only meant for her child.

Mom drops the topic of the billboard and I'm grateful of it. We sit down to eat the best bread pudding I've ever had after mom leaves. She has an early flight home and it turns out she flew in just for my celebration dinner.

No hug goodbye, no 'I love you,' just an awkward 'I'll see you when I see you.' But that's how it is and any other way would make me feel weird.

The days after my dinner I wait on pins and needles for the hospital to officially say I'm now an attending. I spoke to the other residents and they are waiting too. What gives? For good measure I've sent out a few resumes to surrounding hospitals in Illinois. I never thought I'd worry about staying in this state, but the thought of leaving Luke causes me even more anxiety. Of course, Oscar would go anywhere with me, but let's not let Luke know that.

A knock at the door startles me. Who the hell could this be? It's two in the afternoon and most of the people I know are hard at work. Luke and Serena surely are. Glancing through the peephole I'm shocked at who I see on the other side of this door.

"Drake," I swing the door open, coming face-to-face with the best friend who I haven't seen since he got into a nasty fight with my boyfriend. We've been dodging each other at the hospital.

"Ariana," Drakes says, trying to look around me into the apartment. "Is now a good time?"

"Good time for … ?" I ask in anticipation for whatever he's about to say next. I'm suddenly nervous having Drake here which upsets me a little. Drake was someone I was the most comfortable to be around. That's gone.

"To apologize and clear the air," Drake answers.

He doesn't need to apologize or clear the air, but knowing him, he needs to get this off his chest and I can hear him out.

"Would you like some coffee?" I ask, ushering him into the apartment. His face lights up as if the offer clears the air itself. We head into the kitchen as I put on a pot of coffee and Drake takes a seat at the table. It's extra quiet as neither of us knows how to break the silence.

"Well, this is awkward," Drake says.

"Damn straight, super awkward," I say, handing him a cup of pecan pie flavored coffee. "I never thought we'd be able to sit in a room without saying a word."

"Especially because you don't know when to shut up," Drake says before taking a sip of his coffee.

I stick my tongue out at him. "I wish I would have made that coffee just a little hotter."

Drake laughs but his face quickly takes on a serious expression as I join him at the table with my own cup of coffee.

"I'm sorry I kissed you at the club. I'm sorry for everything that went down that night," Drake says, clenching his hands on top of the table looking pretty defeated.

"I accept your apology."

Drake sits in silence staring at me. "That's it? You accept. No lecture about how what I did was stupid? How I shouldn't ever put my hands on you? How I could have gotten myself or Luke seriously hurt? How I made our friendship basically non-existent?"

"Well, you seem to have summed it all up nicely. Drake, I believe you are truly sorry. I know you were drunk, I know you'd never try to hurt me, and I know you weren't going to back down from that fight. Neither was Luke. I'm glad that it is behind us now."

Getting up from the table I start slicing a loaf of banana bread Serena made yesterday. Bringing it back to the table, I place a slice in front of my always hungry friend. He doesn't miss a beat as he digs in.

"I'm also sorry I missed being at your dad's funeral … and your celebration dinner. I fucked up and I didn't know how to say I was sorry sooner. I wanted to be at those things for you."

Drake looks as if he's in physical pain admitting all of this. I place my hand on top of his. "It's okay. I promise. We're cool. And you didn't miss much. I know you were thinking of me."

The front door slams shut and I quickly pull my hand away from Drake's. We both look towards the entrance of the kitchen as Luke strides in with Oscar in his arms. Spotting us at the table, his face takes on a different expression. A look of anger.

"I didn't know you were having a lunch date?" he asks with the words laced in ice.

"This isn't what it looks like," I say, bolting up from the table to take Oscar out of his grasp.

"You have a dog?" Drake asks, clearly not caring that Luke is angry that he's in my kitchen.

"*We* have a dog. And I think *you* should be going," Luke responds.

Drake looks at me like I should say something, Luke gives me the same expression, and I stand in the middle looking like a damn fool with her mouth wide open but no words coming out.

"I don't know what to say. Why can't we all get along?" As soon as the words are out of my mouth, I know they weren't the right ones to say.

"Are you fucking kidding me? You know why we can't '*all get along,*'" Luke mocks me. "This guy wants to fuck you and I don't want to be friends with guys who want to fuck *my* girlfriend."

"Okay dude, you don't need to talk to her like that. She didn't do anything wrong. I showed up here unannounced," Drake says, getting up from his seat.

"Don't tell me how to talk to her," Luke hisses. His hands clench into fists at the side of his body. Drake notices Luke's fists as well before he takes on a defensive stance too. "Now it's time for you to leave before I kill you."

And it's then everything Luke told me about his father comes to my memory. He thinks he's just like his dad and right now he's acting extremely jealous.

"Don't tell me to leave a place that's not yours, you piece of shit," Drake yells.

"Okay boys, this is getting a little overly dramatic," I say, putting Oscar down so he can scamper out of the kitchen to find a toy. "Drake didn't tell me he was coming over or I would have discussed it with you Luke. But he came over to apologize for everything and I accepted. It's not a big deal."

Luke doesn't lose the look of rage even after my calm explanation.

"Drake, next time you want to hang out please send a text beforehand. Out of respect for my boyfriend, I want to tell him."

"Ariana, what the hell kind of relationship are you in? You need permission to see your friends?" Drake asks, looking at me like I'm an abused woman or something.

Luke grabs Drake by the shirt collar with a look of pure rage, "Don't speak to her like that."

"Or what?" Drake spits out in Luke's face.

"Luke, please," I plead touching his bicep, "don't do this. You're better than this. Please. Both of you; knock this off."

With his fist still clenched near Drake's neck, Luke looks at me with a completely different expression after hearing my pleas. Gone is the anger and rage, replaced with a look of sad understanding. He lets go of Drake's shirt and backs away. Luke doesn't say a single word; instead, he leaves the apartment in a flash.

"What in the fuck just happened?" Drake asks, just as confused as me.

"I have no idea," I say, falling into a kitchen chair before putting my head in my hands suddenly exhausted.

A few squeaks cause me to lift my head and smile. Oscar trots back into the kitchen with a dinosaur stuffed animal bigger than him in his mouth. He squeaks the toy and wags his tail, as if he's trying to break up the tension in the room.

I'm thankful for this little guy.

Now I need to go find his daddy.

CHAPTER THIRTY-ONE

Luke's penthouse is empty. His office at Vulcano Enterprise is as well, which perky intern Chelsea was happy to let me know.

Where the hell is Luke? I need to find him to make sure he's okay. I can't even imagine what is going through his head right now. All I can think about is the look of shame and conflict in his hazel eyes when he told me about the death of his parents.

He needs me to fight this battle with him. Maybe even for him.

I've got one more idea and then I'll have to suck up my pride and call Lisa or Eric. Walking into Molly's Diner, I look towards our booth. As I slide into the seat my heart feels confused.

"How are you?" I ask Luke, who is holding a cup of coffee between both of his hands.

He doesn't look up but answers my question with one of his own, "Why are you here?"

Kathy walks towards our table, but I shake my head to alert her that now is not the time to take our order. She catches my signal and heads over to another table.

"Why wouldn't I be here? You are my boyfriend. You were just thrown into an extremely uncomfortable situation that I did not make any easier for you. I'm sorry. I am here to fight for you."

Luke looks up from his black coffee with a blank expression across his face. He's hard to read, and I don't know what words to say to ease this situation. I can't imagine what's happening inside his heart or his head. The struggle to break the chain you think your father holds on you.

"You're sorry? You don't need to be sorry," Luke responds.

"Of course I do," I say, reaching across the table to touch his hand.

Please don't push me away again.

Tears collect in my eyes but I refuse to let them drop. My instant reaction is to guard my heart too, closing off my feelings to protect myself from the pain I know all to well.

But another part of me can't do any of that. If I close my heart up I don't know if it will ever open again. I want to love. I want to love Luke. I do love him.

He faces battles too, deep and grave, but you need each other.

Fuck this. I will be our fighter.

Getting up from the booth, I slide into the same side as Luke, invading all of his personal space. He flashes me a bewildered look before scooting over just a tad so we aren't uncomfortably pressed together, which I didn't mind.

"Luke, you made me proud," I say, placing my hand on his thigh under the table. The bewildered look does not leave his handsome face.

"Proud of me? How can you say that, Ariana?"

"You had the look of rage and murder in your eyes when you had Drake in your grasp," I start saying as he cuts me off.

"Exactly! How can you be proud about that?" he asks, getting worked up. His face turns red and he moves even closer to the wall. Pretty soon he'll be pressed against it just to get himself away from me.

"If you let me explain," I say, giving him an, 'I dare you to cut me off again' look. "I was scared you were going to kill Drake. But whatever I said to you, you heard me. You let him go. The look on your face was conflicted, embarrassed, I don't even know how to describe it." I'm now rambling. I need to get to the damn point before he loses his mind. "Luke, you are nothing like your father," I say squeezing his thigh. "You were able to handle your emotions and push your jealously aside. I'm proud of you for that."

Luke lets out a breath before running his hand through his thick hair. "Ariana, this was one reaction. Next time, I could go off. How do we know? It's in my blood."

"Oh Luke," I say as I lean over and kiss his cheek, intertwining my fingers through his. "You have your battles, so do I. Would you give up on me if I still didn't let you touch me? Would you have ditched out on our relationship if I was struggling?"

Luke is silent for a just a second too long. I'm nervous he's gone mute. "I would not ditch out on our relationship."

"So then why do you want *me* to be a quitter?" I ask with a whole lot of sass. He tries holding it back, but I see a smile slowly creep across his face.

"You're a piece of work, you know that?"

I cuddle up against him and kiss the small scar on his temple. "And you love me because of it."

Luke turns towards me as much as this tiny booth will allow. Cupping my face in between his hands, he leans in to kiss me. And not just any old kiss—the most passionate kiss I've ever felt. If I were standing up, my leg would do that stupid lift like girls do in the movies. I moan into his mouth, not wanting this to end.

And like déjà vu from our first kiss, we hear someone clearing her throat standing next to us. Pulling apart we forgot we are in a family diner. Now would be the time to feel embarrassed, but everyone seems to be minding their own business, except for Kathy who's smirking at us.

"You kids want me to get you a room at the hotel down the street?" she teases, putting down two glasses of water on our table.

"Ha-ha, Kath. You know I have a penthouse now. I don't need to hide out in hotels or random houses anymore," Luke says laughing, but the comment reminds me that he hasn't always had this silver spoon. No spoon at all. He's a man who built himself up from absolutely nothing.

"I know sweetie. And I'm proud of you," Kathy says, truly beaming at Luke. She uttered the same words I just did to him. I feel a sensation like I'm meeting his mother or grandmother—an older woman in his life who has seen him through the worst and now is looking at all he's become. "I'll give you two a few more minutes and then I'm coming back to get an order. Got it?"

"Got it," we say in unison. Kathy doesn't seem like the kind of lady you want to piss off.

When she walks away, I plant one more kiss on Luke's luscious lips before returning to my rightful side of the booth.

"Are we done with all this bullshit about how you are going to kill someone because of me?" I ask, trying to play it cool even though I know what I'm asking means the world to him. He truly doesn't see himself the way I see him, but I'm going to make it my mission to get him to. It will take time and I will be patient.

"I can't say that I won't stop fighting for you if I think you need my protection ... but I can work on acting my jealously out in anger."

Wow. What he just said means the entire world to me. I don't have much experience with men, but the ones I do know hardly ever admit their faults, let alone say they'll work on changing.

Just then Kathy shows up to break up this serious topic.

"Alright kids, what are you having?"

We place our orders and keep the conversation light for the rest of the meal. We need light—we really do.

Back at Luke's, we cuddle up with Oscar on the plush brown couch before throwing in a movie. At some point Oscar jumps off the couch and waddles to his little doggy bed to pass out.

Luke makes it halfway through the movie before he starts running his fingers up and down my arm. He moves from my arm to rub slow circles across my back as I'm lying on his broad chest. Luke's hand gets a little more adventurous, moving from my back to slip inside my yoga pants squeezing my butt.

Luke leans me back into the couch. Now lying on my side, he slips his hand into the front of my panties where he teases around my clit.

"I love how wet you are," Luke hisses. He runs his fingers through my wetness but refuses to touch me where I'd just love him to.

Enough is enough. This teasing can go both ways. Grabbing his arm to remove his hand from my panties, I climb on top of him, heading straight towards his belt. I have his length in my hand in a matter of seconds. Luke leans back, taking me in with heated eyes.

With his boxer briefs still on, I run my fingers up and down his muscular thighs, making my way closer and closer to his cock. I watch it grow to its massive size under the white cotton briefs, straining to be let free.

Not yet.

I stand away from the couch and strip off my black yoga pants before turning around to give him a little shimmy. Luke growls out from behind me. He's right where I want him.

Climbing back on top of him, I lick his cock through his boxers. Planting kisses up and down his manhood before gripping his waistband between my teeth, pulling them down. Luke's cock springs free, and as much as I want to keep teasing him, I need him in my mouth.

Licking his cock from base to tip, every glorious inch meets my tongue. He's absolute perfection. Swirling my tongue around the tip causes him to emit a low growl. That's just what I need to hear to encourage me to keep going. Pressing my lips to his balls before I take one into my mouth and suck on it just enough to drive him to ecstasy.

"Fuck," Luke hisses.

Grinning up at him, he looks at me with hungry eyes—I'm sure my own reflect the same pleasure. Intoxication.

Luke reaches down to pull me up towards his mouth. I cry out at having to leave his cock behind, making Luke laugh. I never thought I'd be comfortable with a guy laughing during sexy time, but you know what? It makes me happy that we are this comfortable in our own skin around each other. I laugh too.

"I'm glad you're having a good time," Luke says.

"Who said this was any good?" I tease.

Luke's hazel eyes go from happy with laughter to dark with need in just a few seconds. If it weren't so fucking hot, it would be a little intimidating. He pulls my T-shirt and bra off in a hurry. Sitting up, Luke takes one of my breasts into his mouth before sucking on it with such force, causing me to throw my head back in a mix of pleasure and pain. He cups the other breast and massages it at the same time. Sensations spread through my body like electricity; all of my nerves tingle with delight. I grind my hips into his rock hard cock as he continues to rub my nipples.

"Take off your underwear. Now," Luke commands.

Jumping off the couch, I strip off the rest of my clothes and climb back on top of him. Luke lost his shirt in the process and we are both naked. I'm ready to ride my man, that's for damn sure. Placing my hands on his strong chest I steady myself before lifting up to find his cock waiting for me. Rubbing myself against him, I create a magnificent friction as his wet tip hits my clit in just the right spot.

"Oh fuck," I moan breathlessly as my speed picks up. Luke grabs my ass and rocks me into him. "I could come from just doing this."

It's as if fireworks are exploding inside of my body. But as much as it kills me to stop this grinding, I want him inside of me. Angling myself in just the right position, one stroke and his cock enters my needy pussy.

"Yes," I scream out as I sit down taking him deep inside of me. I truly think his penis hits the back of my cervix and a gateway of pleasure explodes through me. I've never felt this kind of delight before.

"Let yourself go, Ariana. Feel free," Luke says, encouraging me to take the indulgence I need. And I do just that. I let go of all the bullshit I've bottled up inside of me since I was a little girl.

"Good girls don't do that."

Being forced into trauma.

A few bad lovers.

All of my past sheds itself from my skin as the goddess inside of me strips herself free. Looking into Luke's eyes, I know that it's because of this man. I've found the right man for me that I am able to truly feel sensual.

I wiggle myself around on his cock before he slaps my ass. With my hands still on his chest, I bounce on top of his manhood, pounding myself into him over and over again. Each thrust hits the cervix and the pressure inside builds.

Before I know what's happening, Luke switches our positions with us both on our sides, him behind me.

"Wrap your leg around me," he commands, lifting my leg up allowing him to enter my pussy from behind. Luke reaches around me to rub his thumb over my clit as he continues thrusting into my pussy. I press my hips back, grinding into him.

"Oh Luke," I pant on the brink of climaxing. My body shakes uncontrollably. Luke kisses my neck as he rubs my clit even faster.

And that's when it happens. I have an out-of-body experience. My eyes feel like they roll into the back of my head. I dig my fingernails into the couch and scream out in pleasure. Luke grips his fingers into my hips as his cock pulses inside me; we bliss out together.

We stay wrapped up as one unit on the couch as our bodies come down from their high. All of my muscles relax and I feel like Jell-O.

"I don't ever want to leave this couch."

"And you don't have to," Luke says, kissing me on my temple.

CHAPTER THIRTY-TWO

The hospital finally pulled through and guess who is the newest attending? Move over resident. It feels so good to be an official staff member and receive a few new perks. I'll no longer have to introduce myself as the physician "working under" anyone else anymore.

"Bellisano, congrats," Ben says as he walks by the computers. "Now get to work!" He laughs as he rushes past me.

"I'm going to need help over here," Chief Pitters says as she rounds the corner out of nowhere. I swear, she's a ninja. "Let's go, let's go!"

Jumping into action, I hurry towards her. "What's going on?"

The Power of Salvation

The Power of Salvation

She looks me up and down before smiling and saying, "Congrats Bellisano."

"Thanks chief," I smile up at her a little embarrassed by the special treatment. "Now how can I help?"

We head towards one of the rooms we try to keep open in case of trauma.

"The paramedics are bringing in a man they found in a field. They say he's pretty frozen."

Dr. Pitters finishes talking as a few residents join us and now the paramedics bring in the frozen man on a stretcher.

"Isn't he a frequent flyer?" Lauren, a resident, asks. And she's right. This guy is named Steve, he's about 40 years old, and he has been in here quite a few times in the last year with a vague history of drug abuse.

The paramedics fill us in on what they know—he was found in the middle of a field, and his temperature indicates he's severely hypothermic. This guy should be dead from his temperature alone but his body seems to be fighting for life. His heart stopped in the field and a machine is giving him CPR as we look over his vitals.

"I don't think I've ever seen anything like this," Lauren exclaims. "His sugar is at 20."

"What?" Dr. Pitters asks as she looks at Lauren's findings.

He's frozen, his sugar has dropped to deadly levels, and his heart has stopped once already. How the fuck is this guy still alive?

373

"We have to warm this guy up," I shout, grabbing what we call the 'bear hugger' and put it on him. "We need to get warm saline in him."

"We can't get access to his veins," Ben defeatedly says. "I've never seen anything like this."

This man is so dirty and cold; his body is acting out against us.

I've got an idea. I remember my first year of med school when I drilled a hole in a pig. I can't believe I'm going to attempt this. Quickly washing the dirt from his shin I grab a small drill and then drill a hole into his bone where Ben slips in an IV to get warm saline into him.

Please work.

"Fuck. That's intense," Ben says while staring at the hole. Fuck is right but I don't have time to think about what I just did.

"This machine is about to die," Dr. Pitters shouts as the paramedics remove it and her hands move to his chest to apply manual CPR.

"Don't go! Please!" A voice frantically screams as two women push their way through the door and into the room in a panic.

"Who are you?" Ben asks towards the women as he helps a resident insert a catheter to flush Steve's bladder with warm fluids.

"My son. Please pull through," Steve's mom screams at the top of her lungs as she tries to hold his grimy hand.

"You can't be in here," the chief says in the calmest voice I've heard her speak in. "Someone get them out of here."

While a resident deals with getting these women out of the room, I insert another catheter into his abdominal cavity. I feel like we are working on Steve for hours, but it can't have been all that long. Our team gets him stable enough in the ER that he can be taken to the ICU floor. I remind myself to keep an eye on his chart; I truly have no clue if he'll pull through this.

While I busted ass working as part of Steve's team I wasn't the best physician to my other eight patients. I make my rounds checking in on everyone, and when my shift is over, I bolt out of the door at lightning speed.

I'm absolutely drained and can't think of anything I'd rather do than curl up in bed with my man and my puppy.

Glancing towards the usual spot where Ryan parks, I'm shocked to see no one there. This has never happened before. My instinct is to think of all the terrible things that could have happened, but my doctor brain tries remaining calm. They could be running late or stuck in traffic, or he could have worked longer than he planned.

But this has never happened before.

Pulling my phone out of my purse, I check to see that I have no missed messages; that only makes me sweat even more. Dialing Luke's number, I wait patiently as the ringing carries through until his voicemail picks up.

"Hey Luke," I pause not really sure what the hell to say, "it's me. Ariana. Call me back when you get this, please?"

I hang up and hold back tears. Why am I freaking out? Collect yourself, Ariana. My immediate response is to walk towards Luke's penthouse but I don't have a key. I've always gone into the penthouse with Luke, never on my own.

Why don't I have a key?

Maybe I should call Ryan.

I don't have Ryan's phone number.

Instead of worrying about what not having a key or Ryan's phone number means for our relationship, I think of what my next steps should be. Walking in the direction of my apartment I dial Lisa's phone number. Yet again, another voicemail. Why can't anyone answer their fucking phones? I don't leave her a message because I don't want her to panic. If she sees I called her, I hope she calls back. That's what people do right? I have no clue because I never answer my phone either. Fuck.

My legs carry me at super speed, and I'm at my apartment quicker than I've ever made that walk. Sprinting up the stairs, I throw the door open. I spot Serena cuddled up on the couch with Jack. Chinese takeout food is littered on the coffee table in front of them beside two empty wine glasses. They look a little disheveled, as if they weren't just watching the movie on the screen but instead making out. I don't have time to tease them.

"Hey girl!" Serena shouts a little too loud, "What are you doing here?"

Walking into the kitchen, I grab a bottle of water realizing that my speed walking took a lot out of me. "I live here, remember?"

"Oh you do? I had no idea. I haven't seen you here in weeks," she teases me with a wink.

"Shouldn't you be cuddled up to your million dollar boyfriend?" Jack asks.

I chug the entire bottle of water and then pace back and forth wearing a hole in the floor. "I should! But he wasn't there to pick me up when my shift was over, and he's not answering his phone."

Both Serena and Jack hear the panic in my voice I was trying to hide. That sentence came out entirely too scared. They both sit up a little straighter on the couch.

"Okay, let's remain calm," Serena says. "Being late one time doesn't mean anything bad happened."

"Who said anything about bad things happening?" I shout back at her a little too loudly. Why can't I get a handle on my words right now? They are flying out of my mouth.

"Your face looks like you think something bad happened. Sorry for saying that," Serena says as she runs her fingers through her long blonde hair. "Why don't you go take a shower and we will make some calls around for Luke?"

"I can't take a shower at a time like this!"

"Leave your phone with us and we will keep calling Luke," Jack instructs, reaching out to grab my phone. "Trust me, you need that shower. It looks like someone died on your leg."

Glancing down at my scrub pants, I see they are indeed filthy. I look at my phone one last time seeing there are still no notifications. I hand it over to Jack before walking towards the bathroom. I will take the quickest shower of my life because there's not a chance that I'm going to be in here while Luke is … who the hell knows what Luke is doing.

Not even giving the shower a chance to heat up, I throw off my scrubs and jump in. I shout out as the coldest water hits my skin, making me think of Steve's frozen body in the emergency room tonight.

Great, now I'm in here thinking of a patient.

Can this night be over?

Shampoo, conditioner, soap. Done.

Jumping out of the shower, I throw a towel around my body not really caring if it's mine or not. Sorry Serena. I move to the living room where I expect to see Serena and Jack making out on the couch.

Instead, Oscar is wagging his tail looking up at me.

"Oscar!" I shout rushing over to him. He throws his little body into my lap while I pet him. "How did you get here?"

It's then I notice the room is a little dim with a few candles flickering about. Before I can question where everyone went and why my dog is sitting here all by himself, Luke strolls out of the kitchen carrying a bottle of champagne.

"Luke!" Both Oscar and I jump up from the couch running towards him. Engulfing Luke in a hug I feel all of my tense muscles relax. "Wait. Where the hell have you been?"

Pulling myself back from this lovely embrace, I playfully punch him in the arm for all that he put me through.

"Ouch," Luke says, pretending to be hurt and rubbing his bicep. He walks over to the coffee table, which is now clear of takeout and wine glasses and sprinkled with red rose petals.

"What's going on here?"

"Oscar," Luke calls towards our dog, who is now lying on his back hoping one of us rubs his cute little belly. "Oscar, can you show mommy your new tag?"

"Oh no! What happened to his tag?" I ask, walking over to Oscar. Getting down on the floor to get a closer look at his tag and that's when I see it—engraved in the silver nameplate I see the words that stop my heart.

"Can my daddy be your husband?"

My husband. Luke as my husband. Luke wants to be my husband?

Standing back up I look towards Oscar's daddy who is now down on one knee holding out a ring box. That's when the waterworks start.

"So ... will you?" Luke asks as I continue to have my hot mess moment.

Oscar realizes I'm emotional and bolts towards me. He jumps up and down, trying to climb my leg but he's entirely too small. Bending down I pick him up and walk over to Luke, who's still waiting for my answer.

"Oscar, what do you think?" I pat his little head as he licks my face making me laugh. Kneeling down I join Luke on the floor. "Baby daddy, make me an honest woman."

His face lights up in a big smile, "Are you serious?"

"Are you supposed to ask a girl if she's serious when she agrees to be your wife?" I laugh.

Luke leans closer, pulling my face to his before claiming my mouth. I passionately kiss him back; I kiss him with everything I have in me. It's intense, powerful, adoring, loving. I love this man. I never thought I'd say that about any man. I want to devour him but he pulls us apart, making me whimper out a little in sadness.

"Did you just cry?" Luke asks with a laugh.

"I don't want you to stop kissing me," I moan back at him.

"I love hearing you say that. Just as much as I love you. My soon-to-be wife."

"And I love hearing you say that." I plant a kiss on his neck, sucking a little to get a moan out of him this time.

"I don't want to stop, but Ryan is waiting outside. Let's go home."

Home. I'm in my apartment already so …

"To your penthouse?" I ask slightly confused.

"Of course. But it's *our* penthouse," he kisses me, before taking my hand and pulling me up so we are both standing.

"It's technically not *ours* yet. It's yours."

"That will be changing soon."

Luke scoops up Oscar, and I walk towards the door until I look down, realizing during my marriage proposal I was wearing a towel. Oh my god. Only me. I dash into my room to throw on some clothes and meet my guys downstairs with Ryan.

It's good to see Ryan's face too—which reminds me of the panic I felt earlier when I didn't see them waiting outside the hospital.

"Hey," I say, pulling on Luke's arm before we get into the car, "where were you earlier? Why didn't you pick me up?"

"You don't even want to know the mess Oscar made that I was cleaning up. I planned to do this proposal at the penthouse but I lost track of time with this little guy," Luke says as he pets Oscar. "When Jack answered your phone I nearly lost my mind thinking something happened to you. He told me how freaked out you were thinking something happened to me, and I rushed over."

We climb into the backseat of the car and Ryan takes off.

"Now that I'm your soon-to-be wife, I'd like a key to the penthouse and Ryan's phone number."

Luke laughs at my pure sassiness.

"Deal. Now this is burning a hole in my pocket. You should put it on," Luke says, handing me the ring box. Of course, I'd be the girl who forgets to put on the ring … or even look at it … when she's getting proposed to. I did this whole thing wrong.

"Give me that, bad boy!" I exclaim, extending my left hand as Luke slips the most mesmerizing diamond on my ring finger. "Oh Luke, it's perfect."

"It better be. You already said yes," Luke laughs as he kisses my temple while I cuddle into his side with Oscar resting on his lap.

We ride off to the penthouse where we make our engagement night one to remember. The future Mrs. Vulcano was thoroughly fucked.

CHAPTER THIRTY-THREE

Six Months Later

The buzz of a tattoo gun sends chills down my spine. Even though I already have a tattoo, thinking about the needle piercing my skin still scares me. Once you get one, you forget the pain you previously went through. This feels like a fresh fear, which is ironic because the reason we are here is my idea in the first place.

Yesterday Luke and I sealed the deal, officially making ourselves Oscar's married mommy and daddy. We had a Las Vegas ceremony in a tiny, charming white chapel just off the strip with our close friends and family members—Serena, Lisa, Eric, and mom. I never thought I'd get married. And if I did entertain the idea in conversations with girlfriends, I never thought I'd fly off to Vegas to do it.

Yet, it felt right.

I didn't want to plan out some big extravaganza when the only thing I want in this world is to be Luke's wife. Simple as that. I don't care about flowers, seating arrangements, pictures, or any of that bridal stuff. Don't get me wrong; I support girls who want that. I applaud them for having the sanity to put themselves through all that planning. Opening one bridal magazine nearly gave me a panic attack. I closed it and never looked back.

Mom gave me a hard time about the Vegas wedding. I'm trying hard to learn how to handle my relationship with her. Some days I want to slip back into the mode of pretending I don't even have parents, but then I remember the heartache I felt when I knew my chance to build a relationship with dad was gone.

I can't let that happen with mom. We speak but I definitely don't kiss her ass or hold back my thoughts; however, I include her as much as she wants to be included. Turns out, she wanted to see her only child get married.

"Ariana, you sure about this?" Luke asks.

"Hell yeah!" I cheer as we take our seats in chairs next to each other. "Why? Do you want to back out?"

His arms and chest are covered in art, but I've learned those were all his own designs. This was something I asked him to do. Maybe he changed his mind?

My heart sinks at the thought that he wouldn't want to put this on his body too.

"I'm ready. I love this idea," he reassures me before leaning over from his chair to give me a kiss. "I have a feeling this will be my new favorite tattoo."

Walking into the room are two tattoo artists covered in masterpieces themselves ready to give us some new ink.

"Mr. and Mrs. Vulcano, you guys ready to do this?" Sam, the guy doing my tattoo, asks.

"Let's do it," Luke says, and I nod in agreement.

The second the needle hits my skin I curse under my breath, which must have been louder than I thought because Luke laughs at me. He doesn't even flinch considering this tattoo takes about ten minutes and he's been worked on for hours before. I don't care who you ask, it still hurts like hell.

After thanking Sam and Jeff, we leave the tattoo parlor hand-in-hand.

"Let me see yours again!" I order in pure excitement.

"If I knew getting a tattoo with you would be this fun I would have came up with the idea myself months ago," Luke says as he shows me his left hand.

Both of our ring fingers on our left hands sport new tattoos. They can easily be concealed by our wedding rings when we are allowed to slip them back on. Right now we can't wear them as our tattoos heal.

On Luke's finger—a 'K' on top of a heart.

On my finger—a 'Q' on top of a heart.

Like a deck of cards, King and Queen of hearts.

At St. Francis, I won't wear my wedding ring because who the hell knows what each day will bring and what gross body part I'll be sticking my hand in. I don't want to ruin Luke's gift, but I want him to be a part of me.

Forever. Just like our vows. We vowed to love each other forever and always.

And that's what we'll do.

We'll struggle. We'll fight. We'll want to scream at each other.

But we'll also love each other deeply. Truly.

He's the man who has rescued my heart. And I hope I've done the same for him.

We saved each other from our dark paths. He's made me believe in the power of salvation.

We'll start our own family and give our future babies the love we never had. I know we will.

We'll live Happily. Ever. After.

The End

If you or someone you know is in need of help, please contact The National Domestic Violence Abuse Hotline:

(800) 799-7233

www.thehotline.org

Reviews help new readers fall in love with this story!
Please take the time to head over to Amazon and leave
a review today.

xoxo
Caterina

CATERINA WANTS TO HEAR FROM YOU!

To visit Caterina's website & join her email list, head to:
http://www.caterinapassarellibooks.com

STAY SOCIAL:

Find Caterina on her Facebook page at:
http://www.facebook.com/catpassarelli

SnapChat: @catpassarelli

Instagram:
http://www.instagram.com/caterinapassarelli

EMAIL: catpassarelli@gmail.com

WITH LOVE

My amazing readers, thank you for allowing me to tell my stories. I am honored each and every one of you take the time to read these words.

To my parents & siblings, thank you for all your support in everything I do. For believing in me, guiding me and always having my back. Love you guys!

AD, thank you for being my muse. Your mom would be extremely proud of the man you've become.

To the people responsible for helping me bring this story to life. Duncan Koerber for editing my words and helping me brainstorm ideas to make Luke and Ariana's story shine. To Najla Qamber for her patience & extreme talent in designing this beautiful cover.

To Team Movement, without the support of my fun loving fitness family I would never have the guts to go after any dream. And to Beachbody, who if I never partnered with to be a coach I would not have the freedom to spend time writing.

To Lauren, thank you for letting me pick your brain about all things medical & emergency rooms. I greatly appreciate all the time you took to explain your career with me!

46532120R00222

Made in the USA
Middletown, DE
02 August 2017